P9-AFW-489

THE OTHER PLANET

A NOVEL BY

ASCHER/STRAUS

McPherson & Company

THE OTHER PLANET

Published by McPherson & Company, P. O. Box 1126, Kingston, New York 12401. Designed by Bruce R. McPherson. Typeset in Linotron Fairfield. The paper is acid-free to ensure permanence. First edition.
1 3 5 7 9 10 8 6 4 2   1988   1989   1990

This book has been published with assistance from the literature programs of the New York State Council on the Arts and the National Endowment for the Arts, a federal agency.

Library of Congress Cataloging-in-Publication Data

Ascher/Straus.
   The other planet : a novel / by Ascher/Straus.
     p.   cm.
   ISBN 0–914232–93–2 : $15.95
   I. Title.
PS3551.S3308 1988
813'.54—dc19   88–4991   CIP

∞

for Arnold and Bessie with love:
the best this planet has to offer

THE OTHER
PLANET

ONE

MEADOWS

The laboratory where Valeria worked was taken over by a large conglomerate and the plant was transferred to a new industrial park (one that resembled the ideal industrial districts of the future, a sort of low, open city of plazas, water, grass and all-but-concealed structures) in an unfamiliar, more attractive region of the state, near the Pennsylvania border. Many chemists were laid off and new ones were hired. Rumors circulated and multiplied, growing daily in both plausibility and inventiveness. It was said that the take-over and transfer were linked to a change in the nature of the laboratory's research and the source of funding. And that while, like everything else, the new project was being passed off as cancer research, in reality it was something quite different. It was military. It had to do with Space. Germ warfare. Mind control. Genetic programming. Microscopic entities, alive in a new way, that had been retrieved or brought back inadvertently from Space. Or something so secret it had yet to be named.

Several of Valeria's colleagues were fired without warning. Valeria looked out one of the broad windows and saw three figures walking away from the horizontal office tower, crossing the medium-sized plaza whose diverging perspective lines made it look more spacious than it was, a computer chip of infinity within its park-like frame of lawns. Cool sunlight stuck in coarse, tinted little bandages of clothing to their bodies, which moved forward without apparent locomotion, growing smaller in the usual way, each body sliding into itself as if into a toy railroad tunnel. She recognized the airy shine of the red, billowy hair of one of her fired co-workers. An emotion, inexplicably painful, overwhelmed her. The earth of the wide meadows beyond the industrial park looked green in a cloudy way, the air was smoky with possibilities, and the bark of the aspens had taken on the pale tint of young peapods.

It seemed to her that what she felt had something to do with the meadows, the air, the space and with her fired co-workers, yet nothing to do with "spring fever" or with her colleagues as individuals. She'd always thought of them as ordinary people with ordinary minds, ordinary goals; while in herself a different set of possibilities—the possibility of the extraordinary, the super-human—existed like an equation whose validity had yet to be tested. Therefore, she reasoned, it had to have something to do with the fact, in and of itself, that her co-workers had been fired. And with the way they looked crossing the plaza: not them, but this image of them.

The emotion was so penetrating that she gave up her job at once, without calculating the future and without pangs of doubt or regret.

Someone said that she was brave. Someone else spoke fearfully about the times, the difficulty of finding a decent job, the terror of destitution. Still another was reminded of Katherine Hepburn's light-heartedness in *Holiday*, when she leaves home and sails off with Cary Grant and Edward Everett Horton. And still one more said (with a friendly sort of envy Valeria was certain she *didn't* feel) that Valeria had let go of the baited hook that draws all of us through the endless, horizontal shallows of work. While Valeria said that she felt just a little bit like a shirt when the cardboard backing is removed.

Now that she was driving away from the laboratory for the last time, it seemed to her that the truth was that until you actually *did* something, it was possible to say anything about anything. She was feeling neither brave, frightened, light-hearted, nor free, but simply mildly deranged—the way an aerialist might feel at the instant just after landing in the springy safety net, consciousness not quite having caught up to her as she takes her first rubber-legged steps. She thought of a child on school holiday, the first derangement of days without classes in June. Perhaps the family driving into the country for an outing, with a picnic hamper and a dog, the circumstantial craziness induced by leaving the city. But, in that case, everyone else would be let out too. Whereas she was alone, like a child who's sent home because of a fever, a dizzy spell or a fall in the playground.

A few seconds later, she found herself driving off the road, scraping yellow paint along three dull strands of barbed wire, smashing one headlight on a fence post and braking to a stop in soft earth.

The whole thing happened smoothly and calmly, with only the smallest amount of noise and violence: the thud and tinkle of the bumper and headlight striking the post.

Her hands felt weak and were trembling a little, but beyond that she felt as unruffled as if her car had simply slipped out of her hands, through a tiny hole in things that could just as easily contain five seconds or a year.

She sat there collecting herself so that she could pull back onto the firm, grayish roadway and set off again for home.

The day seemed to be going by peacefully, sounds and incidents recurring and altering, mapping the surface of the planet so that everything could find itself again tomorrow, like a round heavy clock with a green face.

Two men in green coveralls were gardening in the middle distance, beyond the plane of soft and fuzzy spring grass, near a fence of white painted slats. One of them was pitchforking earth, digging out a circle around a small tree while the other, on hands and knees, planted pale yellow, tulip-like flowers, each of them discrete on its long stalk, and white flowers in foamy clusters.

It seemed to her that these two gardeners ought to have been near enough to have heard the little crash of her headlight. Yet, as far as she could tell, neither of them looked up or showed the slightest interest in investigating what had happened over on the road. They simply kept on with their work, which soon turned to hammering at the ground, shifting squares of turf from one spot to another.

Already it seemed impossible that she was here because she was out of work.

"UNBEARABLY LOCAL"

Anyone who has an accident, is struck by even the mildest illness, loses money or is recuperating from anything at all, soon discovers that this condition is like a magnet that draws thousands of apparently similar stories to the surface.

After word got around that Valeria was out of work it was only natural, therefore, that the phone kept ringing. Close friends, second cousins, her Aunt Elena and Aunt Grete, Uncle Sylvan, this one and that one—all of them armed with anecdotes about being out of work, having quit or having been fired, bad bosses, even job possibilities.

Her mother called and spoke about Valeria's new-found unemployment as if it were an illness, something from which she needed to recuperate. She suggested that Valeria might spend at least part of the spring at the shore with her next oldest sister, Nadja. Of course it would have made more sense, she said, for Valeria to stay with *Martina* (the eldest sister), now that Martina was doing so well and had bought a spacious house in East Hampton. Much more room for her there, naturally, than in Nadja's little apartment at the shore. But it seemed that Martina was still in Japan, buying fabric. Of course she wouldn't have known any of this (no one ever *heard* from Martina) if someone hadn't told her. A man had called, sounding utterly desperate, as if his life depended on it, asking if she knew whether or not Martina had returned from the Far East. No, she didn't know a thing, she'd said. She would be the *last* person to know Martina's whereabouts or anything else. She'd managed to draw him into conversation just a little, found out a few things about Martina, but not what the man wanted so desperately, what Martina could possibly do for him; or, for that matter, how he came to be trying to get in touch with Martina through her family. The point was, that until Martina returned, Valeria could stay with her or with Nadja. Or she could go to Grete's or to George and Elena's.

Valeria lost her temper.

Perhaps because she was the youngest of the Florescu's four daughters, and the smallest in stature, with girlish good looks a shade darker than Audrey Hepburn's in *War and Peace*, Valeria came in for an unusual amount of belated family advice and coddling. It sometimes seemed that her parents (whom she saw infrequently—not quite as infrequently as Martina and nowhere near as frequently as Marika, the second-eldest sister, who was married one might say in principle as well as in reality) couldn't get it into their heads that she was no longer eleven, might wander around the corner, lose her way and vanish.

Her mother was able to locate a wonderfully appropriate moral fable that had been passed on by some member of the family pyramid whose job-in-life it was to have worries and suspicions so deep-dyed a thousand rinse cycles couldn't fade them. Someone's daughter, "a brilliant young woman just like Valeria" who'd also lost an excellent job (she was one of the people responsible for a recent, extremely effective series of headache commercials) and ended up very nearly killing herself. Recuperating in Key West, she became entangled, with near-fatal results, with one of those attractive guys with dark little curls and tired eyes who are never-never what they seem to be, or even the third or fourth thing you uncover after that.

Valeria talked with her mother a bit longer and they ended by arguing.

Valeria woke up and saw that her pillow had no pillowcase. She wondered if she'd gone to sleep with the wrong pillow, possibly the new baby blue one her mother had given her recently, but which should still have been in its oversized bag of exceptionally crackly paper, on the upper shelf of the deep bedroom closet.

She looked in the closet and saw that the pillow was, in fact, on the shelf, wrapped in the triple shade of closet, shelf and paper bag. Then she saw her pillowcase on the floor near the bed, just about *braided*. Somehow or other she'd wrenched it off during the night. Was it possible that, without knowing it, she was worried about being out of work?

The bed also looked oddly disarranged: a spiral shadow, like the imprint of a nebula, was clearly visible in the white sheet.

She considered the possibility that she might have dreamed. She did have a memory of *something*—but it was very lucidly and certainly a memory of having been somewhere. Not of having *dreamed* of being somewhere, but of actually *being* there and seeing things.

She was bicycling along a tree-lined suburban boulevard with two of her sisters, Martina, the eldest, and Marika, the next eldest. Only Nadja was missing. Martina was several yards ahead of Valeria and Marika, the little wicker basket attached to her handlebars piled high with a tempting mound of whipped cream. Valeria wanted this whipped cream and bicycled as hard as she could to overtake Martina, yet, no matter what, she remained the same distance behind. While Marika, who bicycled with total tranquility, not straining at all, still-and-all remained perfectly even with Valeria.

Then Valeria came to a spot where a red tour bus was parked and waiting to take a busload of people. She hid her bicycle in some tall grass and boarded the bus with a group of nurses.

As soon as the bus began to move she could tell they were in a foreign country, somewhere in South America. They came into a city that looked like Buenos Aires, or her idea of Buenos Aires: white hotels in the distance, near a body of water, above narrow and depressing streets, more like dark, irregular pyramids of wooden shanties than anything else. The nurses were talking about the new hospital, how happy they were that it had no *wards*, only private and semi-private rooms. How *wonderful* it was, they said, that here in this new hospital (so new it had just barely been erected) something urgent would be cured. Something everyone longed to see cured would, at last, be cured here. They didn't seem to notice how *ugly* everything was. Children were playing, but there was no green anywhere. Then they turned onto a wide street—trees and green lawns—very much like the street where she was bicycling with her sisters—and Valeria thought, Thank god! But it closed up again and there were the same wooden tenements.

The bus stopped in front of a solitary, pale highrise.

Could that be the new hospital?

Everyone got out. The nurses disappeared and she was with a woman named Tina she hadn't seen since childhood, a girl she'd been best chums with but who, for some reason, her parents never completely approved of and who had eventually vanished in the usual way, leaving a tiny, melancholy trace that didn't reappear until now.

The two of them went down some basement stairs into an old bookshop, where, instead of books, there were stacks and stacks of shining dishes. An old man in a blue smock was painting flowers on a dinner plate. Tina wanted to examine the plate, but the yellow paint was still wet, thick as egg yolk. Valeria was looking at a freshly painted landscape on a large serving platter: a peculiar sort of wooden tunnel, something like a covered bridge, in the middle of a forest. She parted some shrubbery and there was the tunnel: a mine shaft with wooden supports or a railroad trestle, and all around it dark woodland. She started to go through it, but for some reason Tina had stopped in front of a small, round mirror. She was doing something to her face. Applying cosmetics, perhaps, and she said, "I'm trying to *change*."

"But you can't change like that," Valeria said.

"No, it really is different," Tina said. "I really feel different."

That made her angry, as if they'd argued about the same thing a thousand times.

"You're a fool!" she said and Tina revolved away from her, leaving Valeria alone in a still darker tunnel than before, with the feeling that there was already someone there, moving noiselessly behind pillars.

She called out, but the concealed figure didn't answer. She hurried forward through zones that were as cold as Atlantic currents, like a deep subway tunnel with its sudden drafts of air, its hidden vents and gratings.

On the other side she found herself in an open, dark meadow. A broad tree emptied itself of thousands and thousands of butterflies, so many of them, in fact, that it sounded like one enormous set of wings flapping. Then it was morning (hot trees in the distance, leaves talcumed with light) and she was on a wide but shabby boulevard, near a large house that had burned. The upper stories were charred and still smoldering and the river of water that had been pumped through the roof and windows could still be heard rushing down the stairwells. A chandelier was sending off sharp, prismatic sparkles through a dark space where a section of wall had been torn out.

I don't *like* this! she thought, and instantly she saw a beautiful woman on a terrace somewhere above, leaning on a railing and looking down at the shabby streets below.

Then *she* was up above, in an expensive garden cafe—and there was Tina, looking at a menu, which was in Spanish. She couldn't read it (Spanish was *not* one of her languages) so she had to sit close to Tina, on a kind of glass bench, while Tina explained the menu to her.

She said: "I can't *afford* this."

And *Tina* said: "At the bottom of the menu there's a list of sandwiches. *This* one is quite good—$2.16—you can carry it *with* you —a sausage sandwich."

She ordered one.

Tina was staring at her. So she said: "What's wrong?"

And Tina said: "There's something we have to *talk* about. We have to clear something up—we never really *understood* each other. We could have been much better friends. . . ."

She felt uncomfortable. Tina's face was very close to hers, like a child's. She could feel her breath, look into her eyes. . . .

"You're thinking of someone else," she said. "You're thinking of my sister, Martina. Martina never got along with you. Martina never gets along with *women*. . . ."

The waiter brought her a sandwich. The sausage looked a little odd, almost black, perhaps a *blood* sausage, but she bit into it. It was hot and juicy and spicy.

"This is very *delicious*," she said indistinctly, while eating.

Tina gave her a strange look, not quite a look of horror, and stood up suddenly, overturning the glass bench.

It was this sound of glass shattering (on a vast scale, as if a sort of watch crystal that covered things had cracked from one end to the other) that woke her up. And when she woke she knew for a fact that this place—the overhead cafe with the glass tables and benches and the charred house with the chandelier visible form the wide street—really existed *right at that instant*, somewhere in South America. And that she had actually *been* there.

"I need someone to *explain* this," she thought. "I need a little instant dream analysis, like Gregory Peck in *Spellbound*."

She looked at the illuminated blue clockface. It was 2:16. Who would be willing to talk at that hour? Who would be willing to meet face to face, rather than remain concealed, secretly yawning, behind the remote intimacy of the telephone? The only one near enough at hand was her utterly self-absorbed, not-very-close acquaintance, Denise Oliveros.

Denise sounded groggy. She'd dozed off, she said, only to be awakened minutes or hours later by the resounding clink of china in the kitchen—having forgotten completely that she had someone in the apartment. That is, the usual someone-who-is-also-no-one. Now this someone/no one was in the kitchen making himself something to eat and watching *Niagara* on Noel's 12" black-and-white portable. *Niagara*! In black-and-white *and* in miniature. The guy owned a hardware store, so maybe you couldn't really blame him for seeing the world in shades of aluminum.

"I *know* the plot of *Niagara*," Valeria said, longing to talk about her dream and secretly wondering if she wanted a friend who spoke film as a second language—or for whom the first language of reality was fundamentally secondary.

That was the one, Valeria said, where Jean Peters and her husband are a couple of corn-fed clucks who, for some reason, never took a honeymoon. Now the husband's won some sort of contest, so they drive to Niagara Falls, where someone gets murdered and there's all sorts of spectacular stuff with the Falls, the rapids and Marilyn Monroe.

Not at all! Denise said. *Niagara* was about the contradictory possibilities of Jean Peter's face and body, the latent eroticism of the girl-next-door.

Valeria couldn't stand this way of talking. She cut Denise short, suggested that they meet for a drink somewhere, say in The Subway Club over by the park.

She dressed hurriedly.

A mild pulsation, hardly stronger than someone blowing on her cheek, carried a whiff of early blossoms, or of something darkly fragrant brewing in the earth like tea, through the two or three feet of space between window sill and sash.

The moment was thick with nothing but itself: the world a dark jam of impasses that added up to the here-and-now, releasing the heady fragrance of the exact present, like the spice of weeds in vacant lots or the cultivated wildness or basil and tomato vines.

All at once things felt so unbearably local that Valeria found herself wondering where the exit routes from any given situation lay—let alone the tiny entranceway into the idealized distance she imagined her co-workers entering.

NO ONE KNOWS ABOUT US

She'd dreamed about her sisters, Valeria said. And then the scene had shifted to South America. That is, only the part that was about her sisters seemed to her to *be* a dream. While the South American section wasn't like a dream at all. What it *was* like was a little harder to say.

She described the part where she was bicycling with Martina and Marika, the futile pedalling after Martina, the basket filled with whipped cream.

What bothered her, she said, was the underlying tone of envy. She'd never thought of herself as envying *any* of her sisters. Martina was undoubtedly the most successful of the four of them. And not only in the local, family and idiotic sense of pure money-making, no matter what that means, but in the slightly more real sense that people in the general population had heard of her. Marika was the only one who was married. That sort of life had nothing to do with success. By definition, everything was already achieved at the altar. And Nadja was simply out of the running, exactly as lazy as she was athletic.

Perhaps there was a *little* envy of Martina's extraordinary beauty. Could that be the meaning of the whipped cream basket? Could the whipped cream be Martina's beauty. . . ? This possibility seemed plausibly stupid.

Denise wasn't even bothering to pretend to listen. She was trying to persuade the bartender to flip the television image from a Las Vegas-style floorshow—plumes, mirrors, a revolving glass stage and dancers in tiny, tinsel-bright costumes, their thighs, long hips and exposed asses powerful enough to gallop through miles of sexual pantomime or real screwing—to a movie on Channel 9 called *The Projected Man* that *TV Guide* said was about a scientist who turns himself into a weird electronic monster.

The bartender refused and they ordered their drinks.

"Now I really *have* heard everything," a guy further down the bar said to the bartender.

"No you haven't," the bartender said with absolute authority, pouring out Denise's bourbon. "There's absolutely no limit to the things you can hear. There's absolutely no limit to *things*. Things produce *new* things. Multiplication is the basic law of the universe."

"Stand in one place long enough and everything that already exists will pass you by," the guy at the bar disagreed. "'Sooner or later everything that already exists appears in the mirror of waiting,'" he added, as if reciting a well-known homily.

"What we already *know* exists may be infinite," the bartender argued, "but what about what we *don't* know. . .?"

Denise seemed to be looking beyond the two men, toward something or someone visible to her in the cobalt blue bar mirror, between the duplicated pyramids of green bottles, at a point invisible to Valeria. All *she* saw was a dark blue version of the red walls, a distant patch of carpet, red and wet-looking as blood, and herself—really existing at least one more time without limit. The place was more of a "cocktail lounge" than anything else—not the dive Valeria had expected when she saw the lurid red lettering from across the street, glowing in a way that made daylight seem improbable.

Valeria tried to follow Denise's gaze. She turned her head to look directly into the dark, red depths of the room, but it was no use—she would have had to lean back, make an obvious show of peering around Denise's back to get a glimpse into the hidden corner.

"Let's drink to my birthday," Denise said, loudly enough to be heard by everyone. She'd turned and was holding her glass aloft to be clinked by Valeria's glass in a toast.

Valeria struck her glass to Denise's without conviction. She knew Denise only a little better than she knew the lanky bartender. Who was she? She stared at her. Short black hair with auburn highlights apparently tinted into it. A very subtle red-brown that appeared in the black and glossy haircut only because her head was interposed between Valeria's gaze and the irregular flashing and suction of the television.

Dark eyes. Brown and enigmatic: coffee with an unidentified something dissolved in it like strong liquor. Mouth more or less free-floating, a puddle of water that floats on ice, making it slippery. A friction coefficient of zero.

A black silk blouse. Dark gray skirt, buttons slightly off center, buttoned to a little above the knee, the rest of the buttons undone. Dark, smooth-shaven legs.

Good-looking, and yet. . . . What did it all add up to? Nothing more revealing than a map you look at hurriedly while driving through an unfamiliar region of the state.

Her brother called her yesterday, Denise said, and hinted that the family planned to surprise her, whisk her away to the family compound. Candles, birthday wishes and birthday songs, presents so extravagant they would nail her down to another twenty years of gratitude, photograph albums, six or seven tears, gluttony, reminiscing, a catered trough by the pool. Nothing would be missing.

For the first time in her life she'd said no, she already had plans, what a pity they hadn't asked sooner. Ten seconds later Roland called and turned her lie into something as true as the truth. Someone at the office had told him it was her birthday, he said. Why didn't they have a party.

She knew that "party" was code for "orgy."

To her surprise she said *yes*, giving herself this astonishing present.

Later in the day, her mother and brother showed up in her mother's bottle green Continental with birthday cake and enough food to keep a rocket crew alive through a voyage to another solar system.

Valeria found herself beginning to accept the fact that they weren't going to talk about her dream. She had to admit that there was something to be said for *not* being able to tell the story you supposed you wanted to.

Someone had slipped out of the hidden crevice into which Denise Oliveros had been staring—crossed the room rather quickly toward the exit. A dark blue jacket and the lower part of the face (apparently quite handsome in a slightly convex and thrusting sort of way) approached Valeria in a double way: five or six feet in front of her, in the mirror, yet approaching her back from the depths of the real space of the room, optically logical but otherwise mysterious and disturbing.

He veered off sharply and disappeared without coming fully into view.

"What a terrific-looking animal!" Denise said, downing a good part of her second glass of bourbon, following the man with her eyes.

"He turned and looked back at me from the door—our eyes actually *met*. I looked into his eyes (it was as if he was right *next* to me) and I knew that I would have gone with him in a second!"

Valeria didn't answer.

"You think I'm joking," Denise said, "but I'm not. I used to be a moron. A hamburger like three hundred billion other hamburgers. But I've changed! I do what I want!"

Valeria found this odd, since she had no idea what Denise used to be like. Still, she said she wondered what it meant to say you'd changed. Everyone said that. But what did it mean? To change meant to transform yourself completely, to become someone else. But no one had ever done that. The self was a compact and porous mass of habits and they never deserted anyone, completely or otherwise. They simply ebbed and flowed over the years. Certain traits, which one took to be absolute necessities, laws of one's nature, diminished under certain circumstances, while others became exaggerated. In this way life consisted of an endless succession of deranged states, during each of which you were convinced you'd awakened from something—till you felt yourself waking up still one more time, looked back and realized you'd been "deranged" again. Right now, she was well aware that she could easily mistake the circumstantial strangeness of her condition for an inner change in her nature.

Head tilted back, mouth open, Denise wrapped her lips around her third bourbon as if her aim were to unfasten her mouth from its weak mooring in the face. She could tell right off what Valeria's big problem was, she said. She thought that she was smarter than other people. She thought other people were stupid. Even if it were true that people were stupid: so what? No use feeling superior. Sooner or later you found out that you were stupid too—more intelligent than some, stupider than others, a mole tunneling in higher ground. Life *made* you stupid, a natural process. She herself, while not really intelligent, nevertheless had given certain things a lot of thought. For example. She knew that every age had its dominant principle, something that pulled you forward, even if only to a tiny degree. In bygone ages this dominant principle had been an ideal of beauty or of order, goodness, freedom, will, knowledge, consciousness itself. What the dominant principle of this age was she had no idea. Were we, for example, still in the "age" we were born into? Perhaps someone knew, but not her. Or it had yet to make itself clear. But something did pull her forward. *Had* been pulling her forward over the years—had *changed* her, no matter what Valeria said.

Once upon a time she was married and a moron. A familiar story, but hers nonetheless. She chose to be an idiot, married a dope, spent her life in office, kitchen and bed. Her reasoning then was that she was dropping below Culture, the everyday blather of civilized conversation. Not one day passed without getting high. They'd return home from work filled with as much enthusiasm as a bus returning to the garage, wash up, eat, turn on the tv, get high. Or drive over to a friend's house, horse around, and get high. Make love and get high. Through it all there was a glimmer of awareness that all this was exactly as exciting as getting electrocuted in your own bathtub.

Then a few things happened all at once. She got sick of feeding her husband his roast chicken and 12 x 16 pans of frosted devil's food cake. (There were just so many times you could get a thrill out of seeing a well-fed face.) She became depressed. It dawned on her for the first time that there really was such a thing as wasted time, a wasted life. It actually went by, dumber and dumber with every day. She met Noel, divorced her husband and his mother, went to business school, moved in with Noel.

In her relationship with Noel she began to discover her real nature. Or to feel that something was pulling her forward. There wasn't an ounce of sentiment in her nature. Not a grain. All that mattered to her, what she wanted out of a relationship, was someone who could screw her gracefully from the rear, someone who was sufficiently self-possessed to stroke her breasts and enter her at the same time. Someone who was able to satisfy her while she stood up or leaned over a soft chair back. Someone who didn't mind being on bottom. Someone who could, with a reasonable amount of consistency, provide orgasms of at least one full minute's duration.

All that meant more to her than birthday presents, companionship, flowers, someone to cook for, cute greeting cards, someone to watch tv with and bring to family gatherings.

Then, not long ago, she noticed a remarkably beautiful young man working as a file clerk in her office. In the less or more real life he led outside the office he was a model, kept in an expensive apartment by a middle-aged designer named Zerka something. His friends were good-looking people who had ill-defined connections with fashion, records, movies. She didn't dislike him and didn't admire him any more than she would a good glass of beer. Their relationship was simple. It consisted of nothing but sex. Nothing outside it and nothing inside it. She hadn't broken with Noel, but what seemed liberating before now felt bound by the familiar hoop of faithfulness.

She wanted to know what Valeria thought. Should she tell Noel about Roland? About the guy back at her place right now watching *I Married A Monster from Outer Space* and eating a late night snack? Keep quiet and continue to do what she wanted? Break it off? Or what?

It seemed to Valeria that Denise's mouth (she'd lost count of the number of straight bourbons Denise had put down while she nursed a solitary gin-and-tonic) had arrived at the free-floating state it tended toward. She took that to mean that it didn't matter one way or the other how she answered.

She turned and looked into the room: small cocktail tables, red banquettes, mirrors, a small stage with red curtains, a familiar, cheesy modernity (the saloon dragged toward the 21st century) and over all a reddened soup of smoke. Looking into only one reality, the moment narrowed down, lost its savor.

"Know what I think?" Denise said, articulate as raspberry Jello. "Know who I'm like? I'm *exactly* like Jean Peters."

"Like Jean Peters? How do you know what Jean Peters is like?"

"Like Jean Peters in *Niagara*! She's married to a middle-American jerk with an Eagle Scout chuckle, Hawaiian vacation-wear and a Kodak necktie who works for a shredded wheat manufacturer. He's come up with a prize-winning shredded-wheat turkey stuffing recipe and that's why they're in Niagara Falls. They've driven to the Falls to meet the big boss and they've turned the trip into a second honeymoon. While they're waiting for the boss and his wife to show up the husband passes the time by reading *The Collected Works of Winston Churchill* and Jean Peters (girlish-looking, sympathetic and trusting) is drawn into Marilyn Monroe's weird relationship with Joseph Cotton.

"*Niagara* is about Jean Peters' education. It's about innocence and experience and Jean Peters growing up. At the end of the film the husband's the same dumb cluck as before—nothing's pulling *him* on, life is irrelevant to whatever it is he's doing. But Jean Peters is transformed, sexually alluring, going down the rapids with Joseph Cotton, stripped down to red lipstick and wet underwear. Or it's about water. Or it's *not* about water. It's about the color *red*. There's a secret red code—Marilyn Monroe's red lipstick, the red rainbow colors of her jeweled lipstick case when she's murdered, red light on blonde hair, red dresses, shoes, blood, fingernails, kisses. . . ."

"You know so much about *them*," Valeria said. "And no one knows anything about *us*."

On the way out through the electric-eye-operated heavy steel, imitation subway doors of The Subway Club, Denise thought to ask Valeria a question.

"Never been married or *wanted* to be married. . . ?"

No, Valeria said, she'd never been overcome by the desire to make a nest for some Don or Bobby. The decision to get married (insofar as it *was* a decision) had always seemed to her a very peculiar one. The very first time, perhaps, that you peacefully accepted a panoramic view of your own future, as something flowing into a sort of basin. Marriage seemed to her an extremely odd condition that people simply got used to. Acceptance of something—beyond one's own habits and someone else's. A mutual pact to remain the same within a jointly improving or deteriorating shell of life. Undoubtedly there were reasons for her attitude. If you looked into things, you found that all your cherished notions were someone else's.

The reasons we did things were never the reasons we did things, Denise said as they crossed the street at a long diagonal toward the spot near the green bank of the park, in view of a near-distant railroad cut, where Valeria had parked her car.

Blue morning was already being pulled across the sky by a noisy little plane with three sparkling star blue lights. On the ground evening was still dark blue, more luminous than the blue trousers or blue short-sleeved shirt of a white-haired man hurrying toward an all-night pharmacy. And astir with the cool, breathless wind, the negative south sea dreaminess of outer space.

During the drive home, house fronts began to light up, to glow, almost yellow. The air began to feel sultry with the vegetable fragrances that signal the birth of amazing numbers of winged insects out of the earth, the green bark, the low-lying meadows blue with ground water.

Valeria thought: while you more or less prided yourself on your freedom, your intelligence, others, many others, more than you'd like to think, were already living more freely than you. Or not simply more freely: according to new principles, as if they'd moved on to the next century while you lagged behind for all the reasons you could and couldn't name. She found herself wishing that the car could go faster—faster than the fastest supersonic transport—at least 55,000 miles an hour, like a space vehicle—through one sleeve of light, then another—giving her the feeling of being on stage at the instant the curtain over the unknown is drawn up.

T W O

NEW PRINCIPLES

Valeria set off to visit her sister Nadja at the beach. It was a windy day and waves of light blew through the early grass. Trees and shrubs, their buds and leaves no bigger than green peppercorns, shook—but not at all in a way to suggest that the sky would soon become as dark as a shade tree, shedding one flat sheet of rain after the other.

The horizontal force of the wind seemed to increase as she drove and the sky continued to drop down blue sheets of water with the regularity of television images.

None of this mattered to her. She was in one of those moods when movement equals something like happiness. When your original plan is washed away it seems of no importance. It even felt pleasant to be driving along the small, secondary road which ran parallel to a set of railroad tracks in the middle distance, the other side of thin and scattered stands of birches and broad tracts of mud that may once have been meadows, where puddles as big as ponds showed up an odd chemical green.

She turned on the radio with the thought that it might bring a pleasantly thoughtless state to perfection.

She listened indifferently to the first voices she found on the FM band.

Two or three men appeared to be arguing bitterly about a subject hidden behind the one they were talking about calmly.

"It no longer means the same thing to talk or write about Paris,

Honolulu, London or Lake Placid," one voice said. "The speed of transportation is catching up to communication. Planes are as fast as sentences. Rockets almost as fast as television images. The world can actually be traversed in the time it takes to leaf through the pages that separate Bucharest from Uruguay in a good-sized atlas. . . ."

Another voice said: "Everyone longs for surprises. When they don't arrive on your doorstep, you go travelling—an attempt to squeeze destiny like a sponge. . . ."

And still another voice said: "The *safest* way to travel is simply to get into bed. But what's the most *dangerous* way to travel. . . ?"

This wasn't at all the sort of thing Valeria wanted (it actually *diminished* the pleasure of driving) and she turned the dial until she heard a man's voice singing hoarsely about the depressing thrill of loneliness.

It was then that she noticed that her car was filling up with smoke.

She continued driving, feeling certain that in this region that did, after all, have the stained and littered, automotive look of a body shop, she would come across a garage in no time at all.

But no garage turned up, the road climbed a bit, grew more narrow, hilly and multiply curving through real woodland, and the smoke, which at first seemed white, almost transparent, no worse than the smoke of a couple of cigarettes, began to turn yellow and acrid. She pulled off the road onto the dirt-and-grass shoulder. Her head covered with a Mexican straw beach hat (one of the aunts had brought a flock of them back from one of those shopping binges disguised as vacations; one for each woman in the family and each with a different colored ribbon around the crown) she ventured out into the downpour.

The storm was a hundred times more intense than she'd thought. In the time it took to take the few steps to the rear hood where the engine was housed, she was as soaked through as Jean Peters when Joseph Cotton's boat capsizes and she's clinging to a rock just above Niagara Falls. It was impossible to stand out there for more than a few seconds without an umbrella or a slicker. The straw hat sailed away like a model airplane.

The wide, golden disc of the hat skated along the wet road to a

point in the middle distance, where it came to rest as if stuck fast.
She hurried to retrieve it, wondering why, when her sister Martina
hadn't even bothered to collect hers, she should be feeling anything
like sentimental attachment. Still, on the rare occasions in summer-
time when the family converged at the beach (her mother, various
aunts, and Nadja or Marika) they all wore their straw hats. It was
amusing to see all the women of the family arrayed in their hats over
a picnic lunch, each with her blue, red, green or yellow ribbon hat
band. Just as it was amusing to hear her mother and the aunts laugh
together: they had the same thick-as-syrup yet singing tone—so
that someone was bound to remark that they sounded as alike as five
geese, five crickets, five Russian wolfhounds, five clarinets. Even
Nadja shared a little of that common voice tone, like an extra strand
of genetic allegiance that appeared only when she laughed. Valeria
and Martina didn't.

The hat began skimming and flying again as she approached, at
last lifting off completely, its red ribbon hatband spinning like the
rim of a flying saucer over a bank of wild, just-budding shrubbery.
Standing on tiptoe and peering over the bank of hedges, she saw the
hat riding away on a narrow, swollen stream that ran on for a bit in
a channel roughly parallel to the road, before forking off sharply
into real woodland.

On an impulse, Valeria stepped through a break in the shrubbery,
forded the shallow but swift-moving stream, and, with short,
muscular steps, dug her way up a little hillside, hoping to catch sight
of the vanished hat on the far side of the slope. On the other side
she saw nothing but more brown and muddy woodland, a gray cabin
in the deep distance. No sign of the hat or the stream. A deep chill
rose from the earth, into the relative darkness of the woods.

She hastened back over the low slope.

From the ridge, the yellow double blot of her car and its image in
the black macadam looked impossibly far away. The atmosphere had
darkened: wherever there had been a smudge there was now a dirty
cloud, wherever there had been a dirty cloud, more rain now
descended, obscuring whatever might be pleasant and scenic and
giving the road the look of something tunneling into a dark and solid
substance along a slight uphill gradient.

Just as she reached her car a set of orange headlights dipped up and down several hundred yards along the road, outlining the crest of a hill. The car plunged into the downslope, disappeared, and appeared again, brighter and nearer. She'd no sooner jumped into her car and locked the doors than a red Mercedes sedan swung in next to her, so close that the driver of the red Mercedes had only to slide across his seat and open his window to look her straight in the eyes.

The man had begun talking, but she had to roll down her window a little (not so far that he could reach in and seize her by the hair) to make out what he was saying.

"We were wondering," the man said with disarming diffidence, "whether or not we might be of some service. One of my associates spotted your smoke—it looked like a red flare in the glow of your taillights—as we came over that large hill."

"No," Valeria said instinctively (and at the same time wondering if Denise Oliveros would have said *yes*), she wasn't in trouble. On the contrary. So many people complained about the foulness of her strong European cigarettes that she sometimes drove out to the country to smoke five or six packs.

"I see," the man said simply. "We're intruding. You came out here to be alone. To sit in your car and look at nothing. And here we thought *we* were being American," he said, turning and looking over his shoulder, apparently addressing his companion or companions in the back, concealed not only by the rain-streaked windows but by the atmospheric darkness condensed in the car's interior. "We thought we were driving like real Americans. That it was really American just to be *driving*." And, turning back to Valeria, "Here the predicted, the longed-for 'disintegration of values' has taken place 150%. Each thing for its own sake, each value system divorced from every other and attached to none higher. Driving-for-driving's-sake. A great idea. So—we thought it was fantastic that we were driving through the American countryside and couldn't see a god-damn thing."

When he said "like real Americans," Valeria heard his accent for the first time, hard to place, perhaps the accent of someone who's lived in more than one country. Moreover, he'd rolled his window down all the way, leaning out a little in order to make himself more easily heard. She saw that he had a strong nose and one of those aggressive mustaches whose popularity comes and goes, but generally in a darker, more Zapata-like shade than these blond bristles, just about the golden hue of Sultana raisins. The strong nose, prominent moustache and sloping upper head combined to lead the face into a pronounced and somewhat bony convexity. His hair was thoroughly concealed under the hood of a yellow slicker. He reminded her of someone unpleasant she couldn't quite place.

The only way to be American, Valeria said, was to stare at things. Americans were famous the world over for staring at things. The snapshot, for example, was a technological means of immortalizing the American habit of staring at things. Whole regions were set aside just so American families could drive out there and have a look. All this might have prepared the way for television. Years of gazing dumbly at landscaped vistas and ocean sunsets extended naturally into staring at the square meadow of the tv screen.

The man stared at her with an unsettling intensity, out of proportion to what they were saying.

"You remind me of someone I know," he said. And, turning again to his hidden companions: "Doesn't she talk just like *Bianca?*" (Since his head was turned away, she couldn't actually make out the name "Bianca," only a sound that resembled it.)

"She might almost be one of us, except for that stupid remark about television. I don't trust *anyone* who talks that way about television."

"Why are you wasting time on a civilian?" a sharp little voice barked from the depths of the interior.

"Ask her if we're on the right road and let's get out of here!" another voice rasped, either masculine or feminine—the voice of someone in a great hurry to get from here to there, someone used to gobbling things up quickly, whether food, ideas or distance. A cut-off angle of a flat, dark yellow hairdo, a pale crescent edge of a long, dish-shaped face, also impossible to identify as male or female, showed up dimly over the shoulder of the yellow slicker.

Valeria rolled down her window, hoping to have a better look.

"I have to apologize for my friend. She has no feeling for the magic

of the mountains, the solitude of a forest road. Her idea of an
excursion into the country is this: you drive up, look at nothing, eat
a good lunch, drive home and eat again. For her the world is so
much dinnerware. But it is true, I'm afraid, that we've lost our
way. Somewhere near Atlantic City, I think, we veered off the
beaten path. Now we have to get back on the main road north—
toward Canada. Ultimately we want U.S. Route 87—through New
England—to Quebec—Route 289 through St. Eleuthere. Arne's
boss has a beautiful place on Lake Pohenegamook."

"He's no more *my* boss than he is *yours!*" the concealed man hissed
from his corner (without coming at all forward to a point where the
weak daylight would pick up a few features.) "I'm accountable to
no one! I continue my research, as before. If others make use of it,
that's of no consequence to me. . . !"

"You see what sort of people I'm travelling with," the convex-
faced man in the yellow slicker smiled, his rather pale blue eyes
looking straight into hers. "I myself have been in the States a matter
of days. Four days ago I was standing on a bridge in Zurich. Can it
be only *four days?* Yes, four days ago! So much has happened since
then, it seems impossible! And now we're headed for a meeting in
Quebec—where I'm told there's a magnificent estate overlooking
the lake—*and* a wonderful laboratory. It sounds very much like
Scotland up there. . . ."

"She doesn't care where you were four days ago or where you're
going," the woman with the deep, rasping voice cut in, "she wants
to get on with her driving and staring, her wet road and murky
window. *She* may not know, but I *do* know that when you're *in* the
mountains you don't *see* the mountains. You see trees. You imagine
forests. But never the dark bulk of the world that makes itself visible
as you approach and depart. Now, let's stop frightening the child
and boring ourselves—and get onto 87 North before we find
ourselves back on the coast."

"I see on the map," the hidden man laughed in a twittering way,
"that we aren't at all far from Boy Scout National Headquarters and
Museum. That might be pleasant. A very short drive—if we're
anywhere near where I *think* we are. And then, if we take a
northwestern route, we can spend the night somewhere near

Swartswood. I like the sound of it. There's a *town* called Swartswood, a Swartswood *Forest*, Swartswood *Lake* and *Little* Swartswood Lake."

"You would never guess that these are intelligent people, would you? Perhaps among the top billionth percent of intelligence in the world. If you know anything at all about physics, for example—and if I were to tell you the name of the man talking like a moron in the back there—you wouldn't believe me! You would say it's impossible! But it's true. My own credentials are a bit more modest, perhaps, but I make up with diligence for lack of genius. He, on the other hand, cares much less for the field of endeavor that's made him famous than for his real interest in life, his true profession. Lust in all its forms is all he really cares about. If it were possible, if there *were* such a thing, he'd throw everything over and give graduate seminars in lust and related phenomena. A nice little secular evangelical program peddling the virtues of lust on public television would suit him fine. Do you deny it?"

"No, I certainly don't deny it! Why should I deny it? 'But even for lust it takes strength, and the ones who want to deny their lust out of sheer weakness, out of sheer inability to lust, are the worst of all.'"

"Yes, yes, we can all recite our *Child's Garden of Verses*—that's all very interesting—but *more* to the point is what you're thinking right now. What you're thinking right now (correct me if I'm wrong) is that you'd like to get into this young woman's ridiculous little yellow eggshell, drive to the nearest motel, spend several days and nights under assumed names, go at each other with no holds barred, nothing too low or too filthy, nothing prohibited, no delving too deep, all secrets exposed, then separate and never see one another again. If I have something wrong, now is the time to correct it."

"Now you really *have* frightened her," the woman said with mock sympathy. "Her face is still easy to read—not yet like a book too many people have read before you."

"You'd like to get the hell out of here—am I right? 'Get the hell out of here'—is that the correct American idiom? I speak perfect *English*—but I'm not proud of that. I have a *facility* for dead languages. What I'd *really* like is to get the hang of *American*—New

York American, southern American, black American, Puerto Rican American—those are the really *difficult* languages."

There was some truth to what they were saying, Valeria thought. She *was* experiencing fear for the first time since the red automobile pulled in. And yet, despite that, absurdly, Denise Oliveros crossed her mind as well. Was it possible that even in *this* situation fear or anything like it was a kind of backwardness, an inability to ride on the actual current of the times. . . ?

In the instant it took to have these doubts a hand flashed out of the wet sleeve of the yellow slicker and fastened on her wrist like a handcuff.

The man's face had gone white around the cheekbones, his eyes seemed a darker and drier blue, his lips narrower and pale, but he continued to talk in a more-or-less friendly way.

"You'd like to get the hell out of here, but I haven't finished telling you about my friend, the genius in the back there. It isn't every day you run across a creature like that, believe me. Something happens to these guys when they're stuck in the laboratory too long. I look at him and I see my future. Arrested development. The guy's arrested at a seventh grade level, emotionally speaking of course. Or it's more complicated than that. He claims that what he feels is the 'pure lust of childhood.' But I don't at all know what that means! It's *adult* lust, but it's stuck somehow at the seventh grade level.

"The day before yesterday (I hardly *knew* the man at the time), when we were horseback riding down around Cape Hatteras, I actually found myself telling *him* an incredible story about *myself.* Something I'd forgotten about completely. A sufficiently disturbing memory, I suppose, for me to have lost hold of it over the years, but also the most intense erotic experience of my life and one that governs my desires even now.

"When I was in the seventh grade and living in Montevideo, where my father was in the diplomatic corps, a distant female cousin was beaten up by a slightly older girl. Naturally it was nothing serious. Very difficult for children to actually do one another serious physical harm. Still, I got it into my head to take revenge."

As it happened, his parents were going on vacation for a week or so and he would have the large house virtually to himself, with the exception of a few indifferent members of the household staff. So, one dark Friday afternoon, when school let out for the weekend, he followed the girl and waylaid her on one of those pleasant streets that wind uphill among banked lawns as broad as mountain slopes and ranks of tremendous oaks or chestnuts. A district where driving is such a universal habit that two pedestrians passing in the same half hour constitutes a crowd.

He kidnapped her. Managed to terrorize her to the extent that she allowed herself to be half-dragged to his house, made her call home and convince her parents to let her stay the night at such-and-such a friend's. Then he took her upstairs to an unused guest room, gagged her, stripped her down to her underwear and tied her to the bed. She was a big, adolescent girl, with a body like a stand of cherry blossoms in full bloom. When he saw that, it filled him with inspiration. Rather than sticking fast to his original program—which consisted of rather conventional threats, psychological torment, and so on—he decided to reduce her to a kind of second babyhood.

To this end he started out by giving her a good spanking, first with her pants on, then with her pants off. Later, when she complained of being hungry, he went down to the kitchen, warmed up some milk, filled a baby bottle and made her sit on his lip and feed from that, sucking on the nipple like a baby.

Next time he refused to let her hold the bottle—had her lie in bed while he held the bottle and she sucked.

He repeated this procedure at every feeding, until, to his surprise, she began to like it. She would lie there like an enormous baby, happily wiggling her toes and hands.

Things were taking a slightly different turn than he'd expected. He began to feel that he wasn't tormenting her at all—while he himself was on fire with a sensation he'd never felt before, violent and free of sentiment, yet oozingly all-consuming, like a big window fan rotating in mud. Lust! Every time he fed her, watched her lips sucking at the bottle, sat close to her and smelled her clean, sharp smell, almost like laundry, his head became as hot as a radiator at full steam.

At last he made her take the bottle of warm milk with its rubber nipple between her legs, while he knelt over her and gave the bottle rhythmic squeezes and pushes as if it were part of his body.

Even at that age, and as blind and over-heated as he was, he could tell that she was aroused. So he untied her completely and they fell on each other—struggled with each other more like wrestlers than lovers—yet nevertheless squeezed out of one another something delirious, ecstatic.

Naturally, the spirit of revenge evaporated. They became, as the saying goes, passionate friends, met secretly, played their games that always led to the same vertigo.

Unfortunately, it lasted no more than three months or so—his father was transferred to Caracas—and he was left with a permanent scar of longing. . . .

Valeria said that he'd told her the wrong story. She had about as much desire to be babied—to be someone's *baby*— as a silver fox had to be someone's little fur jacket.

"You're wrong," he said. "You have a real *baby* face. The kind of face old ladies like to eat for dessert with a little heavy cream. Just the kind of face I go for."

Valeria pointed out breathlessly that there was no way he could get out of his car without releasing his grip on her wrist.

"Quite true," he admitted as the back door on the far side snapped open. "You're about to learn a very important lesson."

Another set of bright headlight beams came drifting rapidly down over the hill, refracted and diffused through the bottle-blue atmosphere.

The back door slammed shut immediately.

"*Move!*" the woman said with irreducible certainty, leaving no room for contradiction.

The man in the slicker delved through Valeria's eyes with one last stare and then the car, flashing lusterlessly in the dull light, wheeled in a sharp little arc backward and jumped away onto the road, very nearly banging into the big car (apparently an old, sea green wagon) that had pulled up on the other side of the narrow road.

BRIEF CONSIDERATION OF THE FUTURE

As the green station wagon went over the top of the hill, Valeria watched the driver of the red tow truck detach hook and chain from the fender of her yellow VW. The straw filling of the wrenched-out back seat was still smoldering, sending up a yellow flare of smoke by the side of the road.

It would be pure luck if she ever found her car again, Valeria said. She'd left it in that out-of-the-way garage that looked like a tiny, deliberately concealed Howard Johnson's.

The driver didn't answer. He stared straight ahead through the half-blind sluice of the windshield, as if he didn't understand a word she was saying.

He doesn't *look* stupid, Valeria thought, giving up on conversation and switching on the radio. In fact, he was rather good-looking. Skin as clear and pink as the skin of a girl in a plaid school uniform, curly hair the color of straw with the subtlest hint of red in it. His face looked somehow at odds with his forest green shirt and pants, the emblematic uniform of years of workaday boredom.

The music that came over the radio might have been from another century. A syrupy tenor sang a lively but sentimental ballad over a rudimentary dance band (accordion, drums, clarinet and another instrument she couldn't identify), couples somewhere probably dancing to its forceful rhythms as if they had something to celebrate.

There was no need for her to worry about finding her way back to the garage, the young man said without turning toward her. The garage lay below the mountains with all their confusing turns, loops and side paths and he knew the district below the mountains rather well, having passed through it many times on the way to the home of such-and-such a relation of his sister-in-law's. He was returning to New York after having been there last night, in fact, for a party that had dragged on beyond the orange circle of the barbecue stage into real night. He'd had too much to drink and very little sleep. Some had stayed the night (though god knew there was room for very few, and even they were cramped and uncomfortable in that little dump). Those who had to get to work had dragged themselves off (neither alive nor dead, like himself) and those who were able to stayed. His brother was out of work, so *he* was still there with his wife. He lived with them on Long Island. He had his own apartment, that is, in the basement of their house. His father had, so far as he knew, deserted his mother before he was born. His mother died before he was three. He was raised in orphanages and in a succession of miserable homes, a very early sampling of human greed, stupidity and indifference. He'd run away from these places any number of times and lived like a wild animal. It wasn't until he was in his teens that his older brother (he hadn't known until then that he *had* a brother) tracked him down, found him quite miraculously.

He stopped talking as abruptly as he'd started, like a difficult talk show guest. He concentrated on steering the car as if it were a motorboat.

They drove on a bit longer, while the radio gave off a sequence of tunes all to the same lively and unhappy effect.

After a while he said that he had a confession to make. He was feeling extremely uncomfortable. There was something about her that made him want to talk to her. But he had no facility at all for keeping up a conversation in the usual way. Speech seemed to come and go in spasms. The story went (according to his brother, Ambrose) that one day, when his mother was still alive and he was an infant, Ambrose looked in the carriage and said something to him and he didn't answer. Ambrose went to his mother and said: "Something's wrong with baby Liam. He doesn't talk." "Nonsense," his mother said, and she came over too. But he wouldn't make a sound for her or for anyone else. Everyone was terrified. And someone said: "This one isn't going to learn the secret." And it was true. He never did. Hadn't said three words all weekend.

The house was a dump, a three-story mess with sagging porches. It had one foot in the grave and the other in mediocre woodland. Lanterns and food on picnic tables covered with green-checked tablecloths under trees. It went the way of every barbecue and family outing he'd ever been to. Someone's birthday and "It's Your Birthday" played three dozen times. After a while drinking changed voices into other voices. Jokes became meaner and stupider. An argument or two. Ambrose (who was in a bad mood nowadays

because he was out of work) knocked the brand-new Stetson hat off
the Beatle-playing cousin's head.

"You're an *ass*hole for buying a stupid thing like that!" he said.
"You and twenty million *other* assholes with their *cowboy* boots. . .!"

They very nearly came to blows. He saw the blood in Ambrose's
eye and stepped in, accidentally getting caught with a feeble punch
on the ear.

Nora, his sister-in-law, took the occasion to cut Ambrose up.
Who was he, she said, to talk about the stupid things someone else
bought? She told the often-told story of the hairy biscuit he'd bought
her for Christmas because she'd seen a drawing of a mink hat in a
Macy's advertisement and said she wanted one.

Ambrose woke up under-the-weather. Not even up to slapping
some paint on a porch or putting a few nails into the rotten boards
of his run-down property. He felt guilty because his regular work
kept him from lending a hand as much as he ought to. He had to
repair an elevator this afternoon in still one more condo complex by
the Hudson. People lived in them, people lived everywhere, and yet
the world looked like a no-man's land.

Valeria wondered aloud what he meant by a no-man's land—and
whether every age felt so much like a trough between one thing and
another. The more truly modern things were, the less they had to
do with the way people were still living; and the more one had a
sense that they were imposing a way of life not-yet-here. She
thought it would be a long while before anything like a livable future
architecture turned up. A long while before people agreed to live
according to different principles. Perhaps new people were needed
first.

"Come in and help me off with my boots," Valeria suggested. Her
voice sounded like someone else's. She felt distant from herself, as
if a tiny second self could be seen performing on a tv monitor.

No, he said, he'd just finish his drink and get going. He still had
a long drive ahead of him. He was standing by the window, looking
down at the street she knew by heart. The usual dull angles of gray,
white, brown, brick red and chalky black, darkened, moistened and
globbed together with rain, here and there a block of green or bolt

of yellow. There was a pool of yellow on Valeria's lawn where the heavy rains had beaten the forsythia blossoms from their green wands, a few yellow rings of daffodils in isolated front gardens. A milky, tender green billowed in distant trees.

It seemed to take her an age to tug off one tight-fitting, red-brown sheath. One leg lifted, knee bent, drawing the leg in close to the body, pressing it slightly into the vegetable green bedspread, her lightweight skirt slipped down below the round, amber shadow between her thighs.

She lifted her other leg and looked at him.

He came forward, took hold of the second boot and drew it off.

"Kneel at my feet," she said.

He looked surprised, as if her panties were the black eye mask of a highwayman (a narrow black band, a little pointed arrow at the center), possibly the one worn by Rock Hudson in *Captain Lightfoot*, and he were a startled but good-natured passenger.

He did as she said. She wound two hands in his curly hair and guided his head. His face was as hot as melting wax on her bare skin.

His eyes had a wild, tired look as if, abducted from the coach with all its gilded curlicues, he were clinging to the broad, lathered rump of Valeria's horse, holding on to her and experiencing a breathless sort of heart failure as she drove the horse like a motorcycle up a steep green hill.

Liam was dressed and ready to go. He hesitated as if hoping for speech to overtake him once more before he left.

"We've met before," he said.

Valeria began to speculate on what that might mean (she was on the verge of telling him about South America), but he stopped her. He didn't mean that they once might have been in the same stadium together or in the same bar in Sunnyside. He meant that their lives were braided together in some essential way. That he was in love with her before he met her.

Valeria couldn't think of a thing to say.

Later, when she was alone and putting away the things she'd set out with, she found a black Subway Club match pack (the red lettering a cartoon rendering of the bar's neon sign). She hadn't smoked while she was sitting at the bar with Denise Oliveros and didn't at all remember having helped herself from the bowl of match packs on the bar. She flipped open the cover. Someone had scribbled a message inside in red. Might have been a name and telephone number or an address, but something had spilled on it, dissolving everything but some tracks that looked like v's and e's, 8's and 1's.

MEADOW AND FOREST

Valeria was bicycling in the park near her house and eating a rocket-shaped Moon Shot. The park was the usual low, circular region of light, full as a lake, that could be entered at thousands of points, traversed along any number of routes. Clouds seemed to be anchored more here than anywhere else, transmitting purple shadows and cold slopes under a golden, upper zone of tiny leaves.

After she'd bicycled round and round the various loops and down the various hollows that bound the park together in the usual way like a broad, soft net that could expand and change shape as one fell into it, she began to feel as if she'd bicycled a hundred miles from the streets where spring was shining. The deeper she went the colder it got, as if the loops of the park were like the imperceptible spirals of a parking garage, a frozen reservoir concealed at the bottom.

She came around a particularly dark stand of trees on a violet bank of earth. A frozen plane of water did not come into view, but a meadow, its new grass no thicker than a film of algae, a tiny inland sea of golden shadows.

The place was so appealing that she dismounted, stretched out in the grass with the intention of planning out her life, but dropped off at once into a light sleep. She slept briefly, one stroke of a paddle sending her skimming across the full length of a lake or the span of a dream or of her life or of something else she couldn't name—and she awoke to find a squirrel approaching in the usual zig-zag way from the circumference of trees. It came quite close, no more than two yards away, and waited on its haunches for something to be offered. She saw that it was an unusually handsome one, fat and sleek, with a large, well-developed head and pointed little ears, a white belly, eyes that were nothing but opaque and glistening pupils.

She remembered a little sack of stale cookies in her saddlebag, fetched them and held one out. The squirrel jumped forward—took the round cookie between two sets of bony nails, swiftly transferred it with a scraping sound to the firm clamp of the mouth and made a quick dash—two, four, six long bounds flattening to a gray streak in the new grass—for some place of concealment.

It returned in a minute or so, from a different direction and appeared next to her in the warm yellow shadows. Valeria thought: there was something admirable, even to be emulated, in this persistent, fierce darting about. Nothing was enough. One motor force above all others: a familiar, endless appetite—satisfied, forgotten, until it presented itself anew. Without that appetite could one accomplish anything? There were those who had it, billions who didn't.

She held out another round cookie. The squirrel again leaped forward—but something frightened it—a particularly loud crackling over where dried leaves lay under the trees, or a shadow that swayed too suddenly and violently—it grabbed at the cookie with a sort of hysterical aggression, as if it were ready to climb up Valeria's arm, and dug its claws into her hand.

Valeria jumped back, frightened.

The squirrel's little mouth looked red, like a tiny smudge of lipstick.

It flew away through the grass in a few skimming bounds, its gray-brown fur blending into the landscape's darker shadows.

The shallow scratch had already swollen into a round, livid welt.

THREE

EVERYONE MATURES BUT NO ONE CHANGES

On her way to meet Nadja, Valeria made a wrong turn and walked east instead of west. By the time she became aware of her mistake (the correct number in the wrong direction was a small, run-down television repair shop), she'd walked several blocks out of her way, though still only a shallow distance into the district of dark storefronts and locked commercial buildings. The error seemed to have led her into colder temperatures. The evening felt un-Earthly. Things might all be squares and right angles, paving stones, building blocks and plate glass, you might be walking at the bottom of man-made channels, yet it was neither more nor less than a mirror of space, an endlessly receding plane of frozen debris and black ice.

She gazed at herself for a moment in the black photo bath of the shop window, her image half-formed against a bank of dead television screens. The transparency of the image uncannily reflected a certain weightlessness. The weightlessness of meeting Nadja?

"You're thinking about *time*," she heard someone say and turned to see two very old women passing slowly, one in a brown overcoat with a red-orange hat, the other in a gray overcoat with a midnight blue hat. "Thinking about the past gives you the chills," one of them said. "Right now it isn't spring and it isn't winter. So I can look either way. But if I forgot to look in the right direction, if I looked into winter by mistake, I'd want to kill myself."

"There's nothing in the past that bothers *me*," the other woman said, as if offended. "*I* can look back with a clear conscience. . . ."

"There are *always* things lurking back there, Grace, and they'll eat you alive if you let them. No way to crawl through life without them. *Some*one has to bury the dead—so we have our creatures, just like those beetles they have in the forest. But you mustn't fall back among them. You must let them do their work—leave them alone—or they'll eat a hole out from under you just like this."

"Yes, I suppose that's so. You have to run, keep going forward just to stay ahead of them. The secret to a long life. But the trouble is, just as you're approaching the danger point, it gets harder and harder to outrun them. You slow down just a little and you feel them gaining on you."

"Even that one there, young as she may be, will have them sooner or later."

Their voices became inaudible and Valeria hastened back toward the west side.

The streets grew livelier, warmer and more populated. Shop-windows were newer and were still lit up, displaying an utterly different class of merchandise, all the up-to-and-beyond-the-minute stuff that didn't seem so much like merchandise as a brilliant ramp that lowered like the back of a truck permitting you to approach whatever was far-off and desirable.

Those walking in the street gave the impression of belonging to one large party dispersed into smaller units—headed for the mirror dispersion of one large interior, a horizontal hive or space station.

As she drew abreast of one of these clusters, she was surprised to recognize a face or two. One of the men Valeria knew (a Hungarian formerly called Georgi, now preferring the pedestrian George) recognized her and said that he'd just seen Nadja at Marceline Black's opening. Everyone was headed to Becky Andropolos's for the opening night party. Nadja was already there helping Becky.

Someone was desperate for cigarettes, so they stopped on a corner while a few people made a party of going into a coffee shop in search of a cigarette machine.

While they were waiting, "George" (who'd heard about her bad luck from Nadja) began to commiserate with Valeria. You never could tell what was good luck and what was bad luck, he said. One downward slope under all. For example: he was no longer teaching biochemistry at the university level, but biology in a vocational high school. And he'd had to *plead* with them, convince them he wasn't over-qualified. Of course they were right. He *was* over-qualified. And a man working too far below his capacities was a dangerous animal. So he'd taken the civil service exam. If things went as badly as he expected, he'd score phenomenally well and accept the job—a miserable business that had to do with passing judgment on work-men's compensation cases—and that would be it for him. He'd vanish off the face of the human universe. Since one was human, after all, only so long as there were possibilities. He'd seen enough to know how quickly a life without possibilities eroded one's so-called humanity. Weekends and longings, that was to be his fate.

Valeria said that her story wasn't as terrible as his. She certainly didn't feel as if she were headed for an abyss. In fact, there was nothing much to tell. Or, in the usual way, what could be told easily was hardly worth telling. As he probably knew, she'd taken a very early PhD—and at once felt disgusted with the university. She'd had certain extremely promising projects underway, one of which, for example, showed real possibility of yielding results that would revolutionize the image-making and image printing processes of which "photography" was a very limited, mechanical example. She took a very good job at a commercial research laboratory that soon proved disappointing and for which, in the profoundest sense, her training was utterly irrelevant. She wasn't able to accept the idea that (as a colleague put it) it was "a life like any other." It seemed she'd been waiting for a reason to leave and now she'd done it.

"Yes," George said. "But there is such a thing as History. What can we do about it? Sooner or later it kicks you in the face, just the way it kicked our parents. It's a horrible thing to say, but I think I've begun to believe that the moment you accept that is the moment you grow up. Being a child means exactly being pre-historical."

"All that happens as you get older," Valeria replied, "is a) you get older and b) everything weak and fearful in your nature begins to have serious consequences. The 'kick in the face' was delivered long before you can remember it—and after that the imprint is always there, waiting for something to stick its foot in. . . ."

The little group came out of the shop already lit up and smoking, everyone set off again, separating her from George until they arrived at the correct address, where she was squeezed in next to him on the unusually small freight elevator.

A dark woman in a black velvet blazer came over to the elevator gates to greet the new arrivals and show them to the distant area of the loft that had been enclosed as a bedroom, where the coats were being stored. Protruding eyes and an odd way of talking, thick and unfriendly, as if something were clamped to her tongue. A strangely depressed sort of hostess, possibly one with a missing piece and a bit of money, willing to foot the bills for food and drink in order to have a place among these performers with their attractive, extra bolt of vitality.

On the way to the bedroom Valeria thought to herself that the allure of these lofts had gone flat. What once seemed like an adventure, a fresh proposal for living (a tribe camping out in the abandoned warehouses of heavy industry) was now just another easily reproducible style.

The small crowd she'd arrived with dispersed toward the various zones that had been established within the large expanse of floor boards—broken only in the deep distance where the bedroom had been boxed off and a curtained opening seemed to lead to a dark other space. Some headed toward friends and others straight for the food or toward the oak table that served as a bar. Others, happy with a bit of music as a background for living, were over by the stereo, and some were already peering at whatever lay against the laundered white of the walls, as if at the fine print in things.

All in all it seemed an unlikely place to find Nadja.

George touched her arm. *"Two* of your sisters are here," he said. He, apparently, had actually been *looking* for Nadja.

George guided her across open spaces and through smoke-laden crowds under gallery lights toward the dark panels of the windows, where a little crowd was centered around a long white couch and a blue rug.

There, in the center of the white couch, in something blue and flowing and flanked by men, was Martina. Nadja, half blocked by shoulders inclined toward Martina, sat at one end. It didn't surprise Valeria at all that this was Nadja's idea of getting together. Nadja had never known the difference between one kind of talking and another. She doubted if Nadja even suspected that there was a kind of conversation that couldn't be carried on in groups, or while hiking, canoeing or sunning yourself in flocks. What *did* puzzle her was Martina's presence. It was astonishing to find Martina in a place, among people, where Nadja might also be. The effect was the same as always, simple and overwhelming. Valeria had seen this retreat, this "eclipse," too often not to recognize it. No matter how good Nadja looked (as she did tonight, in white ski sweater with red and green bands, a green velvet blouse showing out at the collar, dark green knickers tucked into orange-gold boots, and her auburn hair cut the length that made her resemble either Margaret Sullavan or a young West German actress who showed up now and again in dubbed Klaus Kinski movies on Channel 9), Martina was more beautiful still. Dark with warm eyes and full lips, her outward being an inward swirl that drew men in effortlessly at every point. Tonight she looked remarkably like the model in a sequence of French perfume ads that had been appearing on television and in magazines, over and over for half-a-year or more. So that many men, without quite knowing it, were longing to meet someone who looked at least a little like that warm, graceful woman, wearing something blue and strolling across a bridge in Paris.

Nadja saw Valeria and came to life. She tried to make room for Valeria to wedge herself into a narrow space on the white couch. Valeria went over and sat on the padded armrest, with her arm on the couch back around Nadja's shoulders. She felt a familiar discomfort: wanting to take Nadja's side, while realizing that there was no "side" to take. It caused Nadja no discomfort to drift into the background, no more present than one of the pillows on the couch. *She* was the one who thought, self-consciously, that taking a seat on the couch meant assuming a place in the margin, like one of those adoring non-entities in sacred paintings.

A slender man with a brilliant tan, rather youthful-looking, prematurely gray, the hair worn just long enough to suggest certain values, preferences and tendencies, but not so long as to suggest other values, preferences and tendencies, in a very well-tailored blue-on-blue pinstriped suit and black boots, both of which went extremely well with the gray hair and the tan, seemed to be in the midst of responding to something Martina had said. He was sitting on the edge of a high-backed, green velvet chair, with his fingers interlaced.

He said that he thought that was a rather depressing point of view. It seemed to him to leave no room for the idea that people could change. One frequently ran into trouble in long friendships for the very reason, he thought, that people changed in slow and subtle ways, while one's perception of friends tended to remain fixed, to lag behind. For this reason it was impossible (wasn't it?) to say where reality stepped in in any human situation. Everyone was perpetually undergoing changes that no one else could appreciate.

Valeria marveled inwardly at the wonders of conversation. Nothing was simply itself. This apparently self-assured man in the handsome suit, who seemed to be genuinely disagreeing with whatever it was Martina had said, was really begging for something. The words meant nothing, beyond a certain effort to isolate himself from the others with language. All he really wanted was to kiss her, get closer to her, receive a different sort of glance. And ultimately, of course, to put aside his blue suit and her blue dress, find himself side by side with her.

We knew the truth about others from the very beginning, Martina said—the first few minutes, first days—but ignored it for all the reasons that could be listed. Until, sooner or later, one simply forgot what one had once known—and then had to re-learn it very slowly and painfully.

"Yes," Valeria said, "life is a big waste of time."

Martina ignored her and told a story that purported to prove that life proceeded by knowing and forgetting that one knew. A friend had told her this story only last autumn, she said, though she couldn't remember who the friend was: whether it was little blonde Corrine, with her reversible personality, so hard-nosed in business but soft as an ermine collar with men, or tall Katha with her large eyes, her wisecracks and her depressing way of falling for the cruelest, most indifferent types.

Arriving for a brief vacation in France, Corrine or Katha met a man in the airline terminal. He had a kind face and an easy-going midwestern manner, slim and early-thirty-ish. He'd lived in Paris many years, flying for a small air-freight line. She figured she could cross him like a bridge: on the other side, a sense of comfort with an alien city. They shared a taxi into Paris, had dinner together, spent the evening with his friends. She made it clear that she'd be happy if he stayed the night. Too bad, he said, but he had to take off for Hamburg at 4:30 a.m. Absolutely had to grab a few hours sleep. He'd be back in three days.

The next morning, feeling abandoned, reduced to tourism, Corrine or Katha had breakfast alone in the hotel dining room. Two Frenchmen, who, from their style of dress she took to be business-men, offered to show her around Paris. For some reason (her French was rather spotty) they were both free for the day or for several days and could devote themselves to showing her a good time. She couldn't believe her luck. After a day of sightseeing, they invited her to dinner at a *relais gastronomique* a little beyond Versailles. Katha or Corrine sat in the back seat, while the two men sat up front together. It wasn't until they'd been travelling quietly outside the city for half-an-hour or so, with very little conversation, quiet inside the car and outside as well, that she began to have doubts about her situation. The longer they drove, the more she began to feel that her disappointment had propelled her into a situation that was at least as stupid as it was dangerous.

Unfortunately, Martina couldn't remember how it turned out. Several versions seemed possible—one of them authentic and the others from films and books. In one version their destination turned out to be a chateau and a party. Very good and very potent cocaine. Pulses of erotic tension from the drug, through the music, into dancing. To be kissed by one's partner, a complete stranger, seemed completely natural. Or thrilling because it *wasn't* natural. This happened to the woman, who was paired with an elegant young lizard in white. It was odd and disturbing, but the wave of everything that rose up through the stranger's ardent kissing brought her close to orgasm while moving upright, legs scissoring across the room. Later she found herself somewhere on the dense lawns of the chateau, being undressed under a blanket. Her orgasm was easy, rapid and violent, as if a starling-sized bird were trapped in a thick, deep puddle, thrashing its way out or deeper in. In the middle of the night she awoke to find herself in bed with the two men from Paris, one nestled in front ass to belly, the other tongue-and-grooved to her behind, hands loosely clasped around her breasts.

Other versions were too horrible to think about.

The slender, suntanned man on the green chair asked how old Martina's friend was. If she was young, she was lucky. "You mature when there are certain things you'd never do again, things that are behind you, for good. Most of us don't begin to grow up till we're hitting thirty. . . ."

"The problem is that everyone *matures*," Valeria said, facing Martina's blue dress and everyone on the white couch, "but no one *changes*."

"I don't at all understand what that *means*," Nadja frowned, looking both cute and ugly. One of those people who seem attractive until they begin to talk, Valeria thought unhappily. Nadja complained that she'd never understood a quarter of the things *Martina* said or *three* quarters of the things *Valeria* said.

"But I like to listen to them anyway." She shrugged. Her smile was moronic.

Valeria said that she meant something very obvious. Sooner or later life supplied us with a second or third replica of ourselves—very similar to our original sense of self—but with certain fine adjustments, a bit of heavy ballast dropped here, a sharp edge rounded off there. Eventually presenting us with something so apparently different from before (a little like the first time you see yourself in the mirror in a first-rate piece of clothing and admire the way that image ought to be able to succeed in the world), that we feel we can settle down with it. And that's when we become convinced that we've finally "changed" in some fundamental way—that all those tiresome struggles of childhood have lost their energy.

"Gee, I hope you're wrong," Nadja said. She began to talk

uninterestingly about her relationship with Andy, the guy she lived with out at the beach. How Andy demanded that she make the bed every morning.

"First I have to tuck in the green sheet and smooth it down. Then I spread the Moroccan blanket over that and smooth *that* down. And then I cover the whole thing with a white, tassled bedspread. After that, the big burgundy pillow and a couple of little pillows."

The strange thing was that she never wanted to live like that. And you wouldn't think Andy was like that either. Did it mean that they'd both settled into their second selves that were really their *first* selves? Was *that* what she meant?

"Don't worry, Nadja," Martina said soothingly, as if to a child. "Valeria is a pessimist, that's all. The possibility for change is endless. It really is. Next year you'll be making someone else's bed, you'll see."

Valeria began to walk away. It sounded to her like they were practicing a routine. Someone said that the three of them sounded like the Lane Sisters.

"Are you sure you mean the Lane Sisters?" someone else asked.

"I thought there were *four* Lane Sisters."

"Yes," someone else said, "there have to be, because they were in a film called *Four Daughters*, with John Garfield."

"No. John Garfield's in the other one, the gloomy sequel. . . ."

"In *Four Daughters* one of the sisters gets married—and the rest are sad—and look out the window while it's snowing. Not *Priscilla* Lane, but the dark-haired one who looks like Kay Francis. . . ."

"Sounds more like *Little Women* to *me*."

"Yes, but the original or the re-make. . . ?"

Valeria passed out of earshot, away from the little furnished zone under the dark windows, and wandered over to the makeshift bar.

A man with a bony, convex face, receding blond hair and a blond Zapata moustache, cut across the open, map-like expanse of Delft blue and putty-colored rug, moving swiftly, as if he were being chased. He sidestepped one person gracefully, jostled another and vanished by some palm-like floor plants.

It took Valeria a hundred times longer to cross the same expanse of rug. It was crowded and noisy over in the constellation of things by the floor plants (someone was feeding records to the turntable, couples were dancing, struggling to talk as if they didn't speak the same language, a woman she recognized from the street was laughing and playing patty-cake with an Indian man with a heart-shaped melancholy countenance). There was no opening hidden behind the floor plants and the only exit route in sight looked like the door to the kitchen.

THEORY OF LUST

The kitchen was a shallow oblong narrowed off from the vast space of the loft proper by a symmetrical bulking inward at right angles of the whitened facing walls. Earthen-colored floor tiles, the usual dreary kitchen fixtures and cheerful garden of appliances. An aromatic ring of domestic or communal pleasure detached itself from some substantial reality she couldn't begin to guess at and wafted from the stove, where two women were doing things with red saute pans and steel stock pots. Three more women—a red head in green plaid and purple, a Chinese woman in white sweater and dark glasses and a blonde in magenta—sat at the table, blindly throwing vegetables into a salad bowl and craning their necks over a coffee-table-size book of photographs.

"I've always *envied* breasts like that," the Chinese woman pretended to pout.

"No—they're *too* large. They lack *warmth* or something."

"They don't look *real*."

"I imagine that's her purpose. To hint at that unreality."

The blonde in magenta and the red head in green and purple went back and forth in this way until Valeria, out of curiosity, went over to have a look at what they were talking about. The large book was laid open to a photograph of a Las Vegas dancer with a silver gown and silver hair, sitting quite upright on a wooden chair in a shabby, glittering dressing room. The gown was very shiny, like so much water, very tight-fitting: a wasp waist and rounded hips. The breasts were bare, perfectly round, luminously pale and (it was true) extraordinarily large.

"I don't think so," the argument continued without animosity. "I don't think she means to say something about the unreality of the breasts—or of the woman—or even of the *milieu*. She's beyond that. She's *using* the unreality of the breasts (they actually *look* as if they're loaded with silicone) and of everything else to say something about the nature of *reality*."

"But isn't all art critical in that way?" the Chinese woman said. "Art is a criticism and a correction."

"That isn't true. Some art simply exists. It's just another reality, more magical than this one."

How could one talk about the unreality of reality, Valeria asked, when reality was simply the name we gave to whatever happened to exist. Nothing could be unreal, nothing synthetic. Once something existed it was real, whether we liked it or not. Things simply came into existence in different ways, in the test tube or in nature. And each new real thing that ruptured our fixed idea of the real we called "unreal."

Everyone looked at her oddly. Who was she? What strange doctrine was she propounding? Valeria found it strange herself. She'd had no more control over it than Ray Milland had had over what he saw in *Man with the X-Ray Eyes*. Her head felt as hot as a solar panel.

"What was that?" one of the women said. Valeria hadn't heard anything, but she went out of the kitchen with the others. The loft was almost quiet and the dark backing of every head was turned toward a distant point where the enclosed bedroom lay and, beyond that, a second space that was unused and curtained off.

A woman's sobbing was sharply audible. It sounded weirdly out of place. Horrible. No one moved. Then it died down a little and a man's voice, hound-like, muffled or further away, could be heard baying and barking curses. The sobbing started up again, more desperate than before. A wave of idiotic laughter erupted by the stereo and from that point noise flowed back into the room.

Valeria was one of three or four people who headed for the bedroom.

The unfriendly hostess was leaning against the wall and sobbing. She had a story to tell.

A friend, an early arrival, was leaving, and she offered to unearth his coat from under the daunting mountain of coats that had been heaped on the bed. About to go in, her hand on the knob, it struck her that the bedroom door was closed. That was odd. Then she heard the low, coarsely grated notes of a voice. Someone was using the telephone, she figured. Still, she *did* have to fetch her friend's coat, so she slipped the door open—not enough to see in, but to listen for a second to find out whether or not it would be ok to intrude—and she heard this weird conversation.

"'Haven't you ever wondered *why* a man feels pleasure in picturing a woman as his captive?' the voice said, hoarser, more spitting and guttural. 'That the woman has been *coerced* in some way? That her resistance has been overcome, her will melted away. That she feels pleasure in *spite* of herself, as you are now. That a cry of pleasure is, as the expression goes, "wrenched" from her. The drugged woman. The woman dizzy with drink. The abducted woman. The woman filmed in the throes of agonized passion. In what way does a man's pleasure enter into all this? Don't you ever *think* about that?' he hissed. 'Don't you ever think about *anything*? In what way can a man be *aroused* by such images, seeing that, in all these cases, it's the *woman* who is fondled, kissed, penetrated, from whom pleasure is either compelled or drawn out.'"

Her ear was getting red and hot, stuck uncomfortably in the opening. The light of a lamp was visible, something twinkled like an orange star, and the longer he kept up his hoarse and hissing monologue, the more the bed began to yield its song of mechanical sighs and wheezes. And then a woman's moaning—a little sound with every in-and-out—began to twine through his harsh gutturals.

"'Is it even remotely possible that the exquisite shadings of lust aroused in men by these images can be accounted for by the impulse to conquer? The unthinkable truth is this: that, however blindly, the man must pass over into the woman and feel in himself the peculiar ecstasy of the seduced, the dominated, the conquered. A secret panel must swivel open in the man. An ordinary wall on one side, a tunnel on the other. Just as in a dream, where the dreamer is always everyone, he finds himself temporarily in that secret tunnel, wearing the woman's body as a disguise. At that moment, *her* spread legs are *his* spread legs. Her yielding is his yielding. As if the woman's body were a soft net into which they've both fallen. The dark nebula below her belly the only true ground of lust. Not true at all that a man's lust for a woman is objective. I'm wearing your body *now*. *My* will is *yours*—and every move I make I feel through *you*. Like *this*—and like *this*—and *this*. . . !'"

The woman's moans were now more like the cries, the other-worldly groans of a soul in torment. All at once she felt angry—that this was going on in *her bed*, at *her party*. It was escalating to the point where people were going to hear it.

She opened the door. A flash of body-shaped light bounded out of the bed, across the coat-strewn floor, toward the door. A sloping forehead, blond hair and big blond moustache, bared teeth, an expression in his eyes as if he might go for her throat.

Her voice was dry and quivering, but she managed to ask him to leave. She couldn't get another word out. Meanwhile, she was trying to get a glimpse of the woman (she couldn't stomach the possibility that it might be someone she *knew*), but his head and upper torso screened off everything but a bare knee glowing against some brown material.

"'I'll tell you once and I won't tell you a second time,' he said, his face so close he could have swallowed her head like a seedless grape. 'Stop mousing around this door!' She couldn't move. 'You want to know who's in here?' he said. 'That's it, isn't it? I can tell from your stupid expression! You've got a look on your face like margarine melting in instant mashed potato. Well, I'll tell you! It's your good friend, Janine! That's right! It's Janine Klinkowitz who's sighing her guts out in here and leaving her scent on someone's squirrel jacket! You didn't know that, did you! I didn't think so! Now go feed your guests their birdseed and stay the hell away from here!'"

She lost control of herself and began to cry. And the more she cried the more he talked. Janine may have walked in the door a so-called human being, he said, but now she was an animal. Four legs and fur, hungry and dripping. The thing she longed to *be*, longed to find in her dreams. But she'd have to wait her turn. Fifty *years* or more. . . .

He slammed the door in her face, hard enough to crack the wood from top to bottom.

The depressed woman (the longer she talked the clearer it became to Valeria that this was someone who ought to weigh one and one-half times her weight, who dieted to the point of starvation yet still-and-all dragged the lost weight around like a broken leg; and in the same way she'd overcome a couple of breakdowns yet still-and-all etc.) begged Valeria to do something. She didn't want to draw anyone's attention to what was happening, because the party would be a disaster. But they had to rescue her friend!

Valeria agreed without really being sure the friend *wanted* to be rescued and without knowing what she intended to do.

Valeria opened the bedroom door quietly while Becky Andropolos hid behind the curtained entrance to the unused second loft space.

Someone was kneeling on the bed, naked. She saw a tan upper torso, chicken-white, rather flat ass, tan legs doubled up, bent at the knee on either side of other limbs—paler and smoother ones— pinned underneath within a carpet of brown furs and dark velvets. The upper torso of the lower person was hidden from view.

The man was rocking forward and back, massaging into the open legs of the one below. The angle was deep and deliberate.

Valeria was taken aback, but not too taken aback to try to sort out the orientation of things. The palms of the one below—or one palm, the left one—seemed to be turned up. That suggested that the one below was on her back. But, on the other hand, she had the impression that the soles of the feet were *also* turned up, the toes pointed down. And that would put the woman on her stomach, the man swinging into her from the back. It was confusing, visually tangled.

The man stopped moving, rested in the saddle, apparently waiting for something to build up or pass off. He leaned back a little, exposing the woman to view for the first time: a round, strong jaw, strong neck, large, pale breasts soft as ice cream, bright pink nipples. Valeria had the impression of a large, forceful woman completely melted.

The man's face had also become visible, blond hair and moustache lit up, long, sloping forehead gleaming. Her suspicions were both confirmed and put in doubt. There could be no denying that the man bore an uncanny resemblance to the man behind the wheel of the red Mercedes. Yet she had the impression that it was no more than that.

He pulled out of the woman, began stroking her here, insinuating a finger there. That went on for a few minutes. Then he began licking and sucking her between the legs, like a dog grooming its paws, its fur. The woman's breasts grew firmer and more pointed, the nipples taking on a darker shade of hardness. Her hips started doing jerky push-ups. She shuddered, threw her head back, began to give off the usual tormented cries of pleasure, as if from a dungeon within the lamplit shell of things. The man climbed on her again at once, began riding her so violently, like a grown man on a child's rocking horse, that furs and velvet capes flew off the bed. The woman's legs, spread as wide as possible, butterfly style, trembled from the impact. Her hand gripped the side of the mattress.

Valeria could tell that the crucial moment was about to arrive. The woman was about to give out the sharpest of human cries, like the instant when four blackboards of dense calculations yield the longed-for equation.

"Excuse me," Valeria said, "but you're creasing my Aunt Grete's silver fox chubby."

The woman jumped as if stung, made a choked, coughing noise and rolled over, covering herself with a black cape.

The blond man swung himself over to a sitting position on the side of the bed facing Valeria and stared at her while calmly reaching for a blue packet of cigarettes on the nighttable. His gaze, while not filled with the animal ferocity the depressed hostess had described, *was* filled with something beyond the usual range of expressions. He looked perfectly "human," she thought, and yet she found herself remaining silent rather than uttering the threats and ultimatums she was supposed to.

She stood there so long that the man had time to light a cigarette and blow out a good round cloud of blue smoke, all the while staring at her in the same intense, unreadable way. It was only when she heard a commotion behind her that she forced herself to give the man a warning, closing the door on a gaze so physical that it was like slamming a door on someone's hand.

Several minutes later a group of men entered the bedroom. Only the woman was still there, fully dressed, sitting in a chair, putting on her shoes. The blond man had left by the route of window and fire-escape.

The woman had been bundled off in a taxi by Martina. This was both strange (Martina had never voluntarily done anything for anyone) and annoying (while everyone else was guessing and cracking jokes, Martina was finding out what happened). Nadja didn't seem to know that anything had happened. She was content to sit curled up on the couch with her head on Valeria's shoulder and listen to other people talk.

Someone said that the whole thing reminded her of a dream she'd had not long ago. In the dream she wasn't herself, but a friend, a young actress with a pliant, olive-shaped face, full lips, unusual, transparent green eyes, and a nice mane of thick chestnut hair, who'd recently landed a job on a soap opera. A man was making love to her in a coarse, uncomplicated way. She was completely undressed, lying back on a low, wide bed. The man was shirtless, but wearing pants of some rough material she could feel against her leg. He was lying sort of half beside her and half on her. Despite the fact that she was already thoroughly aroused and ready, he didn't enter her but continued to stimulate her, coldly and carefully. His face slipped under her arm, his mouth filled with what seemed to be a whole breast—the nipple hard and radiant in his mouth, almost in his throat, which seemed to be trying to pull it down and swallow it. At the same time, a thick finger was slipped in, sending waves of light through her body. She was like a television. It hardly mattered what he did. Even his mistakes sent bright bands and diagonal shadows across her screen.

She remembered whispering in his ear something like this:

"Nobody—*nobody* has ever given me such—I don't know—such. . . !"

And he said: "Pain?"

She was surprised, and yet it didn't seem *completely* odd to hear him say that.

"Pain? It isn't pain. At least I don't *think* it's pain. . . ."

Then she saw a ten year old boy in a blue bathing suit—one of the neighbor's children, a dark, handsome boy with large warm eyes—standing in the door and watching. There may have been other children behind him, all familiar children she'd seen in the morning on her way out or in the evening, when she returned from staff sessions or rehearsals.

The man looked over his shoulder, turned back to her expressionless, and continued to build up the oval rhythm of his finger, like someone mixing one of those batters where one egg yolk after another gets stirred in. She couldn't resist, despite the fact that they were being watched by children she'd be seeing tomorrow.

Then the door was closed. The children were gone. And the man (naked now, no longer wearing the same rough trousers) slipped onto her belly and proceeded to enter her in the conventional way. Unfortunately, she woke before coming to orgasm. Her face felt odd, beaten up, as if it were black and blue.

Everywhere you go, Valeria thought, people are reciting their dreams. It made her glad that no one had given her the opportunity to recite hers.

Nadja lifted her head from Valeria's shoulder as if she'd been suddenly awakened. It seemed there was a message she'd forgotten to pass on. Mother had been trying and trying to get in touch with her, she said. It had something to do with phone calls from people who hadn't been able to reach Valeria at her own number. One man who'd asked if they were the Florescus who had a daughter named *Valeria* Florescu who lived in Jersey and worked at such-and-such a laboratory and had once published such-and-such a paper. And mother had actually begun to answer, "oh no, she doesn't *work* at that laboratory any more," before it dawned on her that she didn't have any idea who she was *talking* to. Also, Sandor Gura was down from Cambridge with his new wife, who was a chemist and not

much older than Valeria. *Mother* said that *Sandor* said that there
were laboratory jobs to be had up there and healthy athletic
activities and plenty of single *scientists*. The long and short of it was
that mother wanted Valeria to come the night she had the Guras
over for dinner.

Valeria decided to call home at once and went to the bedroom,
where she'd spotted a yellow telephone on the bedside table.

The soft edge of the bed sagged under her with such bottomless
sogginess that she thought of the dark-eyed, gloomy hostess who
slept here—and of the strange way things showed you someone's
essential being.

She began to dial her parents' number, then changed her mind
and replaced the receiver. She leafed through her little red address
book as if searching for god-alone-knew-what. She came across
Liam Lenahan's number, hesitated for a moment, took the yellow
telephone in her lap and called.

A woman answered, out of breath, as if still laughing during some
pleasant exertion. Her voice was crisp and lilting, a shade deeper
than Maureen O'Hara's in *The Magnificent Matador*. Liam's name,
called from one room to another, upstairs, or out a window into open
space, reached Valeria with a peculiar, deadened magnification, as
if the woman had stood back from the receiver, her voice travelling
in the empty zone between one real thing and another.

A man's voice clicked on. Liam was out on the storage shed roof,
he began, tacking down some loose shingles. . . .

The man sounded big, gelatinous, maybe alcoholic. How was it
possible, she asked, for him to be outside fixing shingles at this hour
of the night. . . ?

"Hang up, Tom!" the woman's voice could be heard barking in
the tunnel-distance of the telephone's other-world-in-this-world.
There was a click and a second later Liam's voice came on, oddly
similar in shading to his sister-in-law's.

Liam was so happy to hear from her, so willing to drive into
Manhattan to meet her, that she was a little sorry she'd called.

LOAFING OF A DIFFERENT KIND

Valeria had an hour to kill before Liam could possibly arrive, no matter how he flew above the cracked and gummy roadways. In this way she found herself walking through the chilly darkness with Nadja and two men toward some artists' bar.

"A geographical solution is sometimes the only solution," Nadja said. She'd been talking about Deauville and an opportunity for a life of travel and luxury she'd supposedly blown years earlier. She was thinking about it again because of a phone call from a certain Baron Pauli.

Valeria said that she thought Nadja and Andy were happy—doing whatever it was they did out there by the ocean.

One of the men wanted to know what sort of name Pauli was. Italian? Did they have "barons" in Italy? The guy in *The Barefoot Contessa* was Italian, Rosanno Brazzi—and obviously he was a count.

Nadja was pretty sure Baron Pauli was Austrian. Either Austrian or Swedish. Valeria was certain he was Polish.

Wasn't it possible that the solution to Nadja's malaise might lie (as it often did) in the opposite direction from the one that tempted her? the other man asked. Walking next to Nadja, an outsized mahogany camera case over his caramel leather shoulder, the man (a photographer named Karyl who matched Nadja in what might be called the tanned-and-ruddy physiological symbolism of good health) looked at Nadja with undisguised disapproval. When life began to bore him, when he sensed the approach of that cyclical lethargy that slipped up out of things, a sort of inevitable self-cancellation, a mechanism through which things all-too-rapidly wore out their authenticity, as if absolutely nothing could or should be done more than once, he forced himself to work not less but *more*. Re-examined his professional life to see what had gone wrong. What set of habits he'd slipped into that had drained away the original pleasure.

Nadja had been loafing a long time, there was no getting around *that*, Valeria laughed. She was really thinking: easy to criticize laziness. But how would Karyl's brand of work-as-salvation-ism respond to ambition on a scale not permitted on the part of anyone you actually knew. Permitted, that is, only for mysterious and distant others.

It was hard to make yourself understood, Nadja said good-naturedly, but—could anyone understand this?—it seemed to her there was another *kind* of laziness. Laziness of a higher order.

"No," Karyl said, "I don't see what your solution is."

"Oh, I don't think it's so hard to understand," the other man disagreed. "She's talking about *money*—only she doesn't know it."

It never failed to amaze him, Karyl said, how deep-rooted the human inability to live in reality was. The number of people who truly wished they could live in *Gone with the Wind* was astonishing.

Valeria said that she had to question what it meant to "live in reality." Reality now had to compete with many realities.

They'd long since reached the artists' bar. While the others were too cold to stand outside, Valeria decided to wait for Liam on the sidewalk.

"Call me!" Nadja sang out with an irresistible plaintiveness as she disappeared down the shallow flight of steps that led below street level.

EVERY COHERENT REALITY FALLS APART

Liam was driving a dark green Cadillac lined with green glove leather. When the curb-side door swung open and she saw his yellow-brown curls and pinkish cheeks within the car's green shade she felt as if she'd been offered the antidote to an illness she didn't have.

Hardly a word was said during the drive back to New Jersey. The silence of the green interior seemed profound and wonderful after the evening's talk, the balanced weight of the Cadillac repaving the world with a noiseless black rubber as they drove. She began to imagine that Liam had consciously chosen silence as a method of talking more authentically, more longingly than anyone else. While above, all was clear and artificial, the lucid sky of a planetarium.

Liam turned toward her, his face a fixed point that moved strangely across gray meadows, dark overpasses, factories the color of supermarket bags. He seemed on the verge of saying something he wouldn't be able to say. His eyes were brim full of a warm, dark and steaming substance, like the cups of instant coffee husbands invariably mistake for the real thing. But he shook his head, didn't say anything.

After a while he began to talk about his brother, Ambrose. He told a long story that seemed to explain how his brother came to be laid off. For years his brother had been buying up run-down rooming-houses, shabby bungalow courts, seedy bars. As if it gave him a chance to see his name on a long list of failures. Or to know that someone was driving along somewhere and seeing *Lenehan Bros.* up on some dump. Because he owned all that crap he was always on the look-out for a cast-off easy chair, a table with at least three legs. One day a friend, a certain jerk named Ollie Colleran, told Ambrose about a big, yellow couch some guy wanted to unload for twenty-five bucks. So Ambrose went with Ollie Colleran to this other guy's house to have a look at the yellow couch. When he got there he saw that the couch had been placed, for some very good reason nobody could remember, out on the second story porch. Somehow this pal of Ollie Colleran's had wedged the tremendous thing out there through a narrow door. It looked impossible, but he'd done it.

Ambrose saw that the thing was a little the worse for wear and had just a bit of that sour, vegetable stench you get from leaving things out in the damp of night. Still, he could picture a few good uses for it, and he and Ollie Colleran started measuring and calculating and trying to figure some way to get the damn thing through the narrow door and down the two flights of narrow stairs.

It couldn't be done, not even with the legs unscrewed, not even if they took the door off its hinges. Ollie's pal was just as mystified as they were—couldn't at all remember what the trick was. So Ollie and the pal were scratching their heads and examining the couch, looking for some secret hinge or seam where the thing might bend or separate—when Ambrose came up with the idea of lowering the couch (which really was as big as the king's own hearse, with its moth-eaten yellow velvet and its tassles) from the porch to the street with block and tackle.

He leaned over the railing to size the situation up and—bam!— the railing gave way. Ambrose fell forward. And as he fell he remembered what they taught him in the army. His training in parachute jumping flashed back on him. And he actually managed to land on his toes, to tuck in his chin the instant he felt the ground against the soles of his feet.

The tremendous mass of the earth rose up toward him with all the force of a moon rocket. Something cracked high up in his spine. He felt an unbelievable pressure in his throat, in his nose and ears, through his eyes: the whole body being stuffed into the head. And then he lost consciousness.

The next day, in the hospital, he woke up for a little while and a speck of blood showed up in one eye. Then both eyes were floating in blood like two soft boiled eggs and he lost consciousness again.

He was laid up for months and months and lost his job. Lost it and never was able to get it back. As if, while he was gone, his place in the world had closed up.

Liam left off. His voice had clogged up with emotion the way a piece of bread sops up gravy. His profile darkened against the fast-rolling video loop of New Jersey's oil refineries, factories, discount shoppingt stritps, spacious gas station plazas, its meadows luminous as toilet bowl cleaner, its television relay towers and mysterious installations.

Valeria thought guiltily: the bottomless well of other people's lives. Which threatened to drown you when all you wanted was a sip of water.

The longer they drove in silence the more his face darkened, until it resembled a thick, disc-shaped jellyfish with deep drops of iodine color in it. Something about this dark and troubled cloudiness reminded her of Lana Turner's face, a sort of make-up compact of melancholia (or was it only the expression that seeped into her mother's face when Lana Turner movies were on television?), a generalized unhappiness bound to produce unhappy events.

He seemed to have put himself in his brother's shoes, she said. That was morally "good," she guessed. But what was the point?

Chances are all his brother needed to solve his problems was a little money.

Nobody's problems were ever solved by money, Liam said. If you'd ever known any people who had it, you knew that being like them was no solution. Just because people drank from it gladly didn't mean that the well wasn't poisoned.

In other words, Valeria said, the solution was for everyone to be poor and miserable. The lucky few should throw away their money and their happiness for the sake of the poverty, the misery of others. He wanted to stand the eternal pyramid on its head. In place of the climbing that had gone on over the millennia, a universal dripping of failure and dreariness down over all.

Liam surprised her. That was *exactly* how he felt, he said. He'd sooner see everyone miserable than only a handful happy. The only truth was at the bottom. Everyone above the bottom was a fool trying to earn what could only be given.

Valeria couldn't answer because she didn't understand.

Nothing else was said for miles.

It seemed to Valeria that they'd been following the red taillights of the same dark blue sedan from the moment they'd passed through a certain pleasant mountain town with an amiable New-England-style main street, modish shops, air of casual and happy money, square with duck pond and willows within a surprisingly high crook of green mountains, so unlike the standard New Jersey landscape one's first thought was that the green mountain had been imported like a vine-wrapped ball of cheese.

A car had been following them, she told Liam a few miles outside of town, as they wended their way upward along multiple, tree-filled curves. Or, not exactly *following* them, but fleeing a certain fixed distance ahead as if guiding them.

But how could a car follow them while in front. . . ? And the road was clear before and behind.

The taillights had disappeared quite suddenly a few hundred yards back, she said. Swallowed by a turn ahead of them, they hadn't reappeared. She wanted to double back and have a look.

Reluctantly (he didn't at all understand why it mattered if a blue sedan had been running along ahead of them, following the same scenic route home) Liam pivoted the weight of the Cadillac across the road and turned around. They found a narrow car path.

Liam was all for heading home. He listed reasons.

Valeria listened indifferently. Through the dense screen of trees she saw a round, black stone of water shining below, like another sky at the bottom of the short diagonal tunnel of the path, barely wide enough to accommodate the great width of the Cadillac.

The short, straight line of sight unfolded into a long series of deep and uneven turns, far steeper than she'd anticipated, and mined with profound hollows. The headlights cut such a straight and narrow path and there were so many turns that they lurched downward by guesswork and instant swings. They kept scraping the undergrowth and veering on and off the shoulder. Once or twice animals that were low to the ground, gray and bushy, bounded across their path, virtually under the wheels. Another time Liam guessed wrong and wheeled into a dead end clearing. Four or five deserted buildings stood out in their lights against a solid lattice of vegetation packed with an infinite number of entrance points to the unknown. Darkness flowed out along the ground from under the buildings, filling up all the weak and ambiguous spaces in things.

Circling and re-circling, as if over the same ground, they arrived at the bottom, where the path fanned out and disappeared into a broad tract of mud puddles. There were a number of closed barnlike structures and some derelict machinery but no blue sedan. Beyond the barns the lake flowed out from the here-and-now into the distance, through an hourglass rift between stands of birches, toward a twin, sister lake and far-distant wooded slopes.

The lake was large and spectacular, the sky extending above it telescopically, looking distant and magnified, the way Kansas City looked to Kirk Douglas and Dewey Martin in *The Big Sky* when they saw something like an oval plain of fierce and tiny sparkles as they approached in their buckboard from the zone of low hills above. To them the city looked as far away as a second night sky, a kind of real and man-made other Nature of possibilities. Valeria was overcome with feelings that were exactly the same and utterly different, as if, up there. . . .

The sensation was so insupportable that it instantly degenerated into thoughts about applying to astronaut training school in Houston, where women, scientists like herself, were now being accepted.

She rolled down her window. The earth was voluptuously moist, redolent of bark, wild spices and root stocks, as if it had been shovelled up from five feet down. Something she took to be desire (a volume of sensation exactly equal to the volume of the other, unbearable but hard-to-name emotion?) flooded her skin. She put her arms around Liam and leaned into a kiss. Liam's body gave a tiny but perceptible jump, as if he were experiencing the ultimate longed-for meaning of the kiss, a sub-atomic bombardment of souls.

Valeria thought of the expression: "a little beast." She pictured herself with her face between his legs and his face between hers.

Face down, her cheek resting on Liam's pale yellow sweater, she was a double heart: pale heart of the ass concealing a dark inner heart between the thighs, an ideal animal of perspiration. One animal under another, meeting for the first time on lawn or beach, under trees or black sky, membranes smooth and hot, a slippery salmon rose.

As he bent over her and moved into her, he gave a sigh and a little shudder of surprise, as if god-alone-knew-what had unraveled. She turned her face and looked back at him: his cheeks were pink, almost infantile. It was true that the regularity of their rocking together did evoke the rocking of a veiled baby carriage on a sunny afternoon in summer, the world perfectly full, the dazzling shadow of everything up to and including the vague rustling of space as it defines its horizons, time, memories weaving themselves into your future, the caressing rhythm of a voice that echoes the creaking rhythm of the carriage.

She began to move more athletically, compelling Liam to do the same. Her face lost its contented smile, her body gained the tensile strength of a black rubber ball. She felt herself grow more muscular, as if they were rowing the same fast boat, then less and less muscular with every stroke, more pliant, like a large, saturated cloth being wrung out by unknown hands, audibly giving up dark curls of moisture.

Her convulsions were so strong that she could feel muscles in her buttocks pulsing against his stomach. She tasted the sour wool of the sweater between her teeth, soaked through as if she'd been chewing it for minutes.

She straightened up and leaned back. Her head was on his shoulder. His hands were around her waist. They kissed with passion, she raised and lowered her hips: a mild sensation for her, a powerful one for him. He let out a painful groan like a bent nail being torn from a block of wood.

Valeria stood on the cold grass and shivered as she pulled on her clothes. She felt as if she had less than one dimension. Cold air passing across the back could be felt at the same instant passing across the front. Barely a screen of particles. She thought: every reality, no matter how coherent, swiftly fell apart. A sense of coherent experience lasted only so long as the self seethed up with its own density. And this was our closest, disappointing approximation of the miraculous—the longed-for intrusion of the unexpected, the super-real that, so we'd been told, once-upon-a-time really did walk the Earth, stalking individual destiny.

A profound chill rose from the black earth that disappeared into the forest, carrying bark spices and the sharp aroma of lumber rotting back into nature. It was dark in every direction. The lake below looked like the slope above.

A yellow light suddenly appeared in the distance, gliding laterally. A car (the blue sedan?) on a road circling the other side of the lake? Its two headlights condensed by distance into one yellow, smooth-sailing sphere. Or a boat on the water, the sound of its motor drowned by something one might as well call distance.

Something about either of these possibilities sent a shiver along her skin. She looked over at Liam. He was asleep on the back seat. She slipped in behind the wheel and they set off up the narrow, curving path toward the highway.

F O U R

"TIME ORPHANS EVERYONE"

Valeria spotted an opening and backed in sharply. The tire squealed along the curb and, when she'd parked, she saw that the air valve on the right rear tire had been damaged. She concluded that she wasn't at all in the mood for a family dinner. And, beyond that, that she felt fundamentally displaced. She didn't feel like anyone's child any longer, and not only in the way that time orphans everyone, whether the parents are alive or dead. It was as if everything that one called "The World," the pleasantly overdone furnishings of the lobby and the infinity of familiar surfaces that led the usual multiple life of real places (set of physical memories for you, vacuous corridor of details for others) had an uncanny connection with her parents and all of it adding up exactly to what she hadn't had a hand in creating. Or, still worse, what claimed to have created *her*. The future, however blank and remote, felt closer to her than this.

Her parents' door opened into a bright frame of shimmeringly swollen furniture. A thousand-pipe organ of polished and absorbent textures that unfailingly gave off its one perfect note.

She placed half-a-dozen roses in her mother's hands, cutting short her sourish welcome. Marika and Armand were expected (they were bringing the Guras), she said, Martina *never* came and always had plausible reasons, but something had definitely come over Nadja. It wasn't at all like Nadja not to come down to see Sandor.

Valeria offered helpfully that something had come over everyone lately.

They were on the living room's sea blue rug and Valeria was saying her hellos to and receiving them from Aunt Elena and Uncle George, Aunt Grete, pale, worn-out Uncle Sylvan and an unfamiliar man who rose in several shades of blue (blue shirt, blue tie, blue slacks, each shade a bit darker than the other) from the voluminous black naugahyde reclining chair anchored in a thick aluminum post—a somewhat clumsy-looking piece of no-longer-modern-looking "modern" furniture, but comfortable enough if you didn't mind spending the evening gazing at the point where the ceiling met the wall.

The stranger was introduced (beamingly, by her mother) as Humberto Vilanescu, a fellow Rumanian who'd come their way— through whom? There her mother was stymied—and she turned to the man, saying that she'd forgotten if it was Cousin Leonhard or her sister-in-law's eldest son, Thomas, who he was acquainted with.

"Actually, neither," the man said simply and politely, with a complex accent. "It was your brother-in-law's good friend, Edgarz Lupeni—who I met once or twice in a business way in Montevideo—and then had the good fortune to run into again in New York, quite by accident, in the Westdeutsche Landesbank office on Park Avenue."

Valeria had time to take note of at least three things about this "Humberto Vilanescu" during the brief exchange with her mother. First was the fact (either positive or negative) that he'd been chatting with Uncle Sylvan (whose dark blue eyes were the only element of either looks or personality that kept him from being totally invisible) without the usual yawn or smirk. Second, was the fact that he'd risen to greet her and that he'd then chatted comfortably with her mother. Third, she observed the characteristically aggressive South American head, the vigorous, Cuban-style moustache, above a somewhat soft body in all those shades of blue: a physical contour she didn't find particularly alluring. All of which brought her to a fourth observation: that there was something oddly boring, more-or-less prematurely *aged*, about a man (would one describe him as young? no-longer-young?) who knew, or still worse who *had dealings with*, a business contact of her uncle's.

The man subsided back into the voluminous black chair and Valeria began to explain to her mother that the roses had been delivered to her this morning. Her doorbell had rung and she looked out her window and saw a green florist's truck with yellow lettering at the curb. She was handed a long, white box. Inside, adrift in green florist's paper, were six crimson blots, darker and redder than mouths in lipstick ads. The card inside read:

> "WHEN KISSES BRING BRUISES"
> *An Admirer*

It annoyed her, but the van was gone and she hadn't bothered to memorize the florist's name.

She made a few useless phone calls, but no one admitted to having sent them.

Her mother was disturbed and her father seemed to be disturbed because her mother was disturbed. Uncle Sylvan reproached Valeria for telling that sort of story. They were all like that now, he said. Had to say what was on their minds, no matter what.

The newcomer in blue said that every age had its dominant principles. Assuming for the sake of argument that Uncle Sylvan was right and that sort of honesty-for-honesty's sake *was* one of the dominant principles of our age, then taking offense at such honesty was like being offended by an earthquake. Nature and History had this in common: they were the abstractions that explained everything and made explanations useless.

Aunt Grete said something about the premature old age that had begun in Sylvan's cradle. Her mother wondered aloud if it could have been Valeria's old friend George who sent the flowers. He'd called and left a message, which she'd noted down with the others on the pink pad on the telephone table.

Valeria found herself talking about the damaged air valve. Her father began to get fatherly and automotive and she thought: it was hopeless. In relation to your parents you could never grow up. Never. You could convince yourself that this attitude or that was evidence that time if nothing else had somehow solved the insoluble, but you'd just found a new way of lying. Sentimental warmth, affection, tolerance, amusement, distance, irritation, fury, obsessive grievances: they all added up to the same thing: posing in the face of the inalterably alien.

The stranger offered to lend a hand.

The perfect gentleman, Valeria thought. Boring traits like these were bound to make a big impression on her father, who was a real connoisseur of boring traits, but they left her cold.

On the way down she learned how the Latin-sounding "Humberto" came to be linked with the Rumanian "Vilanescu." While he was indeed born in Rumania, he said, in the delightful mountain city of Cluj, he'd spent his youth in Uruguay and considered himself (aside from somehow appearing) South American. Neither Uruguay nor South America as a whole could be remotely considered the breeding ground of the future. To pursue his interests in communications theory and communications technology, advanced astrophysics, particle physics, gerontology, optics and lasers, he'd been compelled to leave his adopted country and venture to Germany and Japan, China, The British Isles, the Soviet Union, Switzerland and now the States. Our ideas about places (or the historical significance of places, their relative location, so to say, as islands of the past or future), tended to remain fixed—while places regularly switched identities. China, for example, was no longer "China" in the same sense that we apprehended it in the sixties. A certain outpost of possibilities had vanished—no doubt even before Nixon set foot on Chinese soil. Where "China" was actually to be found now was another matter.

Valeria spoke about the potent and melancholy illusion that afflicted the most ambitious spirits of every age: that the future actually lay in a given place.

They came out into the night and stopped to admire the sky (a peculiarly tourist-like posture, heads craned upward as if the world were a museum of interpenetrating panoramas and close-ups). The moon was hidden in white clouds, sailing swiftly through the high, arroyo-like intervals where it shone out briefly, vanishing at once through a lightning-like rift and diffuse rainbow.

The soft-spoken and courteous dinner guest said: now things were in their first flush of green. This surge was so powerful that even the city's deep-dyed sourness couldn't stand up against it. This was the moment that impaled the garden variety stroller-in-the-street with longings from the catalogue of standard longings. An ice pick of cliches that, true-or-false, pierced the heart. He, on the other hand, preferred the second surge of green late in May when cherry blossoms, lilac blossoms and azaleas dissolved into the earth and a darker green began to soak up light.

Valeria was only half-listening. Someone across the street, far enough away so that X^n transparent veils of shade added up to real darkness, threw away a lighted cigarette. It followed a shallow arc over the flat dome of a dark sedan, ending as sparks in the gutter.

It seemed to her that the man who'd thumbed away the cigarette had then retreated into a dark block of something shoulder-high—what appeared to be hedges, though as hard as she tried she couldn't recall any hedged facades along the familiar clean-shaven surface of the building line.

The dinner guest (who was already kneeling at the curb) broke into her thoughts by asking for her tool kit. She fetched it from the trunk and he fiddled around with a wrench and some black tape, then stood up, brushing off his hands.

He'd probably fixed it well enough so that it would get her home, he said.

A cold current of air from the East River passed across the sidewalk square where she was standing. He lit a cigarette while she shivered. The short white cylinder wagged in his mouth under his strong moustache.

She remarked on the kindness with which he'd tolerated Uncle Sylvan's complaints, medical bulletins, helicopter-borne traffic reports.

Not at all, he said. On the contrary. Every shell had its meaty kernel. For him, naturally, Uncle Sylvan wasn't "Uncle Sylvan" but a man, who, for some reason, wanted to talk about his dead wife. He'd spoken rather touchingly of the woman's love of animals. Someone had, for example, once made her a gift of a large turtle, but she didn't know how to feed it. So she called the Bronx Zoo and they said: raw meat and whole grains. The turtle liked these things—seemed to be particularly carnivorous, in fact—and also had a taste for peeled and sectioned oranges. It continued to grow and she phoned the zoo again and they said: "it seems that someone's played a nasty trick on you. What you're raising as a pet, like a common box turtle or painted turtle, is actually a loggerhead turtle or alligator snapping turtle. The thing will eventually weigh a couple of hundred pounds or so. It's powerful and may turn vicious."

She'd grown extremely fond of it and couldn't part with it even though friends had begun to find it rather frightening and though her little cocoa-colored poodle, Pandora, had never taken a shine to it. Ordinarily she took the dog with her when she went out (it was small enough to be carried about in a wicker picnic hamper) but one day she was invited to a luncheon where it was simply out of the question.

She returned home quite late, entered the house and instantly found it strange that Pandora hadn't come bounding and squeaking to greet her. She went through one room then another, calling the little dog's name. At last, in the bedroom, she found it on an oval yellow-and-green throw rug, its stomach sliced open from one end to the other—and ten times as much blood on the rug and the wood floor as you'd think a tiny creature like that could contain.

The turtle was later discovered hiding under a table, with telltale stains on its beak.

She had to have it put to death and mourned her dog and her turtle. Didn't Valeria find that moving?

She almost asked aloud (but thought better of it): had he ever had the feeling that, while he was moving through life to all outward appearances the same as ever, some part of himself had become like a heavy railroad wheel fitted to the endless tongue of a rail—and that no matter what he did, this hidden wheel continued to carry him forward. She found herself thinking about her place in what someone had called "the dense historical moment of the present."

Instead she found herself asking if he didn't find it depressing that still another weary truism was true: one individually could change nothing. The actions that seemed to genuinely push things forward required a cliché of feeling—an emotion that stirred millions in exactly the same way and with at least as much force as the craving for a new brand of cigarette. Yet these mass activities left you feeling empty. Annihilated.

"Right now everyone is depressed and annihilated from that sort of wave of feeling—and a mild one at that. . . ."

By way of answer he puffed on his cigarette, seemed to be studying her, then offered to drive her car to a service station so that she could rejoin her family.

She'd take her chances with the tire and have it repaired in the morning, she said. They could both go back in.

No, he said. He preferred to remain downstairs a little longer—smoke another cigarette—take a short walk. His cigarettes were quite strong and he didn't want to poison the atmosphere upstairs.

He offered her a cigarette from a blue box.

She showed some surprise that they smoked the same uncommon brand.

"I could tell you an interesting story about two people who discovered that they smoked the same brand," he laughed in a way she wasn't sure she understood.

She glanced back from the entrance. His dark outline gave off a mild blue radiance, a tiny orange point between his lips, blue smoke rising into the weird pinkish orange of the streetlamp.

LOAFING OF A DIFFERENT KIND (2)

Dinner had been delayed because Marika and Armand, and the Guras with them, hadn't arrived. Everyone was sitting in the living room, gingerly wading into the shallow edge of Uncle George's strong martinis and talking about Nadja.

Valeria sighed (knowing that at some point she would have to decide whether or not to bother taking up Nadja's "defense") and took her place within the sphere of light of the tall tutu-shaded lamp that was busy drawing everything into the familiar orbit of the visible. Not *quite* as careful and believable, as wonderfully appropriate to what happens in them, perhaps, as the rooms in films and soap operas, but still and all glowing inwardly with a deep-dyed reality she found oddly far-away. It was a little like the dream-feeling of seeing people one knew and loved, yet being as utterly displaced as if one were a traveler from a future time.

It seemed that Valeria's mother and her Aunt Elena (Valeria's father reluctantly in tow) had paid an impulsive visit to Nadja at the shore. They hadn't at all liked what they'd found.

Her father interjected that there was nothing to feel either surprised or disappointed by. The time for surprise and disappointment was long past. He didn't consider sitting on the beach, with a sun visor over your eyes and zinc oxide ointment on your nose, now and again resurrecting some idiot who didn't have the good sense to stay on dry land, an occupation. They had no more thought of the future than a sparrow or a ladybug. *Less.* Seeing that a sparrow or a ladybug had the foresight to line its nest, its tiny hole in the earth, with crumbs for the winter.

Her father, who would ordinarily have been adrift in the deep glove of the black reclining chair, had left it empty in deference to the guest. He was poised, not altogether comfortably, on the edge of a blue-patterned Queen Anne chair.

It was interesting, Valeria thought, that while his face tended to look rather smooth, soft and neutral in memory, as well as in the somewhat more stable memory of photographs, with his healthy skin tone and gray moustache, in person his jaw grew rounder and more prominent, both a real expression and an emblem of an obstinate positiveness of opinion.

"In other words," Valeria said, "the sin that they've committed is that they're not insects." And if they lived without thinking about the future, didn't that prove that they lived without fear? Without the low-grade fear of things that had infected everyone. (Inwardly she knew that she might be telling the truth, but not about Nadja.)

"I'm sorry to have to disagree with you, Mr. Florescu," the complexly accented voice of the dinner guest said from the edge of the Bokhara rug—so that everyone turned to discover that he'd re-entered the apartment.

"I make it my business never to contradict my host," he said politely. "But there are birds and birds, insects and insects. There are other birds than sparrows, after all, and other insects than the familiar little ladybug, with its attractive orange elytra. How some of these other creatures survive through the harsh months of winter, what they line their nests with and drag with them into the depths of the earth, Mr. Florescu, is not necessarily so neutral, so *benign* as you might like to think. And if your daughter isn't living as well as you might like, it may very well be because she lacks the necessary instincts without which one simply can't survive, let alone *flourish*, in the modern world. Not necessarily *predatory* instincts, as some people might say, but simply the instinct to gnaw on someone else, to take sustenance wherever it's necessary, to recognize a ladder upward when it presents itself—to think: 'better *he* should perish than I.'"

He ventured the further opinion that he and his wife had, like all good parents, filled their children's heads with all manner of moral precepts. So he could hardly blame them if they actually took some of these precepts seriously. Of course, if it persisted beyond the age of thirty-two or so, then one could start worrying about something abnormal, something stunted. Time generally solved all that.

Valeria saw her father's jaw subside into the smoothness, the opinionlessness that formed the essential background of his nature. Everyone else also fell silent, though whether in agreement, from trying to figure out what the man meant or from something else it was impossible to tell.

At last her mother burst out that no one understood what she was talking about. She didn't know Andy very well but she had nothing against him. She'd always known that Nadja was lazy and didn't expect her to accomplish anything, as Martina had and as she hoped Valeria would. If she disapproved of their way of life she wouldn't be happy that they'd finally begun to talk of getting married. What bothered her was something else entirely, something she'd never felt out there before.

Valeria made an effort to distract herself by paying attention to Uncle Sylvan, who appeared to have been sitting next to her all along, a teaspoon of powdered milk making the transparent tap water of his being visible.

She chided him for having told the story of Aunt Magda's turtle to the dinner guest but never to her.

His expression softened insofar as decades of looking aggrieved would allow, his eyes shone with sentiment.

He hadn't thought of Magda's animals for years, he explained. But tonight, when he got to talking with that pleasant young man, a few memories worked loose and rose to the surface. Which wasn't to say that he didn't remember things. He remembered so many things that he didn't think memory was the right word for it. So-called waking life was not so very different from sleep and dreams. All day long (so long as you didn't deliberately preoccupy yourself with something else) you passed over all-too-easily into a dissolving set of pictures, just as in dreams. That was, he supposed, exactly how death took you over, little by little your waking life simply merging with your dreaming life.

Valeria thought: it was as if the Uncle Sylvan she was used to, the one who droned on like a radio tuned to an all-day news report, was nothing but a coffin of the palest possible wood—in which *this* Uncle Sylvan was prematurely slumbering, breathing too shallowly to be noticed.

If he seldom thought of Magda's dog and turtle, he shrugged, it was because he chose not to. There were more pleasant memories after all. Just the other day he was thinking about the things Aunt Magda used to collect—the countless magazine subscriptions, the clothing, the shoes, *her* mother's clothing, etc. etc. And how he was still coming across things in the oddest places: not long ago he found a pair of white opera gloves folded up neatly and embalmed in a small blue tin that had once held (and still smelled faintly of) her favorite black Georgian tea.

It was no longer possible for Valeria to ignore the voices of her mother and her aunt, who, in the same thick-as-syrup yet singing tone (shared to a certain degree by Nadja) were in the midst of reciting the story of their visit to the shore.

Her mother was saying that, while Valery set himself up in a corner of the porch (their little apartment was in the back, on the second floor, with a big raft-like porch overlooking the usual gardens and trees) with Andy's portable television plugged into a yellow extension cord so that he could watch the golf match he was afraid he was going to miss, they were opening beach chairs and spreading blankets on the warm boards.

"'Oh good!' Nadja said in that sweet way she had about her. 'You're making yourselves at home!'"

"Yes," Aunt Elena said, "and *I* said: 'I've got to lie on this nice chaise lounge. Maybe *you* feel as young as your daughter—you feel up to lying on a blanket on these boards—but for an old lady like me—no—my back would say no to it. . . .'"

That brought a mild wave of laughter all around, but Valeria's mother went on impatiently, as if the last thing on her mind was to tell a story for the amusement of others.

It was possible to lie on the boards, Nadja said, because Andy had laid down some new ones over the old ones and the surface was pretty smooth.

Her mother said that that was when they found out that Valery was eavesdropping despite his horse race and his weekend newspaper. He said that Nadja ought to tell Andy to make it a general rule never to lay something new over something rotten. It didn't do in the end to try and live on such a surface.

She said that she'd asked Nadja why they were bothering with the porch at all. When they were married they would certainly (wouldn't they?) want something newer and more spacious.

"All Nadja said was: 'I told Andy I didn't think he had to do it. But Andy thought he did. He was up half the night, hammering and sawing. And this morning. Trying to make the place look halfway *something*, who knows what.'

"'You should have told him I wouldn't care.'

"Nadja said: 'Andy thinks you're a little skeptical.' Naturally your father (without putting down his newspaper or missing a volley of the tennis match) had to say: 'We *are* a little skeptical. But what difference does it make?' *I* said: 'Don't listen to him. We both like Andy. We just want you to be happy.'"

Nadja suddenly said she was going to take a sunbath. It was so warm, really summery, why didn't they all get into shorts or bathing suits and take a real sunbath together.

All at once she was very cheerful.

She didn't like that. But she got into her bathing suit (Elena and Valery refused, of course) and lay down next to Nadja on the thick blanket. While they were lying there together, glistening and grilling, Nadja said something to the effect that this made up for many things. For many other things that were lacking. When Andy was at work, in the mornings, she liked to lie here alone on a soft towel. The light shone off the rooftiles then, as wet as grass—blazed in the hot square of the white house front to the north, almost powerful enough to give you a tan. And the radiant heat from sand and water travelled in waves across the square well of the back gardens. The world was peculiar and helpful that way: if you examined a little area of it, a few trees and a sunlit wall, for example, framed off by this and that, you might be anywhere. The world abstracted itself so that you could delude yourself.

She didn't pay close enough attention to what Nadja was saying (it didn't strike her until later that she'd said some things that didn't sound like her), and she said: "I don't want Andy thinking I'm one of those awful mothers. I don't want to be in that position.

"'Maybe there's a geographical sort of happiness,' Nadja said. 'I'm at the beach—I'm not working hard, living like others. If I'm not where I *do* want to be, at least I'm not where I *don't* want to be.'

"Living like *what* others, Nadja? What's wrong with the way people live? Work is not a sin.

"'It's not a sin, but it's not a salvation either. Baron Pauli says that to work means to live abstractly. To work you have to be able to ignore the way you're living, your boredom, your sense of being used, and believe in the future, in weekends, in vacations, in retirement, the hereafter—anything but what actually fills your days.'

"That woke me up. I sat up straight and said: 'Baron *Pauli?* What does *he* have to do with it. . . ?'"

No one heard the doorbell ring, but the sound of fresh voices in the doorway (where the dinner guest, Vilanescu, stood, his hand on the door as if he'd just opened it) submerged the unexpected feeling of communion Valeria was enjoying with her mother. She wanted to say that she too had felt something amiss with Nadja and admired this flash of acuteness (however much it *was* a flash, as if only so much intelligence, so much seriousness, were permitted per evening). She intended to go out there and see for herself.

But everyone had risen and converged around Marika (who was burning bright as a candelabra in a flowered summer dress, orange platform sandals, white earrings and a white shoulder bag with a silver chain), Armand and baby Ian as they advanced into the room—onto the rug and into the light. Sandor Gura and his new wife followed just a little further behind and the blue-clothed, courteous dinner guest, Humberto Vilanescu, was barely visible in the shadows behind Sandor Gura's short, flossy white hair, bright, outdoorsman's skin tone and huntsman's forest-green chamois-cloth shirt.

"ONCE SOMETHING APPEARS IT'S BOUND TO APPEAR AGAIN AND AGAIN"

The tablecloth and place settings were exchanging radiant sparkles with the dining room chandelier. Marika, facing a row of men, sang out with contentment: "Oh yes, the very first grandchild in either family!" She'd been keeping a sort of journal about Ian, an entry a day in the boxes of a UNICEF calendar. The first entry was made in the hospital the day she gave birth. "Childbirth: euphoric experience!" The next day she wrote: "I'm still high. Can it last?"

And had it lasted? one of the men asked.

"Oh, yes. Yes!" She described her new-found tranquility.

They made it easy to despise them, Valeria thought, for reasons

one might be hard put to express. They made a handsome couple.
The likes of them was seen everywhere, in restaurants and theaters.
The good-looking professional man with the case-weary eyes. The
attractive wife, a sticky little program of this or that "look."
Together they succeeded in fashioning a life that was like a
handsomely produced magazine of culturally appropriate attitudes,
neither lagging nor advanced by so much as five minutes. Even their
complaints sounded oddly like bragging.

"Childbirth may very well be euphoric," Humberto Vilanescu
said. "But the childish longing of the bride on her wedding day, the
tragic look of happiness that wells up in her eyes when she turns
her face up to the groom, soft and moist as the first bite of wedding
cake, still has in it more of a cosmic wave of feeling, like a distant
ripple from the deepest ocean basin, then anything she's likely to
feel for the rest of her life."

Armand reproached Marika for making her mother unhappy.
Since everyone knew that a mother's greatest pleasure lay in
worrying about her children.

The dinner guest, Vilanescu, put in his oar. The worrying of
mothers had a deeper meaning than their son-in-law suspected. It
was, in fact, a very practical kind of prayer, a kind of talisman to
ward off bad luck and demons. And it rested on a bit of wisdom
passed on in trivial forms over the ages: that nothing ever happened,
nothing went either right or wrong, in the direction in which you
happened to be gazing. So that worrying was a limited warranty
that everything was bound to turn out alright.

Limited in what way? Sandor Gura wanted to know, almost as
blue-white and freshly sparkling as Marika's diamond ring.

"The person you're worried about may be threatened by something you have no idea of. In which case your worries wouldn't
apply."

Valeria began to be a little impressed: the man had succeeded in
stealing Armand's thunder. So much so that her father uncon-
sciously turned his attention to him rather than to Armand.

"I hear that you're acquainted with my brother's associate,
Edgarz Lupeni," he said. "And that he's in New York, doing

business. You ran into him in the Oak Room if I'm not mistaken, or at the Banco do Brasil office on Fifth Avenue."

"Did I say the Oak Room?"

"No," her mother said, "you said a bank, but not the Banco do Brasil office—another one, on Park Avenue."

"Actually, I think it was in The Palm. He gave the impression of stopping over very briefly on the way to Fort Worth and then on to Caracas."

Valeria found herself taking a closer look at the man's face, lit up by a sparkling rosiness as much as by the thousand thousand reflective points of everything. A long, broad forehead, too rounded to look sloping, a somewhat parrot-like nose, strong chin—yet, in some hard-to-define way, not bad-looking. A head (so unlike Marika's, where dieting as a cardinal principle of existence, a more powerful impulse than eating, sex, breathing or anything else, had robbed the calm and domestic oval of her face of the slightest tremor of vitality), built on elemental structural lines of force. An implement, like a nutcracker.

Armand ventured the opinion that there were so many places called the Palm, Palm this and Palm that, that there had to be fashions in everything. In names, even in diseases.

"Just recently, for example, we've been having a strange wave of *eye* ailments. A regular epidemic—and no good explanation for it. I've been seeing eye ailments that I haven't seen since my student days—and even then, I saw no more than one or two cases. The bizarre case of the woman and the television set, for example—the one that made its way into the newspaper."

Aunt Elena pleaded with Armand not to tell a revolting medical story at the dinner table.

Armand looked startled, as if he *had* been about to relate something revolting.

Uncle Sylvan said that as far as strange ailments—he'd read in a magazine that the Earth was bombarded every day by all sorts of rays and particles—things we'd only just begun to detect. . . .

Valeria's mother remembered that they'd received some postcards from Martina when she was in Hong Kong several months ago.

From the Palmtree Hotel. So it was true that in any city you might travel to there was bound to be a Palmtree Hotel or a restaurant called The Palms.

"Las Palmas, Palm D'Or, Palm Grove. . . ," Uncle George put in, laboring to make a contribution.

Sandor Gura thought that, for obvious reasons, you found these Palm variants in the tropics with much greater frequency than in the north. Here it was a matter of evoking something, while down there the palm tree (of which there were a good twelve hundred varieties) was a significant feature not only of the landscape, but of several regional economies.

Valeria commented that it was apparently necessary, even in the tropics, to make you feel *as if* you were in the tropics.

"It's now impossible for anything to appear only once," Humberto Vilanescu began with authority. "Not only the names of things, but everything. Not one thing can come into being without being reproduced at once. It's not a law of 'nature,' perhaps, but it *is* a law of culture or of communication (which can now be said to amount to the same thing), that once something appears *it is bound to appear again and again*, a million or a hundred million times, in more and more distant ways, until it becomes extremely difficult to recognize. Reproduction is the new law of culture. The notion that one can do, say or create something unique—the unique work of art, the life of quiet and solitary achievement—is finished forever."

"In other words. . . ," Marika began.

In other words, Valeria said, there was no longer a difference between a way of life and a can of diet cola; an idea and a quarter pound of hamburger and pre-shredded lettuce you wolfed down in one of those fast food rhomboids that resembled space stations in the year 3000, when space stations would, of course, no longer resemble our idea of "space stations," would no longer appear strange and "modern," but would be shabby copies of a used-up adventure.

Armand said with feigned weariness that he'd been hearing such ideas for years. No idea was tireder than the one that announced the birth of a new era of alien values—and the obsolescence of all that one lived by. Every few years a new sage seemed to spring up, saying such things less and less intelligibly. But, still-and-all, things persisted. The future kept its distance. Perhaps others lived it—but never you or anyone you knew.

Valeria couldn't restrain herself. She couldn't imagine how they lived, she said. Even in Syosset one or two facts of existence must seep in. Everyone knew that, for the longest time, the age had been marked by a restlessness with the past, a hatred for history and the sense of living out the irrational dreams of vanished centuries. Now this restlessness had deepened. Everyone was restless not merely with the past, but with the present. Living in one's own time no longer felt sufficient. There was a sort of bitter jealousy of the future. The project of space travel had more to do with this emotion than with "space."

Humberto Vilanescu was the only one who agreed. "Yes," he added, "everyone is modern now. Everyone knows instantly everything that everyone else knows. And this can't help but pull us forward, like vacationers on water skis. What we used to call 'longings' are now realities. So that it's a natural step for everyone to feel that to remain on Earth, as Valeria suggests, is to be trapped in a present that merely continues without erupting into something new. Dostoevsky wrote that man fears a new word above all other things. I would add to that that history lurches forward only when a new word is uttered and the present is seen to be closed, a guarantee of death. Poverty and political oppression alone are not sufficient to explain the occasional violent leaps forward of history—since those conditions are ever-present.

"The rapid, multiple flashes that resolve into a single television image, the long-range projection of images, the abbreviated time spans of airplane and rocket travel have given us a taste of something that at least hints at immorality. We know that one day others will live a sort of microfilm existence: five hundred years speeded up and compressed into what we now perceive as sixty. Therefore, whenever space exploration becomes stalled a universal depression sets in, disguised as this or that local economic or political condition. The curse of death is now seen to be the curse of being Earth-bound. The 'Garden of Eden' is, in fact, the Universe."

It struck Valeria that the man with the strong, nut-cracker bone structure wasn't so much agreeing with her as acknowledging *her* agreement with *him*. It was clear that she hadn't said anything he hadn't already thought.

Aunts, uncles and parents looked on with that vacantly interested expression that actually expresses nothing. The outward manifestation of an inner emptiness that wells up with every glimpse into the limitless realm of what one simply doesn't understand. While the younger guests (all of whom Valeria tended to lump into one generation, though Armand was seven years older than Marika, and Sandor Gura was a good ten years older than Armand, despite his glowing skin and athletic bearing) seemed unaccountably disturbed.

Marika said that she'd never heard Valeria talk like this. Who, in heaven's name, had she been spending time with?

Valeria had always talked this way, her mother disagreed. Maybe not *exactly* this way, but always brilliantly and analytically. The scientist's mind, she supposed, was bound to be different from theirs. The scientist by definition ought to be thinking in terms of absolutes, ideals and possibilities. It was true, of course, that of all her daughters, Valeria was the only one she couldn't figure out.

She ended by looking vainly around the table for someone to second her opinion.

Valeria was more-or-less touched by her mother's feeble defense.

Marika said she *knew* that. She wasn't *talking* about that. No one questioned Valeria's *intelligence*. . . .

Armand said that Marika's point was that life as such seemed to hold no interest for Valeria. The daily existence of mere mortals.

No one mentioned the dinner guest, Vilanescu—as if he hadn't spoken. Or had been speaking on a frequency audible only to Valeria, who was shaken by what he'd said. The idea that others *would* live five, ten times as long as she would—perhaps along the purely technological lines of the vastly extended playing time, within a denser plane of fine grooves, of phonograph records slowed down from seventy-eight revolutions per minute to thirty-three. One thing wasn't clear: did he mean that the future lay in something she could *do*? In normal historical, sequential evolution? Or was it something that already lay out *there*, away from Earth.

It was as if a land mine of the obvious had gone off under her feet. Where there had been the reassuring or depressing smoothness of the taken-for-granted, there was now—what? Nothing, or the real possibility of an unimaginable way of life. It all depended.

She sought out Humberto Vilanescu's voice, with the hope of tunneling further out into this new region. But he was merely explaining to her mother that he was certain that the cards she'd received from her eldest daughter, Martina, had *not* been sent from the *Palmtree* Hotel, as she thought.

Her mother was certain that that was where Martina had stayed and written from. They'd had two or three cards, all with the name of the hotel clearly printed on them.

Her father said that Marianna was right.

Humberto Vilanescu insisted politely that, if they would only fetch them and take another look, they would see that it was the Peninsula Hotel and not the Palmtree.

Valeria's mother pushed back her chair and went to fetch one of the cards from its nesting place between the black sheets of the photograph album while her father inquired if this was some sort of parlor trick.

Valeria's mother returned, laid the glossy blue card on the table and said simply, "I don't understand."

Her father picked it up and at once cocked an eye on Humberto Vilanescu.

"Peninsula Hotel," he said and threw it down. There was a bit of a clamor.

There was no trick and no secret, Humberto Vilanescu said, his smile flashing affably. There *were* at least two explanations, one a little more complex than the other. He would leave it to them to choose.

The simpler explanation was that the Peninsula Hotel on Nathan Road in Kowloon, constellation of luxury, was the unofficial meeting ground for the fashion trade. A simple case of deductive reasoning.

The more complex explanation went like this:

Several years ago, at the invitation of a certain newly-formed German-Argentinean consortium, he attended an international telecommunications conference in Hong Kong. They put him up at the Peninsula. One was supposed to expect that. Not to expect it identified you as a stranger to those other worlds that existed in the midst of what we took to be "The World," but which remained utterly hidden from view. Each of them a kind of glass satellite that orbited overhead, beaming ideas and objects into daily life the way breezes once blew through open windows. And those who inhabited those near-distant spheres, while they may or may not have been human to begin with, sooner or later ended up resembling one another and no one else who'd ever lived.

In the particular other-world of the multinational corporation, what one ordinarily thought of as "money" meant nothing. Its existence was assumed, a sort of highway system. The truly priceless commodity in this realm was knowledge of a certain prescient type. Those like himself who could spoon the future on their plates so they could wolf it down before the general population even suspected its existence.

The conference turned out to be the usual pedestrian sociotechnological hash, and he found he had a good deal of time on his hands—time to have a drink at one of the bars, lounge in the lobby, dine in the Verandah Restaurant overlooking the harbor, lunch in the Marco Polo buffet. One person introduced you to another in the usual way, so that life soon took on its most desirable contour, a loosely woven fabric of possibilities, a subtly coherent twining of adventures.

One evening he found himself dining in Gaddi's, in the company of a striking, dark-haired woman in blue. The woman was a designer. While she now owned her own business, she said, it was only short years ago that she'd belonged to one of those familiar acrobatic pyramids: a couple of sharp-witted guys held aloft by the linked, muscular arms of a dozen talented women. Women who were willing to tolerate an astonishing amount of abuse, of out-right *theft*, in the hope of climbing from A to E and sooner or later from E to X. While the sharp-witted guys shifted among the peaks of the various pyramids.

For two years or so her boss had been stealing her designs. She acquiesced in this. It was infantile, she said, not to accept this elemental truth: that the things that were inevitably done to you, the times you were screwed, were *not* done for "evil" reasons, but for practical ones. In its own way, it was all quite fair and impersonal. Meanwhile she went about saving money and making contacts. Her boss must have gotten wind of her decision to launch out on her own, because he suddenly offered her a junior partnership and sweetened the deal with the offer of a trip to Hong Kong. She wavered and accepted.

On the plane he made it clear that a little joust with the bedsprings was on the menu.

The first night in Hong Kong they were in his room sorting out some figures for the next day's meetings. They had a couple of drinks. Next thing she knew everything was being unbuttoned, a cheek was pressed alongside a breast, a hand went under her skirt, hot lips nibbled a warm thigh. But the poor jerk must have put too much of whatever it was in her drink and she just passed out cold, a dead weight. She *assumed* the idea was to have the woman at least a *little* bit awake.

The next day she told him that she knew that he'd slipped something in her drink. He broke down. It seemed he'd never been able to make love to a woman in the normal way. He cried and cried. And the longer he cried, the younger he looked. As if he had been shaved clean from head to foot, his tears a magic depilatory that had removed the dense pelt of everyday business, of phony expressions. Before her eyes her boss turned into a tiny snail out of its shell, innocent and shiny, a glistening *escargot* who could nestle in the palm of her hand.

Humberto Vilanescu said that he kept quiet as long as he could contain himself and then he said: "In other words you're one of those women who have a soft spot for weak men. You reject a forthrightly aggressive nature yet lay yourself bare to some tomato worm, some crawling embryo with its low-grade misery, its caterwauling and weak suction. Five, ten or fifteen years go by and you wake up one pleasant spring morning and realize that you've been picked clean, as if ten thousand tent caterpillars have been nesting in your tree."

He could have said a good deal more. He knew the story of her life from beginning to end. But it was clear that even this tiny dose of the truth was offensive to her. Not another word was spoken through dessert, coffee and cognac.

They parted in the lobby, but not before he'd been introduced to a number of her colleagues. Among them, he was quite sure, there was a woman named Martina Florescu.

Valeria was struck at once by the uncanny consonance of the woman in blue with Martina. Therefore, at the same time Humberto Vilanescu seemed to be going out of his way to tell them that his path had crossed Martina's, he'd also gone out of his way to displace Martina from the center of his story to its margin. An assertion and its denial deftly welded together. But, in that case, why mention Martina at all? It was a little dizzying.

Valeria's mother said that she was confused. If he was saying that he definitely had met Martina in the Peninsula Hotel then how were they free to choose the first explanation?

Uncle Sylvan stirred and murmured: "Lost in space. They've lost another astronaut. . . !" His voice was the hoarse, clogged voice of someone who's awakened from a few hours of death, having slipped from life right at the dinner table.

It was impossible to persuade him that he hadn't been watching the Houston Mission Control Center on tv. Indeed, he was able to describe the Center's banks of video monitors, the exact nature of the messages relayed on the screens and through the speakers of its innumerable tracking devices, in convincing detail.

Humberto Vilanescu apologized for having, perhaps, inadvertently touched on subjects that had no place at the family dinner table, that sanctuary of unreality.

Valeria offered the opinion that what we now called "Space" would become a depthless industrial park where unknown projects already under way on Earth, with Earthly limitations, would be carried out with awesome purity and mathematical abstraction.

SUICIDE-IN-LIFE

Valeria leaned back, out of the conversation. This was the moment Amy Gura chose to touch Valeria's arm with the tips of her fingers and introduce herself. "I've been wanting to tell you for a while now," she said, barely audible, "that I admire the way you talk. You seem to hold your own so *easily*. . . ."

Was it really necessary to say "thank you" in return?

Meeting Valeria was a little depressing, she said. She'd always been able to blame her timidity (didn't everyone have a secret, idiotic explanation for such things?) on her small size. But nobody took those kinds of liberties with Valeria. For example: three years ago her parents prevailed on her to be maid-of-honor at some dopey cousin's wedding. It fell at a time when she absolutely had to master a certain caprice. Her summer time-table of etudes had been running just about on schedule until she agreed to be maid-of-honor. As soon as she said yes her concentration crumbled. Cold fingers, allergies, watering eyes, a swollen nose, anxiety: the familiar symptoms of an approaching bout of depression.

One day her aunt called and said: "Do you have a *pale blue* gown or a *bone* gown?"

"Of course not," she said. "What would I be doing with a bone gown *or* a pale blue gown?"

Her aunt had seen a *very lovely* bone gown at such-and-such a little store mid-town.

"Yes, a *bone* gown definitely. Bone would suit your neutral coloring—you make such a weak impression you'd *drown* in pale blue—and bone will blend in with the decorations."

Then, at the wedding, despite the fact that she'd spoiled a precious summer's practice just to make her aunt and her mother happy, despite the fact that she had actually gone shopping with her aunt for the very lovely bone gown and bone pumps, no one seemed to know she was there.

The next day her violin sounded odd. She examined it and found a tiny crack. She brought it down to New York to have it repaired at Wurlitzer's. They said that it wasn't only the crack, but the entire sound post structure, the structure within the violin complementary to the external bridge, which supports the sound system as a whole, that was amiss.

While it was being repaired friends told her she looked awful. Her face grew white and tiny, her nose longer. She needed a microphone under her blouse, like a nervous talkshow guest, to amplify her whispers. She tried wearing dark glasses, but they only made her face look more insect-like. She had her hair cut short, hoping that would make her face look larger. But it didn't.

After her violin was repaired, she couldn't play herself back into it. It sounded better, but *not like her violin.* The longer she played the less she felt the strings under her fingers.

Days went by with no improvement.

She developed a bad cold and a sore throat. The violin sounded as if someone were playing it in the next room. She felt tempted to go in and criticize the technique, the sheer sogginess of tone. A hopeless deterioration. And at last she thought: "why do I *need* this? Why am I *tormenting* myself? Why can't I simply *accept* the fact that I'm a failure, like everybody else? Or, rather, I've achieved something *unique*: I could be a failure at twenty-five. I could *achieve* failure, the way other people achieve success. I'll buy a wine silk blouse, white riding pants, a panama hat and grow mint in the back garden. Sit on the steps, in the sun, and drink iced tea with home-grown mint. Why not? Or, better still, I'll earn some money and move *out* of this chicken coop."

Valeria laughed with the guilty feeling that there was something wrong with participating in such obviously self-inflicted cleverness; suicide-in-life disguised as a nightclub act.

Her pupils, dark as coffee beans, sent out what might be warm flashes of emotion or strong rope rings tossed dockward from a small, lurching craft. What was there to go by? Sharp ears, a sharp nose, rows of almost fishlike teeth, thin lips, skin as sun-free as Sandor's was a radiant vessel of sun, above a white-on-white, silk-on-linen blouse, close-mown haircut. As much to learn from that as from her mother's exhilarating misinformation (Amy Gura as a model of the well-rounded academic-athletic life in Cambridge!).

"Tell Valeria why you're in New York!" Sandor Gura prompted, a dead give-away that he'd been monitoring their conversation. His white hair and Olympic rower's smile flashed against his tan with exaggerated vigor, as if skin, hair and bone, literally an extension of the ego, had entered into the noisy business of advertising his youthful good health.

Amy Gura was startled by the abrupt, resonant ring of her husband's voice. She recovered quickly, like someone who's used to being startled by things, and said that she was in New York to have her *hair* cut. Whenever she let her hair grow she looked exactly like Lea Massari. She didn't *mind* that, but no one knew who Lea Massari was. The haircut was *supposed* to make her look like Audrey Hepburn in *Sabrina*, but the guy who did her hair was in a hurry to get back to his darkroom—or he had a client waiting for an hour of therapy somewhere at the other end of the loft—or he wanted to get up to his cabin in Orange County—and he did a sloppy job and made her look like Barbara Rush in *Strangers When We Meet*. And no one really knew who *she* was either.

Someone said that wasn't true: Barbara Rush was the one in *Castle of Blood*.

No, someone else said, that was Barbara *Steele*.

"Oh. Then who *is* Barbara Rush?"

Amy was *not* in New York to have her hair *cut*, Sandor Gura interceded curtly. She was in New York to have her bow re-*hair*ed. He added that now that she'd *had* the bow re-haired, her sound had returned to the inside of the violin. One could hear it in the few measures she'd played in the repair shop. And you had to take into account the fact that the wood took time to achieve its full character.

"Charming," Humberto Vilanescu said. "Charming to discover that the age-old ventriloquism of the married couple hasn't died out after all. Other centuries live on in these habits and customs, walk across the surface of the earth in our flesh, have conversations at dinner tables with our voices. A very real sort of immortality—but of *ideas* not of people."

Amy Gura said that, to be fair about it, Sandor was *half* right: while *she'd* stopped playing in any serious sense, her bow and violin did sound better than ever. She felt a little guilty for standing in their way.

Marika thought that everyone ought to leave poor Amy alone. Other people always knew what was good for you. It was never you, always others, who wanted you to accomplish something, to struggle. We labored all our lives, died from sheer stupidity, trying to live up to the expectations of others. What if Amy was simply *tired of struggling with the violin?* Had anyone thought of that? Soon Amy would be a mother. Wasn't that a sufficient occupation? And there was no need to catalogue all the activities and projects that could make life full, pleasant and changeable.

Who cared whether Amy pursued the violin or not? Valeria said. No one believed in struggling-for-struggling's-sake. That was obvious. But people did extraordinary things. People had future-forming visions. Things actually happened because of the visions people had.

She stopped herself. She hadn't meant to say that much.

Armand said that Valeria hadn't grown up. Boredom and restlessness plagued you until a certain age and then they wore out, like whooping cough, wailing for your mother in the night. Sad to say, the visionary ideal she spoke of didn't exist in reality. No one was satisfied. Everyone longed for something else. The more you had, the more you dreamed of having less, as if that would solve something. He confessed that he wasn't immune to such absurd longings. The dream of an adult childhood without responsibilities. Sex and travel, sleep and play, food and bullshit. Once-upon-a-time in the south of France he'd stopped at a farmhouse. Best meal he ever had. Simple honest fare. Natural way of living. The memory lingered to this day as an ideal, a domestic paradise.

Sandor Gura said that he'd always envied his older brother, a cabinet maker. Recently he'd taken up carpentry himself, set up a shop in his garage. He'd built a hardwood cooking island for Amy, had begun to fiddle around with plans for a house over on that wooded acreage they had near the border, in the hills off Route 23. It was satisfying to the degree that he'd been toying with the idea of leaving the university. Amy would be happy. She could stop worrying about the potential effect of his work on the genetic makeup of the baby.

"Is Amy worried about the genetic makeup of the baby?"

"I'm not worried," Amy said. "I liked *The Creeping Unknown* and *Day of the Triffids* and I loved *The Blob* with Steve McQueen. So why shouldn't I like my own baby?"

"What a horrible joke," Marika said, wrinkling her nose sitcom style.

Humberto Vilanescu said that it wasn't entirely a joke. Sandor Gura's secret research on long-distance transmission of high-energy particles (the so-called neutrino-phone, the muon-o-scope, etc.), did involve a certain degree of danger. Monsters had certainly been created out of less promising materials than these.

"What sort of conversation *is* this?" someone asked.

Sandor said that he didn't recall having talked about his work; Marika cautioned that they were frightening baby Ian; and Amy's white little face began to crumple like a napkin.

Valeria said that we all lived wonderfully screened off from the invisible world where the visible world originated and disappeared. As if we were meant to see only what was seen: the tiny visible spectrum and its enormous surface.

She began to feel that she'd drunk a lot of wine.

Yes, Uncle Sylvan agreed (looking like someone who awakens in the morgue, about to undergo autopsy), when something stirred from that invisible realm, like wind in hemlock boughs, then that was the breath of a being one should never see.

Humberto Vilanescu, making a big show of loading food on his plate long after everyone else had finished, said that every birth might be viewed as a strange eruption of the concealed and the invisible into the daylit world. Accompanied by shrieks and agony, a being the color of a human heart, a pale red pulp like condensed tomato soup, entered the world—swiftly inoculated with the trivial, the everyday.

In his own case, there had been two children, though his mother had never given birth. He and his elder brother were delivered by the Caesarean method. His head, even in the embryo stage, had been far too massive for a normal passage through the birth canal. Then the umbilical cord broke, as if it had been gnawed in two. The doctor gave his father a choice: "you can save your wife or the baby."

"Save my wife!" his father said. "I don't know the child! The child's a stranger! To *hell* with the child!"

A logical and natural sentiment. But, as usual, the doctor was wrong: both mother and child survived. An unborn child, so-to-say, who succeeded in clawing its way into life.

Even as an infant he was aware that his parents regarded him as a monster. A tiny beast who ate up their happiness. Later in life he came to see that this was a reasonably accurate definition of the monstrous. A monster was a creature that fed off others: that drew its sustenance from either the happiness or the unhappiness of others. Every other soul was a tiny meal for such a human beast. It sucked them up like algae, swam through life in widening or narrowing circles, nothing but a mouth with fins. Some people felt that things had now progressed to a new phase. That everyone lay in wait for the defeat of everyone else, everyone fed off everyone else. A generalized aggression and hatred with local spasms. And, since what was once considered monstrous was now normal, since accepted political and business systems of values now ordinarily and day-after-day populated the world with "monsters," new and extraordinary actions would be required to lend fresh meaning to the idea of the monstrous.

Uncle Sylvan murmured that all one had to do was drive a few inches off the road. Monsters were waiting in their pools.

Humberto Vilanescu said that everyone was acquainted with at least one monster, but struggled not to recognize it. In one's nightmares one couldn't help seeing the faces of the monsters that one knew—but one forgot them again in the morning.

Sandor Gura said that he demanded a straight answer. And he didn't want to hear any more of this mumbo-jumbo. He wanted to know exactly who Vilanescu was. How he'd come into possession of one speck of information about his research. What agency of what government he worked for. How he'd gotten himself invited to dinner. What was his actual interest in high-energy particle transmission. No one present could appreciate the seriousness of the situation, he said.

All at once he looked older, less a friend of the family, less out-doorsy, more dangerous.

At this instant Amy Gura slipped from her chair. She clutched at the white tablecloth, bringing down a little Niagara of dishes, glasses, food and wine.

Sandor Gura sprang to his feet, jarring the table. Humberto Vilanescu was already at Amy Gura's side. The two of them crouched over her.

"You know very well," Humberto Vilanescu said, looking directly into Sandor Gura's eyes, "that your wife's sole contact with the violin is the research she does for a middle-aged virtuoso who's writing a useless treatise on scales. She's attempted suicide twice in the last six months—she's contemplating it again tonight—yet you persist in these lies!"

The chandelier sent golden highlights flashing through his straight billow of dark hair and outlined a sort of inner, darker and sharper head within the massive outer one. This second, shadow head vanished the instant he stood up, lifting Amy Gura's limp body from the carpet. It didn't reappear even when, bending to deposit her body on the green couch, his head was framed within the glowing cylinder of a lampshade.

It was impossible to tell, Valeria thought, if Amy's face *was* the face of someone yearning for death or if it was simply the utterly worn-out, oddly aged face of someone for whom the smallest social occasion is a torment. Or even the unglued look of a face glimpsed in the frightening inwardness of dreams.

After a few seconds her eyelids fluttered open, a moist little soul shining out through the wet brown irises.

She said that she'd been somewhere where there were women in gold robes, men in purple suits. It was *death* but it wasn't all that bad. A sort of well where life looked like color television. Now she couldn't figure out why she'd allowed them to bring her back. They'd tricked her by bringing her back in two stages. Before this they had her in a hospital. She remembered saying to the woman in the next bed:

"I've been in the hospital what is it now—two months? three months?—and my head is *still* fucked. It gets *stuck*, going around in circles. They say I'm allergic to the medicine, but I think they *brought* me here to speed up my rpm's. People don't understand sickness. They don't know the first and most important thing about sickness. I've got to go back and tell them: 'Sickness is a second world. There really is another place.'

" 'Yes,' the woman in the other bed answered, 'I have my problems too. I promised my mother I'd go to the *beauty parlor* with her. I thought it would be nice, it would be *sentimental*, if we had our *hair* fucked together before she flies south. . . .'

"That's when it hit me that I had to go back. 'I've got to go back!' I thought. 'I've *got* to go back!'

"I couldn't hold on to it! That's why I'm here! I'm lying here, trying to hold *on* to it, and I *can't*! Otherwise I wouldn't *be* here!"

Her sobbing was so violent that it looked as if her body was being thrashed from within.

Sandor helped her to her feet and guided her from the room, his arm around her shoulders. Valeria's mother went to get their coats.

As soon as they were out of earshot Aunt Grete whispered that Mr. Vilanescu was right. More was wrong there than met the eye. In marriage, anything was possible. Every public appearance of a married couple, the private couple speaking a public language, was a lie in the worst sense. The truth was precisely what wasn't and never could be said.

Marika told a story about a friend of hers who almost committed suicide. Her old friend Ellen who'd always been in love with Armand and who married Armand's college friend, Jon. Ellen's mother didn't help. She was always drawing comparisons between Ellen's life with Jon (which was kind of a mess) and hers with Armand. Then Ellen's baby died and Jon walked out and Ellen swallowed some Meprobamate tablets. She learned a lot from that. She learned to take pleasure in what she had. She thought that, in general, you learned your most important lessons from the tragedies that befell your friends.

Armand gave her shoulder a little squeeze and said that that was true. He told a story about the cancer death of a patient at the hospital. Words couldn't describe the effect the man's death had had on the staff. The dignity with which he accepted death, of course. That was always astonishing. But there was something else. As if someone else's death made it easier to live.

Humberto Vilanescu half rose, reached across the table and

jerked Armand forward by the knot of his tie so that food splashed on his shirt front. He flicked at Armand's face with the back of his hand.

"Something was crawling in your hair," he explained and released him. Armand slumped in his chair, white and small. To the table in general Humberto Vilanescu said that he wanted to let everyone know how happy he was that he'd come. "Not healthy to spend too much time in the stratosphere. You lose touch. You really do forget exactly how many morons there are in the world! Just look at those faces!" He stared at Armand and Marika, Uncle George and Aunt Elena.

"Someone ought to give the Guras a lift back to their hotel," Marika murmured.

"Or they might need one of us to call a taxi."

The four of them left in search of the Guras. Valeria's parents were nowhere to be seen. Uncle Sylvan dozed. Valeria watched Humberto Vilanescu eating his dessert.

In this way the dinner party came to a premature conclusion, under clouds of strong cigarette smoke, the near-empty table giving the impression that the family had been wolfed down along with soup, salad, meat, gravy, potatoes, vegetables and coffee.

A PRINCIPLE OF OUR AGE

Valeria woke up on the over-padded and shimmering green couch in the living room. Humberto Vilanescu and Aunt Grete were chatting pleasantly while her parents looked on glumly from their easy chairs.

She drifted off again and found herself crossing one street, then another, searching for something that seemed to be the taste of a certain pastry in a certain pastry shop. The path to the pastry shop was diagrammed as clearly as the field of a video game, but when she arrived at her goal a butcher in a blue apron stood in the window, slaughtering cattle. With a hand as large as a baseball mitt he seized the enormous head of a black-and-white cow and drew a sharp knife across its throat. One cow toppled over, lay in the window; another appeared, identical to the first; its throat was slit and *it* toppled over. This gesture was reproduced ten, twenty, thirty times with no variation. So that the image took on a television-like neutrality. Only the blood that sprayed the inner surface of the window suggested the possibility of a real interior space.

Someone called her name.

The voice was distant, tiny, shrill and desperate. She ran toward it. At the end of a long, white arcade, in a round window, something like a port hole, at the uppermost level of a pale highrise, she saw a woman's white face and round, dark mouth hole.

She thought: "I can see her whole *life* through the window. Years are passing. *Centuries* are passing. Her suffering is growing worse. She doesn't know which way to turn. But can I *help?*"

The frame around the face, and then the white face itself, went pink then orange, as if a fire had sprung up in the apartment.

She boarded the first bus that passed, hoping it would carry her near the still-distant highrise. It flew swiftly over the roadbeds and arrived outside town, in a garden suburb where every street was hedged in by solid banks of azalea and lilac.

"This is *not* where I wanted to go," she said to the driver.

"No," he answered politely, "but it *is* where you've gone."

She disembarked hurriedly, under a vast green parasol of full-leafed shade trees leading into a park. A woman passed, leading a child down an avenue of evergreen oaks. She said that the direction Valeria wanted, where the fire was burning in the post-modern district, lay in the deep distance on the other side of the park.

"I'll help you get there," she promised. "But first we have to sit on this bench and share a ripe mango."

They sat down and the woman cut the soft, orange fruit in two. It dripped on her fingers and on her face.

"All I do is watch color tv," she said. "My tv is old and the color is lousy, just the way I like it. It looks like an indoor swimming pool."

Two young women passed, wheeling baby carriages down the

path bordered with evergreen oaks. Valeria decided to leave the woman with the mango and follow the two young mothers, hoping they would lead her out of the park. She fell in step behind them and listened.

"The more you look into things," one of them was saying, "the more you come to the conclusion that everything replaces reality. Reality is exactly what retreats behind things as you approach."

"But how is that possible? If reality is what retreats behind things, then what is *this*?"

"Real love is mathematical," the first woman went on without answering. "You love the one you end up with and you end up with someone when X number of events lead to a certain point in your life. When the number of events in two lives add up to a similar total, two lines cross—and that's *that*. . . ."

"The great thing about living *right now* is that everyone understands you better than you understand yourself."

Valeria asked if it was true that the future was already on fire, but the women ignored her. She asked for directions, but they took another fork. While Valeria's path led through a region of flowers, butterflies and bees. She was stung and stung again, but the swellings were neither painful nor dangerous.

A few steps carried her deep into the park as if they were the giant, loping steps one takes down a hill. At the bottom she found herself at a high, endlessly wide mesh fence and beyond it deep woodland. An acre of shadow for every broad-leafed shade tree, each mile of trees and undergrowth a massive X like the supports of a railroad trestle.

She thought: "I've been here before—or at least in a *sister* to this place—as certainly as I used to look in the blue dining room mirror or my grandmother's dark apartment—a place that doesn't exist anymore except in memory. But why am I here *again*?"

The fragrance of ripe peaches assailed her senses, like a whiff of the nether end of summer. She saw a broad but solitary peach tree, laden with orange-red peaches, some of which had already dropped to the ground while others had been eaten down to the pit by bird or insect.

A dark butterfly drifted up from the base of the tree, coasted through the fine mesh fence, made a little loop and flew straight toward her face. Enormous wings, like the soft muzzle of an animal's jaw with a spectacular border of turquoise beading.

Something stung her on the forearm and the obscurely woven reality of the forest curled away as if on fire, uncovering a distant, open plain shimmering with heat and white as quartz. Something was clearly drawn there, a city in the form of a bluish circuit. She felt herself flying toward it and as she flew she thought: "what region can that *be*, if it's true that the future is already on fire?"

When she awoke again only one lamp was burning, her father and her uncle looked like bulls killed in the arena, and the barely perceptible horizon of sound that continually arises from the world, percolating and receding along a graph of mass activity, had dropped below the audible.

She was astonished to see that her mother and her aunt were sitting forward on the edges of their chairs, listening attentively to Humberto Vilanescu, laughing, rosy-faced and lively.

"We secretly have contempt for the way other people pass their time," he was saying, "yet we ourselves do one thing after another without knowing why. Things just happen. And what happens seems designed to impress us with life's sheer smallness, familiarity and insignificance. We long for life to be like a waking dream, an adventure whose coherence, whose 'plot,' provides something akin to meaning. Even the nightclub comedian and the stage magician attract us with their ability to organize the moments."

He had a particular liking for the card trick, he said: intimate, baffling and elegant, it manipulated space, light and optics in more subtle ways than larger-scale illusions. He disliked illusions that relied on devices unknown to the layman. While he himself was strictly a gifted dabbler, he had learned a good deal about the magician's art from his elder brother, who, while prodigiously lazy in most things, had mastered every feat of magic known to man.

Perhaps he'd do a little something for them later on. By chance, he had the means of attempting a rather spectacular illusion in his coat pocket.

"Oh, please! *Please!*" her mother and her aunt cried in unison. "Don't wait! Do it *now!*"

"Later," he promised. "Before I leave."

"Make *Valery* disappear!" her mother suggested giddily.

"And *Sylvan!*"

They all laughed.

Valeria sat up to the point where she was noticed.

"Oh, you're awake," her mother said, not altogether pleased.

"I think you should *grab* this man!" Aunt Grete sounded more hysterical than her mother.

"I'm afraid your niece doesn't believe in marriage," he said. "She isn't a romantic, like me. I've been married four times and all my marriages ended in bitter divorces, filthy accusations, no more than half of which were true. The judge who presided over my last divorce complained about the sheer ugliness of the whole business. 'If you don't mind my saying so, Your Honor,' I said, 'you're an idiot. It's a priceless gift to see people at their worst. No one ever insulted anyone else unfairly. The uglier the accusations, the closer to the truth. The things that are said in anger never have quite the same stench of the mediocre and the hypocritical as the endearments murmured in tender affection. Naturally you wouldn't know that. As the old axiom says, what we really hanker after in success is the chance to rise above the truth. The atmosphere up there is a delirious cocktail of oxygen and bullshit. So, if you've lost touch with things it's only to be expected.' For example: not long ago I was walking along the narrow promenade above the East River and I couldn't decide if it was beautiful in a way no other age could imagine or just plain ugly. Ugliness the spontaneous aesthetic principle of the age. The random, repulsive vista, with its panoramic hodge-podge of accident, accumulation and deliberate construction easily overwhelming every feeble effort at conscious, aesthetically pleasurable design. A thousand kinds of smoke, a million brands of filth, billions of flakes and quadrillions of particles swarming in every casual vista. Similarly, every marriage has its unique smoky flavor."

"Its own special ugliness?" her mother asked. "It's special *filth?*" Aunt Grete chimed in.

Aunt Grete's laughter, while on much too long a wavelength to rouse the dead, did cause Valeria's father and uncle to resettle themselves in their deep chairs.

Humberto Vilanescu replenished their drinks, while his own remained full.

Marriage was bound to have a fresh spasm of popularity, Valeria yawned. Every surge toward the future was marked by violent relapses of mystical nostalgia. She'd picked up the idea from two girls on a bus, so it had to be true. They'd also said that we didn't all live in the same century. History occurred at an astronomical distance from everyday life, as remote as a nightclub act one either booed or applauded. Remote from history, it was impossible to say where and when everyday life was actually lived out. Life as we knew it was lived in a peculiar, timeless trough, part museum, part television receiver.

She sank back into the cushions.

Perhaps it wasn't merely a question of mystical nostalgia, Humberto Vilanescu suggested. Perhaps there was something indispensable and inevitable about marriage, like the suicidal lure of Golden Gate Bridge. One had to be on guard against an easy cynicism.

Several months ago he was being wined and dined by someone from the laser division of Bell Telephone. The man was begging him to take charge of a certain stalled project, while *he* was cracking lobster claws with his side teeth. The man (who had a narrow head and a row of weak and tiny molars) followed suit as if he'd discovered a new fashion in table manners—and instantly broke a tooth.

As they hadn't concluded their negotiations, he agreed to accompany the man to his dentist.

While he was sitting in the spacious waiting room of red and silver, reading in some magazine or other about the invention of still another brand new successful personality—someone pinned to the same clothesline of success everyone longed to be pinned to, reeled in out of the daily universe of working-toward-death—a silver-haired woman came in, dressed in red. A second woman entered, her color scheme neutral and self-effacing.

The two women got to exchanging microfiche autobiographies. The woman in red said that she was tasting freedom for the first time. She was forced into it, the way everyone was. She'd been longing to move to Florida for years, but her husband refused to retire. Last year she bought a place in Boca Raton, but he still refused to leave New York. She began to suspect that there was another woman. She confronted him and he confessed. He didn't want to leave his closets. He had a passion for closets. For seeing his miles of suits arrayed in a subtle spectrum from pearly gray to black-on-black. She had to admit that the New York apartment *did* have more closets than any other apartment in the Western Hemisphere. Only an apartment with more closets than rooms would lure him down to Florida. So she moved to Florida alone. At first she was terrified, but now she couldn't be happier.

"But that's *impossible!*" Aunt Grete cried. "That very same thing happened to *me!*"

"Yes, that's *true*," Valeria's mother said. "Grete's told the story of her husband and the closets more times than they've recycled *I Love Lucy.*"

Valeria tried to rouse herself. Their voices had taken on a peculiar timbre, as if the silence of the streets had flowed into the apartment, between one voice and another.

"Is it possible that our paths have crossed before, by *coincidence?* That that silly woman in the dentist's office was *me?*"

"Our world is *woven*," Humberto Vilanescu said, rising to his feet, his dark hair golden against the lamp as it had been under the chandelier, "a web of webs. Still, nowhere is the universe so finely woven that things can't tunnel in or out. Some creature is always able to burrow through and deliver its sting."

He looked at his watch. It was time to go, he said.

Valeria sat up completely. From this vantage point (deep in the green couch, her feet barely, childishly touching the floor) Humberto Vilanescu appeared under the lacy shadows of a life-size artificial fern.

"But you *promised!*" her mother's girlhood face pouted again.

He made a big show of giving in, went to fetch something from his jacket pocket and sent her mother in search of something cape-like.

Her mother came back with something that gave off a faint whiff of cedar.

He commenced a slightly hunched-over pacing, oddly bobbing and bird-like, round the darkened square of the Bokhara rug, all the while keeping up a steady stream of chatter.

The important thing, he said, was to watch him closely. Magic tricks were a test of patience. The performer was like an athlete who won out over the flabby, hopeful mass of the audience through sheer endurance, if nothing else. What's more, the audience participated gratefully in its own deception, a sort of fundamental good will it took a certain violence to rupture. Then there was the human inability to pay attention to things. The magician kept up a steady patter of nonsense, all the while waiting for an inter-stellar pinhole to open up in the audience's collective attention. That was the instant the audience was astonished by the miraculous appearance of this or that.

While her mother and her aunt sat on the edges of their seats, hands clasped expectantly in their laps, Valeria tried to follow Humberto Vilanescu's movements.

Round and round the rug he went, around the wide perimeter and step by step winding his way inward—only to follow the same flattened spiral outward to the margin. His hands were visible all the time, holding the cape-like garment in place.

Once upon a time, on vacation, he met a couple of morons on Basseterre, a little island in the Leeward chain. A guy named Laurens, who looked exactly like a pair of low-budget Italian boots, and a wealthy young woman named Nina Pozzi who for some reason couldn't wait another second to sign over her savings, her stocks, her condominiums and country houses to this guy with a brain like a refrigerator drip pan, a sort of combination red bikini and stainless steel fountain pen to sign all necessary documents.

A couple of months after returning to New York Nina Pozzi called him. She was suicidal, begged him to meet her at such-and-such a restaurant. She didn't look like the same woman. A bright red dress and a worn out face. Her father had killed himself while she was away and his second wife, who was like a mother to her, was moving out to San Francisco to take charge of her father's container shipping interests. Then, on the heels of that, her sister Lilliana decided to marry some numbskull with a farm in Connecticut. She was actually going to sell her gallery, move out to some level wilderness of lawns and fruit trees, have babies and learn to play the piano.

"'But you aren't alone,' he said. 'You have Laurens.'"

He didn't *understand*, she said. She'd given Laurens huge sums of money. He'd lost a small fortune on some phony energy deal. And lesser sums on frozen death, picture phones, holography. He was a sucker for anything that had to do with the future. Somebody knew that and knew about their engagement and was trying to milk her dry through him. She was angry, she was *hurt*, and she broke up with him. But he was so pathetic, he *needed* her so, that she took him back. Something about his eyes coaxed out a milky sap of sympathy. When they kissed the bottom dropped out, like a fragile jar when you pour in hot soup.

A couple of weeks ago Laurens took her to a party. Some guy was trying to get together a consortium of backers to launch a rocket or a satellite or something.

A very weird crowd. Mainly business vultures, she guessed, with here and there some screwball "scientist" thrown in. You could tell that some of them already had their piece of meat, teeth and appetite were a little dull; but there were some real live werewolves, guys with fresh blood on their lips, people using English in ways that sounded like six different foreign languages.

Around 1:00 a.m. things settled down to a bit of quiet dancing and a lot of rabid embracing in corners.

Laurens went into the bedroom and called out to her. He had a sudden, overwhelming need for her, he said.

The apartment was dim and quiet; the amber helix of some sour melody had risen up from the turntable and was revolving on the ceiling; a pink, hypnotic shadow spread from one end of things to the other. So it seemed ok.

They lay down on the big pink bed, glossy as a magazine cover. They kissed. His eyes looked like the sad eyes of a donkey. She called him "donkey face" and undid his shirt. Again he said, "I need to touch you," and her legs turned to chocolate pudding. One thing led to another. She was undressed from the waist down and he was stroking and stroking the long, black path of hair between her legs. Her orgasm was strange—long, hot waves, very low peaks, almost flat—like a dream that seems to go on all night. He kept whispering "this is good for me—I *need* this—this is so *good* for me!" And that and the stroking seemed to keep the hot, level waves flowing out of her, exactly like the overflowing pitcher in the fairy tale.

In the midst of this, something clinked. She pushed Laurens off. Some people had slipped in and were watching. Someone had jostled the perfume bottles on the dresser. Ranks of glazed, flushed faces, slightly sticky, like taffy apples.

She grabbed her clothes, ran out to the bathroom while Laurens shooed everyone out of the apartment.

She cried on Laurens' shoulder, poured out her humiliation. Maybe they should stop seeing one another, he said. What? she said. He'd met someone else. She didn't grasp the point. To be *exact* about it, he said, he was engaged to marry a woman just a tiny bit older than her who had the desire, and the infinite means, to support some of the projects she'd lost faith in. The immortality research. The secret "space ark" project that was already under way. This was, in fact, a sort of *engagement* party. Engagement party and farewell party combined. He intended to be faithful, for once. He'd needed to touch Nina one more time. Now that he'd done that he could say goodbye.

He walked her to the door. Out in the hall she felt suicidal. Came close to killing herself in the lobby. But she ended up going home and watching television. She fell asleep during *The Blood-Spattered Bride* or *Deep Red*.

In the morning she felt happy. All she'd done was to have trusted another human being. If he wasn't worthy of that trust, well, that was his problem. That night she took some pills, but she timed it so the maid would find her. Then, last night, Laurens called and said that he needed to touch her again. What should she do?

"What you need is revenge!" he said. "Forget all this crap they've taught you! The 'Sermon on the Mount' and *Magnificent Obses-sion.*"

Someone gasped, someone else let out a small scream, and Valeria jerked back.

Humberto Vilanescu was no longer there.

Just above the dark rug a creature, about six feet long, that resembled a furry, unraveling cigar, opened a vast pair of wings and circled the room.

The creature was able to remain virtually upright while gliding with graceful undulations just below the ceiling. Its wings (which seemed black and gelatinous) appeared a luminous, chocolaty red-brown, black veined, within a velvety black and white-spotted border, as it coasted directly in the path of the lamp beams. A faint scent of honeysuckle fanned through the room.

"Magda!" Uncle Sylvan cried out, on his feet quick as a twenty-year-old. He took a few steps this way and that, groped as if blind and sank back into his chair, older than before.

Humberto Vilanescu was sitting at the foot of the green couch, next to Valeria.

Valeria's father said that he'd been in Rumania. The Rumania of his childhood. A thatched hut, a dirt floor—water drawn from the lake and carried by horse. Snow so deep you lived indoors all winter. Huge wood-burning stove. Aunts, uncles, cousins who'd been nothing but the most spectral of memories were there in the flesh. He'd seen his grandfather again, the man who'd raised him from infancy, after his own father had ventured to America, vanishing utterly for ten years or more. His grandfather appeared just as he remembered him, just as he'd longed to see him all these years, with no hint of the terrible death he was said to have suffered while pulling a heavy cart from one village to another. Now it seemed to him that of the many versions of the story of his grandfather's death he'd been told, the one that simply had his grandfather vanishing between one familiar place and another, on a much-travelled length of mountain road, was the most likely. He'd vanished somewhere and returned now, unchanged.

He cried now as he'd cried then, when his grandfather died.

"It really was another lifetime," he said. "I lived before—an utterly different person in a different world. And now I've been there again—as if for years."

"Valery, you missed something astonishing," her mother said.

"Near the woodpile," he went on, "one of my ancestors approached and handed me a sheet of paper. There were several names on it. And he impressed on me the importance of remembering them. 'This is a *warning*,' he said. But I've forgotten them already!"

"'When a daughter's eyes grow dark and her cheeks grow pale,'" Uncle Sylvan murmured, "'then she may have drifted into the twilight land where kisses bring bruises and wounds bring sighs.'"

Valeria's mother suggested that it had been a long evening. It was time to go to bed.

Aunt Grete coaxed Uncle Sylvan to his feet and Valeria's mother steered them both to the clothes closet. Valeria didn't move. Aunt Grete turned at the door and begged Humberto Vilanescu to tell the secret of his illusion.

No, he said, the most he was permitted to do was offer a few clues. He was willing to stay a little longer and do that. Valeria, for example, might be able to deduce the basic principle and then she could tell the others.

Grete and Uncle Sylvan departed. And her parents went to bed, reluctantly leaving Valeria alone with the dinner guest who was, when all was said and done, an utter stranger.

FIVE

"YOU MUST LIVE *QUICKLY!*"

Valeria dreamt that she was in a palatial house, cool and hollow as the self-styled baronial mansion of some long-dead financier now open to the public. Vistas of lawns in the tall windows. Lawns leading into meadows, meadows into other meadows and shaded woodland. Bird sounds, numerous and tropical.

Martina was at an easel, arguing about money with someone Valeria knew and didn't like.

Someone told them to lower their voices.

"You're talking about *money*, but what you really need is *time*. Your father is in another room, near death and your mother is crying, inconsolable. Inconsolable grief. Your father looks hideous. No one knows it, but he's been wearing a box for years. They remove it only at night, when he goes to sleep. They *have* to leave it on during the day—otherwise he wouldn't be able to *speak*. His face would fall apart. But now even the box can't hold him together. Nothing but wrinkles. If we put him in a bath, he would melt. Wrinkles come swimming toward everyone, lodging first in the natural cavities under the eyes, and then everywhere, on the smoothest plane. You *think* you have time, but you don't. Others *will* have time. One day time will extend for others in wide and open plazas. Water will flow amidst deep colors. A little like the plazas of 'Las Arboledas' in Mexico City or the Towers of Satellite City on the hillside above Mexico's Queretaro Highway. But you won't see this. You must live *quickly*! Faster than the fastest saxophone solo!"

Valeria went to the window where the atmosphere looked dark in a peculiar way, as if the approach of night had brought a new, more autumnal season: brown instead of green and space between the branches.

She felt that someone was outside the door, able to see, through the thick wooden panels, the outline of her body in its light cotton nightgown. She lay down on the floor, in one of the shallow troughs of darkness that collect near walls, on a soft plane of carpet. She was gazing through a dark thicket of chair-and-table legs into a blue mirror that sank below the carpet.

A beautiful woman who looked less like Martina than like Valeria's mother as she appeared, radiating the usual pathetic beauty, from the black pages of family photograph albums, lay nestled on her side.

Her body was outlined through a clinging black dress with red flowers. The carpet showed up an odd, tomato soup red.

Then the woman was face down, bare legs and persimmon panties against a billow of black, as if the skirt had been torn in two.

Then the woman was naked: naked legs and naked buttocks. Globes of light appeared bound up with shadows, sold and ready to be delivered.

The face of a large, star-like wristwatch sparkled in the infinite box of shadow where the ceiling was hidden.

Humberto Vilanescu approached. He turned the woman over and, passing his hands over her body, dressed her in an orange leotard with a detachable bottom panel.

He snapped the panel open.

The muff showed up dark and shining as a bed of mussels.

His body, thick as a bull's shoulder, hunched over the woman's, a condensed, nut-colored blot between two shining knees.

Hands were on Valeria's breasts.

Her knees were up.

The hair between her legs stood up with electricity, an odd orange-gold.

Humberto's face appeared from below, between her thighs.

She tried to push his head away with two hands, but it was too heavy.

She opened her mouth to complain about the unfair advantage he had, delving into her while she could barely see him at all, but a pair of lips entered hers, kissing her to the point of suffocation.

She felt a series of tugs, as if someone were pulling at the resistant brass snap of a new pair of jeans. The snap popped free and she was orbiting Earth on a tiny, unstable platform.

Radiant particles and vast black intervals passed through her.

She rolled her eyes back, trying to see down to Earth. Her body rotated as well, knees to shoulders, inducing a continuously rotating levitation.

The rounded, upraised triangles of her legs rocked back and forth, resembling two dark wings. These wings grew larger and larger, breathed in and out, like a separate creature quietly fastened on the deep cleft and its warm stream.

How did this *help* her? she cried out. How was this *truer* than anything else? Others, many, many others, had tried to locate the center of things in the body, as if one could make an orgasm a lifelong project. Acquaintances and red-headed actresses you met at parties. Was that all anyone had to offer?

By way of answer she found herself accelerating from a level far beyond the ceiling, landing with a springy rebound in her bed.

A door slammed in the near or not-so-near distance: the door to her parents' apartment or a door in another building.

The darkness in her room seemed unnaturally deep. Something that should have been gleaming wasn't, as if the synthetic amber daylight of the streetlamp had been replaced with an anti-lamp that cast deeper rays of darkness through the apartment.

She lay down again, but couldn't fall asleep. She had done something. But what? Been someplace. But where? It was as if you were continually weaving a second life for yourself and this life was unavailable to you. Or as if, inside the first life, there were a pond, concealed by nothing more than forgetfulness, in which everything from the first life swam without its mask. Every time you swam there you felt, with a thrill of pleasure or terror, that this was your true life, that these people, these creatures, were the true cast of characters of one's existence on Earth.

FAMILY FEELING
AND "THE EXCEPTIONAL LIFE"

No, Valeria said, she didn't think Humberto Vilanescu had shared the secret. She couldn't be *absolutely* sure, because he'd been in one of the hundreds of dreams she'd had last night. But they hadn't actually spoken. She was pretty sure of that.

Her mother paused to watch her struggle with a breakfast meant to fortify her across light years of fast food.

"You look worn out," she said.

Valeria got up and looked in the mirror. It was true. There were dark smudges of sleeplessness under her eyes. She looked like one of the roses already blackening in its vase.

Drifting was fine for some people, dangerous for others, her mother said. Nadja was a drifter. And that was fine for her because that was her nature. But it wasn't fine for Valeria.

She went further. Maybe it had nothing to do with drifting. It was obvious that Valeria didn't intend to go back to anything like her old job. She had grander plans. But the greater one's expectations, the more likely one was to be disappointed. Things rarely worked out as they did in the novels that inspired one's youth, satisfying yet melancholy precisely because one knew that in one's own life things would *not* work out in mysterious ways over decades to fulfill one's deepest yearnings. One simply had to root these yearnings out of one's being.

She spoke about Amy Gura. It wasn't so much that too much intelligence could be dangerous, as that intelligence didn't necessarily save you. You could waste all your intelligence. Easily.

Valeria looked up from her dish of griddle-cakes and sausages.

Whether Amy Gura was a model of what one could be with a little effort or of what one should avoid like the plague, she didn't think Amy's problems had much to do with an over-worked brain.

She went on from that to talk about Marika. Didn't her mother find it suspicious that Marika's friends were always so depressed? So near suicide, on the verge of breakdowns? Didn't that ever strike her as odd? The need to see others fail. . . .

Valeria wasn't making sense, her mother said. Marika's friends were like anyone else's.

Her face had gone blank and unfriendly.

Valeria saw that she'd overstepped the bounds of truthfulness beyond which no family conversation was possible. But she continued.

The moment when certain childhood torments finally slipped away as if we'd managed to outlive them, she said, also seemed to be the moment when something else, something hopefully restless, died out as well. And that dead something. . . .

The yellow wall phone trilled like a child's tricycle.

Valeria pushed away the rest of her breakfast and took her coffee cup with her to the window, where a white, molten plastic filled the square region above the roofs.

"You've lived too long in one place," her mother said with some sharpness. "If someone's windowshade is two inches lower than usual, you call the police. I know what you're like!"

And a minute later: "Then George is worse than you! He had no business doing that! He never *said* he knew Josef or Ana! No—and not the Philadelphia cousins either. Yes? And what would be hope to gain? If this is a criticism I'd make this criticism: a little starved for home and hearth, like someone who's been away at sea for two years, and maybe a little *greedy* for things because of that. Yes. Tell me why I'm naive. . . ."

Valeria went into the living room. Her mother's voice was audible, but not as language.

There were more windows, a wider panorama of the hot street. Far below, a dark blue car went by slowly, drawing Valeria's attention to a solitary tree toward the corner. Little more than a sapling, its tiny leaves yellow-orange, it seemed to have found the secret of dying while remaining alive.

A young woman in a white polo, coral skirt, pale platform sandals, her upper body in sun and her lower body in the narrow strip of shade that lay at the base of the building line across the way, appeared to be heading for the Czechoslovakian restaurant on the corner. Valeria marveled at that. Wondered who this woman was who could eat Czechoslovakian food on a day that resembled one of the days in *The Day the Earth Caught Fire.*

But the woman walked straight to the corner and began to cross the soft gutter.

The side entrance to the restaurant flashed open. Ten billion electron volts of sunlight accelerated toward Valeria.

A woman came out: brilliant green shoes, silver toreador pants, purple blouse, silver hair, walking a long, shaggy dog, silver, not quite as dazzling as the woman's pants, but a little more dazzling than her hair. The hot, white atmosphere gathered around woman and dog as a red aureole. She might have been someone from a planet where everything was silver, trying to blend in unobtrusively with Earthly ways and making all the wrong choices: green and purple, heavy food in hot weather.

Her mother came in and said that she'd just been arguing with Elena about the dinner guest, Humberto Vilanescu. She began to recount the argument and wanted to know what Valeria thought.

Valeria was watching the silver-haired woman with the silver dog walk along the other side of the street, in the direction of her parents' apartment building. A muscular, mannish stride was concealed by the exaggeratedly rhythmic leg-and-hip movement imposed by the high heels.

A few hundred yards away the woman stopped and stared straight toward the spot where Valeria was standing. Valeria was certain that she couldn't be seen. Still, the telescopic accuracy of the woman's gaze was unsettling.

She dropped her coffee cup, made a clumsy grab for it and succeeded in spilling it all over the curtain. The cup shattered and a blot appeared instantly in the neutral fabric.

Her mother, looking dismayed, kneeled to pick up the shards, then changed her mind and went to get a damp cloth.

"We'll have to get the stepladder to take down the curtain," she said from the hall, rummaging in the bottom of the linen closet for a rag.

The telephone rang again.

Valeria glanced down into the street. A workman in a dark blue uniform with FUTURE VENTURES lettered in red on the back was stacking folding chairs in the back of a red van. An old taxi zipped toward the green light at the corner as if it signalled the entranceway to an ideal destination.

Her mother set about taking down the curtain while Valeria dressed.

That was Marika, she said. They hadn't been able to catch up with Sandor and Amy last night. They'd walked to the avenue and then both ways along the avenue, looking down side streets. Then they took the car and circled the neighborhood for half-an-hour or so. Nowhere to be seen. Sandor and Amy must have caught a taxi the minute they hit the street. Or Amy in one taxi and Sandor pursuing in another.

But the real reason Marika had called was to say that before things blew up last night she'd planned to invite Valeria to stay with them as long as she liked. Valeria's being between one thing and another might be a blessing in disguise. They could get to know one another, for the first time. They could talk, swim, play tennis, go horseback riding, picnic, cook dinner together, have breakfast out on the lawn, under the oaks. They'd have a wonderful time.

Valeria marveled that Marika had said all that and that her mother had been able to convey it with such fantastic accuracy that she felt as if she'd already been there and didn't have to bother going.

"You have no family feeling," her mother said glumly.

There was no time for that, Valeria answered. Ordinary life permitted such nostalgia and sentiment. One step forward, ten steps back. But in the exceptional life there was no room for it. This way of living always seemed cold to others. One was always reproached for living too consciously. But the truth was we spent too *little* time trying to live up to the ideal outlines we had for ourselves, not too *much*. All our lives, if we were the least bit ambitious, the least bit capable of self-criticism, we felt unworthy, surrounded by the emptiness of the outline we hadn't managed to color in.

Her mother looked at her as if she were a stranger.

MICROWAVE

Valeria was sitting on her front steps eating a coconut pop and leafing without interest through the *New York Times* want ads while she waited with the flattest sort of curiosity for the round and friendly mailman to make his delivery.

The language and format of the "Help Wanted" columns was so compressed, so reduced and code-like, that one couldn't help feeling that each little half-inch, inch, or inch-and-a-half box contained ten or more years of life reduced to microfilm. One had only to respond to find oneself, *in reality*, on a road in Bayonne or leafy Westchester, about to spend five or twenty years within another absolutely real frame of life.

The large leaves of newsprint crackled and fluttered pleasantly in the mild wind.

The coconut pop was almost finished.

A blue van turned into the street from the wide intersection at the avenue. It was so high and so broad that it scraped the violet asparagus tips of the budding branches. It pulled to a stop only a few houses further along. Uniformed men alighted and began to unload dolleys, padded cloths and the like.

The way the light glowed in the blue paint of the van was in harmony with the warmth of the day, the appearance of pink flowers in someone's peach tree, the red glow of new green leaves in certain hedges, the white butterflies and early buzzing of harmless insects, the tiny, scarlet-edged cabbages of the lilac buds with their layers of pointed leaves, and the unearthly smell of lilacs that had opened somewhere out of sight.

The blue van interposed itself between one side of the street and the other like a window into a second, more intense out-of-doors; a door through which one ought to be able to enter a shallow, pleasant ideal of living.

The men who'd alighted from the blue moving van came out of someone's house with cartons and furniture. Valeria felt a sympathetic stirring—picturing her own things being carted out that way, few as they were, having a wonderful, odd uprootedness out in the open space and bright sunlight.

Her mail arrived (one small, pale blue envelope with no return address) at the very instant Denise Oliveros beckoned from the steps of the house into and out of which the furniture movers were passing.

Denise was sitting on the hood of a dark blue sedan with another woman who looked strangely like her; that is, like a heightened, sharpened, tanned and obsessively stylish version of her. Both of them sat there, talking, smoking, dangling their legs like teenage girlfriends. It was obvious to Valeria that they were stoned, and not only because of the usual bad jokes and laughing, the sense of a trivial inner world that can't survive either the microscopic magnification of drugs or the simple light of day, but because of their stationary velocity. One could feel their electrons racing. Denise and her super-twin seemed to share this fast inner rate of existence as well as a remarkably similar style of laughing (as if their selves, the unique collection of ordinary properties that separates one person, one *thing*, from another, had elected to vanish into a shared cultural type). They also held in common: red lips and red nails, jeans sharp enough to slice bread, clogs with cork heels, black hair and hairdos that instantly brought to mind this model and that actress. What differentiated them was chiefly Denise's relative pallor, her square jaw, the far weaker and at the same time more enigmatic texture of her surface being. The other woman was better-looking but further along the path of cultural mass production. Her name was Holly, she worked as a file clerk in Denise's office, was wearing a blood-red rabbit jacket and had taken part in the orgy on Denise's birthday. Denise hinted that Holly was a prostitute.

Valeria kept quiet.

Denise imitated the way Roland said she looked like a fuckn moron with her fuckn mouth hanging open when they'd told her that Holly wasn't really a file clerk. She said to herself: "I'm not just playing at being out of my depth, I *am* out of my depth."

Everything was always compared to prostitution, Holly said. As if all that was required to prostitute yourself was to work and be paid for it, to work without wanting to, without having your heart in it, to work in the usual way, feeling neither clean nor dirty. But it was one of those rare exceptions: a cliche that wasn't true. Anything that happened to the body was different from anything else. Nothing else came quite so close to equalling your whole and real self. So that it was really possible to say that, no matter how detached you were during the act, it was your soul that was getting fucked. You couldn't exactly make the same claim for office work. Or even for writing advertising copy. Of course prostitution was mainly dismal. These guys tried to tear you along the dotted line just to see what was on the other side. They went at you sometimes as if they'd like to kill you. But it was all a matter of attitude. If you liked the idea that your soul was getting fucked then you were ok. She doubted that someone like Denise could handle it. Denise didn't know who she was. And that was dangerous. She used to be a little like that herself. Married, divorced, re-married, divorced, re-remarried. Not only because she had no *talent* for marriage (which was certainly true) but because marriage was an impossible project she just couldn't seem to keep from trying. The story of her cure was long and impossible to tell. The important thing was that she wasn't herself anymore. She'd gone to court and had her name changed. Her job was stupid and stayed 100% within its own frame, like a photograph she crawled into and out of.

She'd dropped all her old friends and hadn't made new ones. Roland certainly wasn't a friend and neither was Denise. They wouldn't call an ambulance if they found you bleeding on their front steps. She was the only one she knew who lived life the way it was supposed to be lived. She was the only one who'd accepted the world's new sober phase of realism.

It was clear that Holly had made a big impression on Denise. Denise was just about at her feet. She called herself a moron. "It's like you're two people," she said. "You try to go forward, but there's this other self, this moron, who's lurking behind you. And that moron takes over every time you doze off." She couldn't believe the orgy had ended up the way it did, she said, and she began to tell the story of the orgy.

The obvious and most important thing about an orgy was that there were more than two people involved. Things happened that couldn't happen otherwise. While you were bending down, kissing someone from above, another set of hands and lips might spring up in the always vacant space behind you. In sex you always moved forward with a sort of wide-awake consciousness straining to overload itself, to short circuit. You were always looking to pass through the wide open door of another body. But you never got the shock that you yourself had "doors" hidden from view. That you yourself *at the same instant* might *be* a door for someone else. For more than one.

While you were lashing up a tide of unconsciousness in someone's body, someone else was free to lash the same tide up in you.

So that the bed became (if she could convey this at all) a bobbing ocean of half-curves, broken chains, sickle moons, flattened pyramids. Nothing was allowed to die down and nothing was allowed to reach a conclusion.

Women's pleasant sighing and men's harsh groaning. One, two, three or four voices escalating into silence.

The sound of kissing or the sound of hair moving on your shoulders.

A woman's voice would begin laughing sweetly: very sweet and girlish, almost gushing. Very simple delight. The gushing, undiluted pleasure of midwestern girls on European tours.

Gradually the laughter would lapse into murmuring and the murmuring would lose its articulation and flow into whimpering.

The field of excitation was so enormous, that (if you managed not to escalate out prematurely) it was wonderful. But was it better than an overwhelming plunge into one person? She needed to test it again to make up her mind.

Afterward they sat around drinking and making pigs of themselves. The phone rang and Roland answered. It was Noel. She gave him a pitcherful of bullshit mixed with 2% of truth, the middle plane of lying honesty the deceived one begs for.

She agreed to meet him for breakfast the next morning, before work.

He picked her up in his ice blue Mercedes convertible and they drove to the coffee shop (a coffee shop crystal from which other coffee shop crystals could be derived) out in his Florida-style condominium complex—where they could breakfast with a lovely view of green squares melting out between pale towers into the greener-than-green fields of the professional 18 hole golf course, up to a brushy re-forested horizon. You couldn't help imagining your own future retirement. The view kind of relaxed you into a pleasant and premature senility.

While the chef was defrosting a couple of breakfasts in the microwave, they started to talk over paper napkins and glasses of lukewarm water. She decided to tell him about the orgy. If she was going to keep lying to him, she reasoned, she might as well have stayed married.

Something passed across his face so quickly, swifter than a shadow, more like the light that arcs across a roomful of faces off the surface of some vehicle zooming by outside the coffee shop window, that it was impossible to figure it out.

He was calm, as if he were still trying to choose between pancakes, waffles and french toast.

An orgy was no big deal, he said. "You'd *like* to shock me—but I'm not shocked." He reminded her that he'd once been in a situation, maybe not exactly an orgy, but a pretty weird sexual situation. He insisted that he'd told her the story. She didn't remember it at all.

"'I can barely remember my own *childhood*,' she said. 'Sometimes my brother gets in a sentimental mood and he says: "do you remember living on such-and-such a street?" or "do you remember doing such-and-so?": and it's a blank. As if there are a couple of planks missing. I remember a few vivid scenes—and that's all. I remember being on vacation at a beautiful hotel somewhere in the Caribbean—and wanting to go in the pool and not being *allowed* to because my father wanted to take *pictures*. And I remember crossing a suburban avenue with my friend. Not a vehicle, not a *bicycle* within a five mile radius. So quiet you could hear a fly approaching from the stratosphere. I remember the sensation of doing something simple—being with my friend and feeling happy—being spotted somehow by my father or some family spy—the maid or whatever—and being spanked severely. That's just about the sum total of my childhood memories. So why should I remember a story you told *me* about what happened to *you?*'"

"'Are you really that self-centered?' he said. 'Don't you care about me *at all?*'" His expression wasn't hard to read. She'd gone too far.

She ought to have melted like a pink packet of sugar substitute in a hot cup of sour coffeeshop coffee, but she didn't. She became angry.

"Why do you always *say* things like that? I'm not your *mother*, for christ's sake! How many mothers do you guys *need?*"

She felt at once how shopworn it all sounded, as if it were printed on glossy paper, facing a full page ad for Betty Crocker Au Gratin Potatoes. But she didn't care. What she said—or how or why she said it. A wonderful feeling of *not caring*.

His face drooped and he re-told the story of how the sexual triangle had brought him close to a breakdown. How he'd recuperated in the family fold in Greenwich and then met her.

He imagined that he'd re-told the story *not* to gain her sympathy, but to show that orgies were ok with him.

He begged her to set up another orgy with her friend, this time including him. If they did these things together they would be adventures.

"An *adventure?*" she said, her mouth full of defrosted and warmed-over waffle, salted butter pat, bottled blueberry syrup and shrivelled brown-and-serve sausage link.

It seemed he'd worked out some screwy theory about the couple of the future. The couple of the future would have everything: the freedom of a single person and the super-human power *in reality* to take both forks of a highway. No need to choose and to wonder what one had missed on the other road. Wasn't this, in fact, the ultimate mystery of the romantic couple—which other ages had been too earth-bound, too handcuffed by moral precepts, to explore? The idea of one will and one body multiplied by another: each a safe haven for the other and a companion on voyages where only two could venture.

She'd never heard Noel so talkative. He couldn't stop. He was excited. He was foaming over. As if his tongue had sprouted wings. She wasn't so much convinced as overwhelmed. He'd thought of everything, anticipated every possible objection or talked so much and so fast that she couldn't think.

So she agreed to arrange for the orgy.

The next Friday night they gathered in Noel's 21st floor apartment. She arrived with Roland. Holly and a guy named Bobby D'Amico were standing at the window. Beyond the endless, shallow pans of lawn grass, the rounded parking plaza, the other-worldly golf meadows, the imaginative not-quite-blue of the swimming pool, the tennis courts red as bricks, flower gardens, playgrounds, fountains and white towers of the complex, one could see thinned-out woodland above a fundamental bed of marshland, split pea yellow and split pea green, and above them both the lights of highways and industrial installations. The horizon of things already-or-soon-to-be-visible from any slight elevation in the world.

Noel had unearthed some slug and she was helping him set out stuff to drink and munch on.

They swilled champagne, nibbled and chatted. Holly chainsmoked and told a story about some monster who wanted to fuck her even though she was running a temperature of 104^0. "'If you won't fuck,' he said, 'at least let me tie you to the bed posts.'"

The slug did impressions she'd never seen done at parties: an angry rabbit, a sullen codfish.

Roland joked and acted thirteen times more vulgar than usual. Noel and the stranger named Bobby D'Amico struck up an instant hatred. They got into an argument about women, of all things. Bobby D'Amico was saying that women were passive by nature. This wasn't a criticism, he said, it was a *description*. No put down there at all. Far from it. The natural passivity of women was something to be envied.

Noel looked white, as if his face had been slapped. If passivity was really a virtue, he said, then someone ought to fuck Bobby D'Amico. Women were *entered*, Bobby D'Amico said. That was *biology*. So for the woman to get any pleasure there had to be *receptivity*. The woman who fought against receptivity fought against her pleasure. The woman who *enjoyed* her receptivity was the one who had the swooning orgasm others only dreamed of.

Noel said that Bobby D'Amico proved that men knew as much about women's sexuality as a ringworm knew about electromagnetic radiation. He was stalled somewhere before the Triassic period.

Bobby D'Amico shrugged and said that Noel had to rely on what he read or what some jerk concocted in the laboratory. He was talking from first-hand *experience*. He'd seen it a million times. A trap door opened under a woman's feet. It was a woman's fate and her secret pleasure. Easy to spot a woman who resisted her fate. There was an unmistakable flatness.

Ludicrous as it was, they were ready to go for one another's throat. Noel was hot under the collar, Bobby D'Amico was cold and dangerous.

"Well," she said, just to ease things up a little, "if it's unnatural for a woman to be aggressive then that's how a modern woman has to be. 'To be modern means to be at home with the unnatural.' Haven't you ever heard that proverb?"

Holly saw what she was doing and said: "Yes. Whatever is modern in the world is what looks alien, no matter how shopworn. 'Everything alien and everyone at home with it.'"

"The more shopworn and alien the more *modern*. Because the 'modern' is already historical. We can already talk about The Modern Period. It's just that the world lags so far behind what happens that for most people the museum-world of the modern still *looks* like the future."

They went back and forth like that and it seemed to do the trick.

The slug played the piano and sang a few heart-felt love songs in a nasal voice.

A little more champagne and everyone drifted, glass in hand, into the bedroom.

They didn't break up into pairs as she'd expected and didn't go off into separate corners. They fell into two sets: Holly and the slug with Noel, Roland and Bobby D'Amico with her.

Roland and Bobby D'Amico went to work on her as if they'd done some talking ahead of time. Roland had filled Bobby in on all her little preferences, weaknesses and sensitivities. While Roland kissed her mouth and breasts, fondled and touched her, so that in no time at all she was space-walking, struggling for breath, Bobby D'Amico simply inserted himself, deep and firm as a thermometer.

The center of her body, which seconds before felt slightly more humid and buzzing than neutral, suddenly felt like one of those wide-mouthed, two pound jars of wild flower honey everyone brings back from vacations in New Hampshire. It felt like someone had started heating it on the stove and then dropped it—and all this hot stuff was gushing around Bobby D'Amico's penis. The idea that this guy, who she'd never *seen* before, was inside her, that she was wide open to him, as easy for him to get from one end of her being to the other as for a car to get down the Avenue of the Americas on Sunday, had something to do with it. She was aware that *he* had to be aware (he was, after all, taking the temperature of her desire) that every deep kiss, every touch of Roland's only made her flow more heavily. Nothing he had to do but receive in a patient and bowl-like way the sap being pumped convulsively from the tree.

Still more perverse, didn't she have to be at least a *little* bit aware of what this guy had just *said?* It didn't take a genius to figure out what he must be thinking, the pleasure he had to be taking thinking about Noel.

He remained inside for a good five minutes. Then he got rough and had her gasping. Roland kept up his part of it too. They had her body doing S-curves.

Noel went crazy. He lunged for someone—she couldn't tell if it was her or Bobby D'Amico. Just about broke off his prick falling out of the bed. Noel was screaming. "YOUR HEART IS IN YOUR CUNT!" he said. "YOU'RE NOT WORTH KILLING!" and "I'LL KILL HIM! GET HIM OUT OF HERE BEFORE I *KILL HIM!*" and other crazy stuff.

She was crying. Everyone was frightened, scrambling to get out—half dressed, dropping clothing, pulling it on, Roland naked and laughing like an idiot, knocking over chairs in the dining alcove, stumbling down the foyer to the door. She followed them, sobbing her head off. Holly pleaded with her to leave with them. She gave Holly a hug, but she couldn't do it. Noel pushed everyone out into the hall and slammed the door. Holly was cursing him right through the door. After a while her voice got lower, as if the others were pulling her down the hall. Then she heard the elevator doors and they disappeared.

Noel sat down on one of the white couches and cried into his hands. She sat down next to him. They were both crying. "I thought you understood," she said.

"I *do* understand."

"Everything you said in the coffee shop. . . ."

"It doesn't help!"

His voice was filled with such anguish that, even though she didn't at all know what that meant, she put her arms around him, cradled him. She wondered: could she be crying for the same reasons he was crying? Was she crying *because* he was crying? Because she'd never seen him cry before? Because a man's tears contain a universal solvent, weeks of arguing, a woman's body, five years of abysmal failure disappear into them as if they were a vat of lye. Or maybe she was thinking that it was all talk. That it wasn't possible to live in the ideal ways one set out to. And, if it *was* all talk, then what was the point?

Later he asked her to marry him.

She said no, but agreed to move into his apartment—temporarily and on a trial basis. He promised to give her freedom.

Someone called "hello" from the other side of the street and made a beeline in their direction, an enormous pair of garden shears flashing signals as he walked. A familiar neighbor. Denise and Holly went off with the furniture movers and the blue van, on their way to Noel's white condominium complex out in the green bed of the countryside.

Valeria did her best to listen to the neighbor's story—which had to do with the garden shears. He'd just returned from the cemetery where he'd trimmed the low hedges that overgrew the graves of his father and sister. When he got home he started trimming back the freshly budded hedges on his own front lawn. He was at it ten, fifteen minutes before he realized they didn't need it. He'd just about killed them.

While he was talking, and shading the unusual super-clarity of the day, Valeria was thinking about Holly and Denise. It seemed that every time you talked to someone a new model of life was proposed. As if there were no resting point, life continuing to weave itself, not from your inside out, but without regard for you or what you thought. Each person with his eye on the next, memorizing a few words here, divining a possibility there. And, no matter how many maxims and possibilities you assimilated, no matter how far you ventured, you were bound to run into someone who seemed to have passed all of it by.

She allowed the talkative neighbor to bend her ear only as long as she was able to carry forward this line of thought. She broke away from him with no effort to be kind, the only way that's possible in such cases: when there's no sign at all that the speaker knows or cares whether you're impatient to be on your way or that something in the world might be more compelling.

Back on her steps she opened the pale blue envelope. The thin stationery fluttered in a more hopeful way than the crowded blocks of the classified section had, though still-and-all not quite capable of flight.

Dear Valeria,

I'm not the person I was two weeks ago. Otherwise I wouldn't be sitting here in my basement apartment with a green fountain pen and my sister-in-law's stationery, writing a letter.

I have never thought of myself as someone looking to fall in love. I have a friend who calls himself a "love addict"—because he's always in love with someone, *wanting* to be in love with someone, unhappy because he's fallen *out* of love with someone. All I hoped for (as I think I told you) was to meet someone kind and pleasant and make a peaceful life for myself in some untroubled rural spot, perhaps in Ireland. Or if not there, in Maine or Colorado, it hardly matters. I have no particular liking for the country. More of a disgust for city and suburb. And—what else is there? Has someone invented something other than city and Nature? Forest and mountain, desert and ocean. Of all these I find myself thinking of an anonymous life in or near a small, country town, like Robert Mitchum with his garage in *Out of the Past.*

Until now, I don't think I knew what love meant.

I *do* love my brother, of course—and my sister-in-law—who are, in many ways, like parents to me. And my nephews and nieces, the whole family. But that's a very different emotion, obviously.

It seems to me I said very little to you the night we were together. Now that I'm writing to you—with no feeling of confusion—with everything (*almost* everything) clear to me and my heart full—yet *still* finding it difficult to say anything, I understand why I was so quiet then. Can you understand how much it means to me when I say that since I met you I feel rootless, here with my family? That, as much as I love them, as much as I owe my brother, and as much as he needs me, I would leave tomorrow if you'd go with me. I would change my name so no one could find us. I'd live quietly, become a handyman or house painter. Anything you'd like.

When I picked you up after your party, at your friend's place in Manhattan, and I saw you standing on the sidewalk, I had the oddest feeling. Moving toward you in the car, the way the Cadillac has of gliding out of itself as a machine, you seemed to be floating toward *me* along the sidewalk. I felt the most intense longing. The street was dark—there were lights here and there—street lights, window lights, a light in a shop or two—and I thought: this is what it's like to be in a space ship. To drift through space—not to know whether you're going up, going sideways or even falling—and to see a blue light here a yellow light there, a row of white lights and then to see someone coming toward you that you loved and who'd been taken away from you. You feel that you've been alone for hundreds of years—wandering and abandoned—and you think: "there you are at last—you really *are alive!*"

Now life seems simple to me.

There is nothing else.

Nothing else matters.

I could die and come back to life. Find my way across any distance—the empty distance that really exists out there and which is exactly like our idea of death—to see you again.

I would do anything for you. I ask for nothing in return.

Yours,
Liam

Valeria was stunned. She felt as if someone had given her a gift she had no room for, a sort of concert grand piano of feeling.

S I X

SOMETHING THAT RESEMBLES A DESTINY

A strong wind had blown away one world and replaced it with
another. In this second world everything was drawn on glass. There
were days, Valeria thought, when nothing moved and you could just
about see the glue that held things in place. While other days, the
stuff that held the world together withdrew into the deepest
distance, a panel of glass across which each thing scratched out its
separate, random track.

The low heavy body of the dune buggy flew into the hollows and
threshed its way noisily up the shallow slopes, tearing out jets of
sand.

The goggles that hid Liam's eyes also flattened his curly hair with
their elastic strap. The green and yellow bands of his boating shirt
billowed like the banner of a nameless but familiar international
league of physical happiness.

He veered swiftly toward the far-away shore and picked up speed,
only to be delivered by one unyielding hill after another into a sky
whose bluer-than-blue joined Liam's boating shirt in advertising
happiness.

He kept turning around and shouting something and pointing
toward something, but she couldn't make out what he was saying.

They cut across a ridge and churned diagonally down a long slope
toward a broad delta of dark sand near the water. The sky was clear,
a few hard little clouds along the horizon.

A line of rusted pipe, a livid, crusty red orange, four feet or more in diameter, ran parallel to the shore, extending over the near curve of the horizon no matter how rapidly they zipped toward it.

They buzzed along next to it, its massive volume of rust lending the sea air a sour metallic scent. Liam turned again, his words blown straight back in his mouth, and she saw that his face was round as a watch face. That was unpleasant. Memory of something unpleasant that had happened to someone with a watch-like face or an unpleasant memory that had to do with a watch face or watch crystal. They were going fast, she thought, but not fast enough. Accelerated the *rate* of thinking, but didn't cancel it out. Maybe, carried to an extreme, in inter-stellar rocket travel, speeding through years or centuries, acceleration of thought could change the *nature* of thought. But not here.

They settled down on the blue oblong of a blanket in a spot where the rust-orange pipes took a long, sweeping curve, arriving quite close to the shore. At two or three points along this curve the pipes were surmounted by odd, windmill-like devices—large, spoked wheels on tripods that, Liam said, had something to do with regulating the flow of water and sand that were perpetually arriving from somewhere deep at sea. The heavier objects one heard striking hard blows against the inner walls, amidst a river-like, multitudinous gurgling and mineral jostling, were not only rocks, but dead, half-dead and living creatures. Lobsters, horseshoe crabs, sand sharks, and other large fish and shellfish gushed out in the dark geyser visible from where they were sitting. Hundreds of gulls could always be seen circling there.

All at once he stopped talking. He had the stricken look of a murdered murder witness, about to tell all. He cursed himself for always talking about things he didn't want to talk about.

"There's only one thing I want to say!" he burst out. "I wouldn't want to live if I couldn't see you!"

"We assume that the person we're talking to understands what we're saying and wants to hear it. We assume that the other person feels what we feel. Otherwise we wouldn't talk at all. But it isn't true. The other person *doesn't* understand. The other person *doesn't* want to hear what you need to say. The other person feels something altogether different, even if it goes under the same name. You think you say too little, but you say too much."

"You don't understand," he said. "I'm not saying 'I love *you*' so that you'll tell me that you love *me*. I'm saying that I found out that there aren't hundreds and hundreds of others, endless numbers, almost anyone, that you can fall in love with. Isn't that why everyone is miserable? Long, miserable marriages or people wandering from one person to the next, knowing that only a tiny bit of themselves is flowing toward the other. When I first saw you I thought: 'now I know that all my life I've carried around a memory. That memory is a longing, like the soul's longing for a body. As if it were before childhood, before this life.' I feel like someone who'd been abandoned in space, pulled on board after centuries, after death itself."

"When two people are unhappy enough," she answered, "they're ready for love. The romantic moment occurs when two pools of sadness flow together."

She looked at him closely, to see if she'd wounded him beyond what was absolutely necessary.

His head was framed, portrait-style, within the red-orange frame and black circle of an extra length of pipe. She wasn't able to read his face through the dusk that was gathering prematurely there.

Valeria ran a comb through her short hair, which felt dry and salty. The rough chords of an engine could be heard in the distance, somewhere beyond or within the dazzling masses of the dunes.

Liam had gotten to his feet and had taken a few steps away from the blue blanket. He signalled, arms upraised, toward a distant point where a lustrous patch of yellow paint corresponded to the accelerating chord of motor noise.

It raced toward them, at a fantastic rate, making more noise than a pack of motorcycles, which curse the world they tear across with apparent pleasure. Tons of distance were sucked in and threshed out. In seconds a massive block of yellow machinery on huge caterpillar treads bore down on them, right across the blanket they'd been sitting on, its driver hidden behind the windshield like a pair of eyes behind dark glasses.

Valeria tried to pull Liam back out of danger but he bounded forward, leaping with great agility into the cab. In another second he was catapulted out, fell to the sand, rolled over and miraculously got to his feet at once. He ran to the dune buggy, which seemed to jump into motion before he touched the steering wheel.

Both vehicles disappeared, the burr of one motor then another bored into and smothered itself in sand, diminishing into that almost-nothing that never quite resolves itself.

Valeria climbed up on the pipe and sat there, calmly waiting for Liam. The danger seemed remote, like the sensation that passes off when a car that's nearly run you down vanishes down the avenue. These things happened all the time, but came to nothing—as if life consisted exactly of a gluey shield against such possibilities, the ability to spring back the essential principle of normal living. If you failed to spring back, then you were no longer living in any normal sense. Then your life would have the coherent glamour of Jane Greer's in *The Big Steal* or Margaret Lockwood's in *The Lady Vanishes*. Something that actually resembled a destiny: one saw it at first from a distance, like the second track of a pair of parallel tracks that could never touch; and then it drew near, came close to touching. No such destination or destiny without intersecting at some dangerous instant in someone else's affairs. One crossed a path where something was in progress, fell into a net so wide and yielding one never felt it. Someone, foaming over, told you something he shouldn't have. Someone else found out and pursued you.

It struck her that she hoped the driver was the blond man, that he'd reappeared, drawn near like a gold thread in dark cloth.

The dune buggy came into view, parked at the bottom of a shallow downslope. It looked like a discarded soda can. The door was open and Liam was sitting sideways, his feet in the sand.

She came near. There was blood on his lip. He seemed to have shrunk and Valeria thought: "this is exactly the size time will whittle him down to in forty or fifty years."

She couldn't get him to talk about what had happened.

"You look like Steve McQueen when he sees the Blob," she said.

She put the dune buggy into gear and took off in a sharp arc toward the shoreline. A motor boat was skidding over the dark blue surface of the water, in the same direction and only a little faster. The boat's foamy trail seemed to double its size: a second, ghost boat, whiter than the first, somewhere between solid reality and a dazzling form of energy capable of lifting off vertically from a dark, magnetic sea of iron.

THE PHYSICS OF LOVE

Liam wanted to be comforted. With his face laid against her bare leg in a lamb-headed way she found it hard not to feel the desired wave of tenderness. It was as if a straw had been slipped down into her being: nothing she could do to keep the syrupy stuff from being sucked up.

She began to stroke his curly hair, but drew back her hand.

Hadn't he ever wanted to *change?* she asked. Didn't he get sick of doing what he was *used* to doing? Whatever felt natural was exactly the unchosen stuff that added up to an identity without your will. It was exactly what wove every individual destiny into a hopeless common history.

Liam wondered if she understood him. A couple of months ago, he said, he would have felt that there was no way out. No use longing for this or that, life was a matter of putting one foot in front of the other. Now things had changed.

The other morning he had breakfast in the Paragon Coffee Shop, a little dump in his neighborhood, so quiet and dreary you couldn't imagine why it hadn't closed down. Unless its quietness and dreariness were exactly its attraction. It seemed that every neighborhood needed at least one place where people could be miserable away from home.

He sat at one of the dozen or so pearly gray formica tables and ordered breakfast. A fat woman with iron red curls and royal blue dress was squatting on a stool at the counter, drinking the dissolved

Camels that passed for coffee over there and eating a chrome yellow slice of pound cake. He recognized her and she recognized him. They lived on the same street. She was known as Fat Agnes.

He ate as much as he could of the watered and fried griddlecake mix, drained his deep ashtray of coffee, and all at once he felt strangely exhausted. It was very early, of course—not really that much after dawn, before going to work—but that didn't have anything to do with it. It was more as if the table was iron and he was iron and his head simply had to join it. He laid his head on his hands, but didn't fall asleep. That is, he was no longer awake but he wasn't asleep either, almost as if he were a slightly more alert part of the table.

He heard the waitress, who was behind the counter refilling Fat Agnes's coffee cup, say: "Wudja believe it? Don't anybody go *home* any more? Another inch an' his face'll be in the goddamn *griddle-cakes!*"

"I know that shithead," Fat Agnes said. "Dontcha know that shithead? That's wunna those Lenahan Brothers who own all that crap, those bungalows and all that other garbage."

"Yeah? Is he one a *them?*"

"One thing there's no shortage of and never will be is shitheads, right?"

"J'hear about the guy they found *murdered* this morning. . . ?"

"Yeah, I heard about that. So what?"

"Found this guy Guido or Gino—sort of across from the new diner—the one that looks like an airport terminal—behind the gas station, what is it, the *Mobil* station. . . ?"

"If it's the one over there—on the far side—that one to the left of the A & P—if that's the one, that's Getty. . . ."

"I thought it was Mobil. Mobil, Shell or Chevron."

"Getty."

"Well, that's where they found the body. Throat slit from gill to gill, stuffed head-first into one of those rusty oil drums they use as trash barrels."

"One more shithead bites the dust."

"Hey—they oughta scratch that on every headstone in the cemetery."

Later on he realized that he actually *knew* the guy. A dark-haired, sad-faced, puffy-eyed little guy who'd had some real estate dealings (if you could call them that!) with Ambrose.

During their conversation, his strange exhaustion hadn't worn off, it had gotten worse. His head felt as if it was welded to the formica tabletop. And as if, *inside* the tabletop, he found himself in another world, walking down a street that looked very much like a certain avenue that ran perpendicular to the street where he lived. The same familiar linden trees and frame house-fronts, only much wider, emptier, the pavements very hot and pale. On the other side of the street an ugly little old wreck of a man was walking very slowly in the hot sunlight, smoking a cigarette and dragging a heavy shopping cart. A lifetime's worth of crap in dark bundles. It made him feel very old and tired, to the point where he could read the old man's thoughts. "I'm dreaming that it's so hot the air looks dark. I'm cleaning up the debris in a vacant lot. Everything is scorched, vacant lots everywhere, as if the whole district burned to the ground. Someone offers me a tray of thick sour cream. I say 'yes, thank you' and stick in my hand. The sour cream freezes around my hand, a block of ice. I become frightened and I think: 'what am I *doing* here? More alone with every day. How much longer will it go *on* this way? Are they going to make a little tunnel for me in Holy Cross Cemetery, like all the others? Every step brings me closer— better off not walking. . . .'"

He thought: someone might call this a *dream*. But I really am wandering around somewhere without knowing it. But if I'm *somewhere* else (and also still at the table, the way you can be sitting and eating and also be reflected ten or thirty feet away in a mirror or a coffee urn) does that mean I'm *someone* else?

He tried to get away from the old man as quickly as possible— almost to the point of flying. As if *he* were moving ahead on *fast-forward* and the *world* were whizzing backward on *reverse*. A powerful longing was pulling him.

Then he was on a street so beautiful, so *green*, that it was more of a green tunnel than a street. Above even rows of black trunks the leaf masses were round, curved and swirling like fingerprints. A dark green umbra of light reached the slate-like paving stones. A low, blue-gray wall flew along the left-hand side. In the middle distance, under the trees and against a water-like sheet of light, he saw Valeria. The green tunnel was like a raft that carried him from one lifetime to another.

As he walked toward her (it seemed to take an age), he tried to figure out what orange and green had to do with time. "Soon I'll have to confront my own death as something coming very near. It really does happen."

And then he was at her side, overcome by the miracle of having run into her again. That was strange. Why was it a miracle? As if he hadn't seen her for a hundred, five hundred years. She looked more beautiful than ever. A forest green sweater with a wide cowl collar and something orange around her throat. He thought: "I was wrong about the green and the orange. They don't mean *that*. They mean something else *completely*." The mild perfume of her hair made him dizzy.

The next thing he knew, he was actually on his lunch break, sitting in an elevator and eating a sandwich with one of his buddies. He never "woke up" in the Paragon Coffee Shop, never had the sensation of lifting his head from the table and waking from a dream.

She said that there was nothing to say. Even if he felt the depth of love he imagined he felt, and she were able to return that love, then their speech would be unnatural and elevated, like singing: the twined voices along which souls ascended out of their bodies and out of time. Mysterious waves of emotion so puzzling in physical terms—apparently having neither mass nor charge—yet undeniably real. But, even if she *was* that for him (which she doubted), he *wasn't* that for her.

Having said this she felt a wave of tender affection and changed the subject.

A DEATH ON TELEVISION

Two red toenails, then three, appeared against the white sheet. A tanned foot elevated on the bed, the other lowered to the cool floor.

Kneeling on the floor, proposal fashion, Liam painted in a fourth toenail and a fifth. Valeria lowered one foot and raised the other. A second row of flattened red oblongs appeared against the sheet with each stroke of the tiny brush-head.

He levitated to her mouth for a romantic kiss, slightly thrusting out the rounded points of her suntanned knees. Her legs didn't resemble wings and she wasn't able to conjure up the creature who'd paid her a nocturnal visit in her childhood bedroom. Nothing arose to bring the desired rush of sensation until she guided the flat prow of Liam's face into warm cotton. But that wasn't enough. She imagined that he was a muscular high school student coming up behind his math teacher and kissing her passionately on the throat, which seemed amazingly long, exposed, and pale against the blackboard. Hands covered the teacher's breasts, which seemed to double in size at once. The student's trousers dropped away, exposing powerful thighs, an erect and bull-like penis. He lifted the math teacher's skirt, pulled her panties down and let the skirt drop over them. He pressed against her. They began churning at once, the frenzied convulsions of legs and hips swiftly bringing the high school teacher to something resembling ecstasy. She bent over a school desk, supporting herself with two hands as if to keep the muscular high school student from lifting her off the ground—lifting her and lifting her again—the way a car jerks up by steady degrees above the relentless pumping of an auto jack.

Her dark skirt was thrown down over her head, severing the upper half from the lower half of the body. The upper half of the torso vanished through a black plane as if drowned. While the lower half remained exposed, luminous, round and smooth. It was up into the amphora-like ideal of the lower body that the man jacked himself again and again.

Then the black skirt was drawn off and sent sailing. The shoulders, neck, hair and head did *not* return from their black bath the same as they'd departed. Her eyes gave a blind glance from their corners into remote space. Her mouth had a transported, drooling look.

The man was bent over her so far that she was carrying him on her back. Two open mouths, two sets of crazy eyes, cheek to cheek.

Liam was exhausted, virtually asleep. Valeria used the remote control to turn on the tv facing the bed. Some sort of private eye program was in progress. Two guys in tropical shirts were talking in a bar.

"I've reached a point," one of them said, "*I really have reached a point* where I feel I could do anything for money."

"First I'd have to know what you mean by 'anything'—and second I'd have to know what you mean by 'money.' There's money, Ed, and then there's *MONEY*."

"Well, certainly not a salaried income. Long years of being a jerk have brought me to *that* conclusion."

"You say that, Ed. But I know you. You still have moral scruples. A man with moral scruples can kiss serious money goodbye."

"No, you *don't* know me, Tom. I'm not the same person I used to be. Since that fall I took I've changed. I know something I didn't know before. Something I *thought* I knew, but didn't *really* know. I know that we all die. There's no such thing as earning extra time for good behavior. So what difference does it make how you get your money?"

"I have a feeling that that's a very old argument, Ed. I've heard that before and there's a major *flaw* in there somewhere that proves you wrong. Only I can't at all think what it is. . . ."

"Turn the station," Liam murmured, his voice close to the inner, unspoken voice of the sleeper, like the voice of a motor you imagine you hear after it's receded across miles of streets. He knew too many guys like that. Guys whose lives smelled like the air out near the Mobil refinery in Jersey. Valeria didn't know jerks like that. But he *did* know jerks like that. Half the guys in the *world* were jerks like that. Miserable jerks who weren't the sharks they'd like to be.

She switched the channel. The enlarged head of a newscaster (sun-tanned and sandy-haired) crystallized on the screen, pale jacket whipping around in a strong breeze against the deep blue focus of the background. His first words were lost in a blur of crackles, while the camera withdrew into itself to take in the railings, cables, lights and traffic of a bridge. Cars hummed as if they were plugged into the future, when vehicles would travel swiftly from one region to another along beams of charged particles.

The police continued to drag the river, the newscaster said, with particular attention to the stretch downstream from the bridge. The spot where he was now standing was precisely where, at 4:00 a.m. this morning, three motorists reported seeing a woman poised on the railing. The three witnesses (scientists on their way to Washington, D.C.) agreed that there was something odd about the woman's stance: as if she were leaning forward on her toes, so far off the railing that she should have fallen. Yet she didn't. She remained poised that way for several minutes, with her arms away from her sides. Like someone trying to summon up the courage, the *momentum*, for a swooping flight to a lower point. Something crumbled or she lost her concentration. She fell as if she were sliding, like a child shooting down a sliding pond.

A black Corde handbag and a velvet jacket were found on the bridge. The name of the phantom leaper was being withheld pending recovery of the body, but the reporter had learned that an MIT research scientist had been flown to New York. Reliable sources said that the scientist's wife, a concert violinist, had recently suffered a nervous breakdown and had been missing for several weeks.

The image switched to a pretty, exhausted-looking woman at the studio-bright anchor desk and Valeria turned off the set. She found it impossible to remain in bed and left Liam dozing.

A pale blue Cessna passed smoothly across the window's blue subdivisions, its flight from here to there broken only by the lead strips anchoring the glass. The sand in every direction was marked with a deep map of grooves and tractor treads. Gold wires flashed in the water, painful to the eyes. And over everything sunlight still fell in unusually distinct sections of transparent brilliance and deep shadow, as if here the universe had been modelled on clear, mechanico-logical principles. If anything, the more western angle of the sun had sharpened the demarcation lines of light and shade, gilding one by darkening the other. So that the world momentarily looked like a blueprint for the solar or nuclear zone where light for the 22nd century was being manufactured.

"WAITING TO BE USED"

Liam and Valeria had showered and Liam had gone down to help with the packages that would turn into dinner. Valeria leaned out the window and watched from above. A pair of red wings darted across the foreground and alighted in an unruly mass of hedges sprinkled with conical clusters of white blossoms. It vanished for an instant amidst the leaves and re-emerged, detaching itself from the hedge and skating erratically upward, growing in size.

The door opened and closed. Valeria turned and banged her head violently on the half-raised sash. No one noticed.

"Why is grocery shopping so depressing?" a woman with blonde-blonde hair and Silvercup skin asked no one in particular, heading for the kitchen with a red can of coffee in one hand and a quart jar of Miracle Whip in the other. "Why does it get me down?"

Liam and a startlingly identical Bob Dylan lookalike were struggling with supermarket bags that had burst.

The lookalike said that he hated when Lana complained. Everyone got what he deserved. Life was amazingly just in that way. Just the right amount of misery was delivered to each according to his needs.

Valeria didn't like the tone of his bark. He sounded like one of those belligerent little dogs, their leashes as delicate as necklace chains, that darted out at you in their snug plaid jackets, flustering their owners with shame-faced delight.

"Bad mood, baby?" the woman cooed, following him into the kitchen.

"He's *always* in a bad mood, Lana," Liam called after her. "He's been in the same mood since he lost his job down at the Cape."

The Bob Dylan lookalike re-entered the room swabbing off a leaky milk carton.

"If I'm *always* in a bad mood, then it isn't a *mood*, dummy."

Things didn't improve over Denver sandwiches and beer. Liam tried to interest Valeria in his friend, Roger Muller, by getting him to talk about his days at NASA. It seemed that for seven years NASA had trained Roger to service an isolated element of the lunar module's electrical system. It was such a great job, great salary, great place to live that it was like being a perpetual "Dating Game" winner. Condo with patio and swimming pool in Cocoa Beach, motor boats, sports cars, deep sea fishing and women. They changed his idea of life so much that he just wasn't the same Roger Muller. Then the module project ended, his job was eliminated and he was supposed to decelerate back down to the old idea of himself. Try as he might it couldn't be done. He floundered for a while, then landed the job he had now, repairing signal lights and switches in the subway system.

He said that sometimes, not very often, you were really alive. Very, very rarely you felt: the plug is in, the switch is on, the filament's not burnt out. Most times you lived on the memory of that real life, lived *as if* you were alive. Since others were doing exactly the same, no one knew the difference. The trick was not to think too much. Thinking always brought you to the same question: why get out of bed? Why get down into the subway when other guys were still driving their Ferraris around South Florida, Malibu, the Riviera? Very dangerous to think about the teenage millionaires in rock bands, the models and lousy actors pulling down fortunes in prime time tv serials, the incredible sums they were handing out to stupid running backs and peevish tennis players.

It didn't take a genius to figure out that your life was garbage next to theirs. Only ignorance made life tolerable. You had to *not know* how this weird aristocracy lived to survive the uneventful, impoverished and one dimensional life you lived.

Then there were people like Lana. Her life was so shitty before, this seemed like luxury. When he met her she was waitressing and living in a roach motel on Avenue B. She wasn't all that different from the normal lump. The normal lump didn't give a shit one way or the other what his days were like. "A day is a day" was the normal lump's philosophy. He claimed only one advantage over the normal lump: when he was underground he knew where he was, how *foul* it was, and what it said about his life. The atmosphere down there couldn't be described. Every day fresh poisons sifted down through vents and gratings from the streets above: exhaust fumes and particles from every possible vehicle, residential chimney and industrial smokestack, filth of every kind. All this added new bitterness to the accumulated muck of the roadbeds. Electrical fires were commonplace. Even the working slave who wasted one, two, three hours a day travelling from here to there was familiar, in his dull and unconscious way, with the singed whiff of smoke, the smothered yellow fire doused with chemical foam, the bottomless sourness of dirt and combustion.

He knew this. He smelled this. He *ate* this. He knew the taste of his life. Was it *boredom*? Did boredom taste like cigarette ash, like a black puddle that would never dry up? His life was a bore, it was true. You ate, you drank, you slept, you watched tv, you went to a movie, you drove into the country, you danced your ass off and fucked till your cock turned blue, you found ways to make the same things different. One day you scrambled an egg and the next day you fried it over easy. You turned boredom into an activity: an activity you repeated until it became so familiar, so *essential* you began to imagine that if you *didn't* do those things you'd be bored.

That was how the normal lump lived.

He, at least, knew that the thorn was in his flesh, even if he made no effort to pull it out. But he was ready. Ready and waiting. Waiting to be used. He would have no qualms about doing something unheard of, if only someone would tell him *what*! He guessed that Valeria had similar thoughts. (Those with thoughts like that amounted to a secret society and you learned to recognize its members.)

Valeria said that she found it impossible to agree with Roger. She didn't believe in his "normal lump." Everyone was disgusted with everyday life, those who were stuck in it most of all. Therefore the idea of a secret elite built on vague, unfounded feelings of superiority was just more of the same empty crabbing that had been going on since language first crawled up out of the inland sea.

Lana said that she was selling cosmetics. That wasn't too bad. No boss, no regular hours. Still, it was work. She looked forward to getting a cold, climbing into bed, reading comic books and watching television.

Roger Muller said that maybe he'd been wrong about Valeria. Maybe she was just another victim of unconscious, lumpen socialism. The socialist lump sought out what the normal lump fell into. The socialist lump reasoned (and hoped!) that in the new age everyone would be equally miserable, equally deprived and depressed. "Democracy is failure and failure is democracy." Liam, who wasn't at all "political" in any conscious sense, believed this instinctively. A devout distrust of success or even of happiness. No surprise, with Ambrose as an older brother. Ambrose often struck people as a lay priest, a monk without a monastery, who'd taken vows of poverty—or at least of failure—but, unfortunately, not of silence.

Liam stood up, pretending to threaten Roger.

"You know what family life is like," Roger persisted as Liam took hold of his arms and they began to struggle. "A family is a deep fat fryer. Everything battered up, dropped in—shrimp and potatoes, heart and brains—crisp on the outside, mush on the inside."

His last words were shaken out of his throat.

Liam had his hands locked behind Roger's neck. They wheeled around like one four-legged animal.

Lana looked disinterested and began to clear away the half-finished sandwiches and the empty glasses and bottles.

"Whose family are you talking about, you asshole!"

He was trying to mash his friend's face into the rug.

"Yours, dummy!"

Roger's face was pressed sideways and distorted, the mouth misshapen but still able to get out a few words.

"You have to see the Lenehans at the trough! Jesus! The kids are *pigs*—and the brother—I don't even know what to *say* about the *brother!* Three *roast* beefs could fit in that belly! Only one I feel *sorry* for is the sister-in-law. . . ."

"Let him talk about himself!" Liam screamed. He was looking at Valeria but he was blind, wildly red in the face. "Get him to tell you how he tried to kill his wife. . . !"

The phone rang. Lana went to the kitchen, then sang out Liam's name.

Roger went to the liquor cabinet and poured himself a drink. He was flushed under his tan. His eyes looked like they'd gotten a quick coat of floor polish.

He said that in every family there was someone stupider than the rest, one sentimental idiot who kept the whole thing going, and he quoted a maxim to the effect that you never truly knew anyone until you saw him with his family.

"Better off not truly knowing anyone then," she said.

Liam re-entered the room, looking as if someone had pulled his plug. The green and yellow bands of his boating shirt were livid by contrast.

"What's up?" Roger asked, looking unconcerned. He swallowed his drink, the flush almost subsided beneath his tan. Lana's face, while puffy and amorphous as a supermarket jelly donut, looked sympathetically stricken.

"There's trouble at home. I have to go," Liam said in a voice that didn't belong to him or to any other living creature.

She went to the door with him. She didn't want to be left behind, as if going along would be an adventure.

He didn't know when he'd be able to see her again, he said, so he felt it was only fair to tell her something she wanted to know. Nothing had happened on the beach. He didn't know how else to put it. He'd never gotten within ten yards of that thing. And yet, at some point something had happened. There was no explosion, but it felt like one.

He gave her a withered smile and slipped into the hall.

"CAN'T LIVE WITHOUT BEING RECORDED"

Roger and Lana got it into their heads to have a bonfire on the beach.

The street was a solid realm of shadow. Here and there an attic window blazed orange, others smoky with violet clouds, while in the highrise windows warm sunlight still reigned.

The root scents of evening, wild as the smell of animal fur, arose with the plane of shadow. At twilight, Valeria thought as they walked toward the beach without saying a word, a question was posed. Trees opened like dark green blossoms, out of each something sailed off like a black bandana, joining the sky.

Valeria followed the two of them reluctantly, across light years of sand, to a point below the shuttered lights of an old beach house. A meadow-like lawn sloped down to a low sea wall and the beach rolled in a long, pale hill toward the transparent hologram of outer space.

Roger and Lana built a fire and swiftly got high: a thermos of vodka and orange juice and a couple of joints.

Despite the stupidity of being there, the bonfire was pleasant. It singed the air with something tar-like and, when that burned off, with real wood smoke. A real second or third world was generated by the first, she thought. What existed had little to do with those that created it, a collective other-reality. Every day you moved through this world of things and their collective auras. No one made the world. It wove itself out of the materials supplied by all. This lent a strange value (however much one didn't want to become a part of it, continued to despise it) to the everyday processes that made things appear. A universal hive of phenomena, produced by others, invisible to others, forgotten by others, and which, perhaps, utterly drained the lives of others—yet out of which the possibilities that would actually become the future presented themselves to the exceptional mind.

She felt restless and asked when they intended to go back. Liam might call. Or they could drive out there, offer their help.

Roger wanted to know if Valeria really hadn't discovered how hopeless people were. How much harm you did to others and how much harm others did to you. How disappointing everything was. How little we deserved the sympathy with which we anointed ourselves.

He talked a little about Liam's relationship with his brother Ambrose. Ambrose had sunk every penny of the family's savings in worthless property. No way to calculate the number of years Liam had wasted helping his brother. As if he were his brother's father. Incomprehensible anguish.

Of course you couldn't blame the family for asking him to shoulder their burdens. Nothing but rational self-interest, the principle of corporate business practice applied to everyday life. The true moral force of the age.

Lana complained that Roger, for all his talk, did a lousy job taking care of his *own* self-interest. Scored in the top two percent on the subway exams three years in a row, but he never got promoted. All sorts of dummies passed him by. Why?

The more people talked the more they proved one thing, Roger said. There were as many kinds of stupidity as there were leaves on trees. He considered *himself* stupid, otherwise he wouldn't be in the situation he was in. Always others, many others far sharper than you. But he wasn't *so* stupid that he didn't know that no one ever got rich by working. Right now he was worth in the neighborhood of $40,000. That was nothing. Forty thousand was no longer enough to feed a good sized dog. Life was no longer worth living below $500,000.

The hard part was accepting your limitations. He couldn't honestly say that he was convinced that he'd never-ever switch on the tv one day—in the middle of a baseball game, for example, and—where the beautiful shadow of the grandstand curved into the green sunlight of the playing field, intersecting the red-brown earth of the outfield warning track—see the name MULLER in red block letters on a white metal panel fastened to the wall, the way you saw GETTY or HEINZ.

His ex-wife was way ahead of him. At the time she left he was a zero, a neutral particle, an agitated neutrino.

She used to say to him: "How can you be happy just *living*? After you've seen people talking on tv, how can you talk in *private*.

Nothing *matters* anymore if it only happens in *private*. After you've seen a woman walking down a street in a movie, how can you be happy just *walking down a street?* I don't know *why* it is that an empty life really is empty, while a film about an empty life can never be empty and even strikes us as too full of meaning, but it's true—as if one system had drained all value from the other. Maybe there are those who still don't mind being invisible and there are those who can't live without being seen and remembered." And sometimes she would say: "If I'm not *reproduced* soon—if I'm not *recorded and transmitted right away*—I'll go crazy!" Then she left for Hollywood.

Lana wondered if Roger's ex-wife was happy now that she was beginning to show up in a couple of tiny roles in crummy tv movies.

"Happiness has nothing to do with it, stupid!" Roger said. "She's *there* and you're *here*."

The other day, on the way home, he was giving some jerk a lift to the Bronx and he thought, "what a depressing borough! Every city has one living zone—one zone that seems to be sailing some-where—ringed round with all these boroughs of depression, the domain of the normal lump." He thought about fire. All those rows of houses, shoulder-to-shoulder, would go up like this. "Fire is ruthless," he thought. "It has no mercy. It doesn't care what it melts, who it consumes. No sentiment and no exceptions. Much more logical than we are!" How thoroughly everything could be changed! The whole look of the world!

He'd made up his mind, Roger said. If he didn't bank half-a-million five years from now, he'd brand his name across the country, each letter a barbecue grill the size of New Jersey.

The bonfire leaped higher, as if trying to catch hold of a collar or a wave of hair, crackling and smoking, autumnal in both sound and smell.

"Well, I don't know, honey—half-a-*million*. . . !" Lana began.

"Tell me something, Lana," Roger said. "What the fuck do you know about my life?"

"I don't know," she said.

"Do you know who I see? Do you know what I *do?*"

"No, I guess not, Roger."

"Then shut the fuck up," he said. Doors were opening for him.

Big doors. He'd run into this guy he used to know at NASA—a weird guy who he'd never liked very much and who'd dropped out of sight after a nasty alligator hunting accident down in some swamp around Naples. Had his leg slashed from thigh to ankle, down to the bone. Severed so many nerves they had to amputate. Apparently, he'd been mutilated in other ways too.

This old acquaintance had introduced him to certain people. His eyes had been opened. He saw how stupidly he'd been living. No one ever accomplished anything living among idiots. No one was immune to the allure of the lazy dullness of things.

Fortunes were there to be made in new ways. Ways the world had never *seen* before. The man in the street had no more idea what was going on than a dog tethered and yowling in the yard. No idea how things were seething in the invisible perimeter where business, science and technology boiled together to create the future. Many things were underway. Some were known to the usual well-informed few. One could read superficial accounts of certain projects in magazines. Venture capital was already heavily invested in things still considered science fiction by the layman. And many of these things were trivial compared to what *wasn't* publicly known. He himself was still only on the fringe of things, only a drone. But promises had been made. One day he would disappear from all this. . . .

Valeria found it disturbing that she shared something with Roger Muller. Perhaps this desire was now a universal value, she reasoned, like the bygone will to be good or the longing to be in love.

She stood up and said that she was going. She needed to borrow Roger's Alpha to get out to Liam's brother's.

Roger checked his watch by the difficult light of the fire. If Valeria hung around for a couple of hours he'd introduce her to the people who owned the beach house. They were here for a reason, he said.

Lana scrambled to get her things together. She wanted to get back in time to see *Nightmare Honeymoon* with Dack Rambo and Rebecca Diana Smith.

Valeria glanced back from the sea wall and saw that someone had joined Roger, appearing as a dark blot, something like the multiple, globular outline of a jigsaw piece, against the red-orange of the bonfire. And a red light, deep and inwardly glowing, was travelling rapidly over the water, emitting the enormous field of night in one red ray.

OTHER PEOPLE'S LIVES

It felt like one of those summer nights when the heavy bodies of automobiles float in the darkness above the smooth roadways, under the dense trees of garden suburbs, and the red or green lights suspended at the intersections appear a second time, in a spilled, luminous way, on the grayish macadam.

It was a pleasant night, without a trace of the collective unhappiness that occasionally poisons the atmosphere. Yet, as she turned the corner of the street where the Lenehans lived, she saw fire engines, flames, water turning into smoke. An amber light flashed at seven second intervals across the pale facades above the screen of shrubbery and trellis growth, sending planes and cones of darkness flying out of their customary places in things. Broken, amplified and far-away voices on shortwave bands were both commonplace and unreal. Part of the charred roof had been torn away. The green walls were lit up weirdly like a hotel swimming pool.

She pulled up several houses short of the one that was smoldering. Liam was standing on the walk between low hedges and two green wings of lawn. He had his arm around a beautiful woman (red-orange waves of hair, pink-cheeked, childish face, pale, bare arms in a green sheath dress that would have looked out-dated in any zone where the magnetic pull of the future could be felt) as if he were comforting her. A striking similarity in coloring and hair texture made her look more like Liam's older sister than his sister-in-law.

Liam hadn't spotted her and she was certain that he never would, unless she got out and drew attention to herself. Down here, she thought, one experienced the total eclipse of necessity, the complete blackout, the black hole of immediate cares. What was generally taken for reality. She was on one side of this eclipse and Liam was on the other.

She got out of the car. Her short dark wave of hair and pale oval face should have been clearly visible over the low roof of the car. But he still didn't see her. It was uncanny. As if he was staring into a blank spot or looking right through her. The street between them was moving from one horizon to another, a compact ball spinning within a deep, invisible basket. Time was large and separate, lying outside in its own territory, surrounding every lighted window and the sharp edge of every dark roof with a second darkness that yielded into the cosmos. Everything was crowded, concentrated toward an astonishing degree of absorption. Super-dense rings and staggering waves of energy—the ultra-solidity of brick walls and the quickly evaporating waves of human voices, the strange half-materiality of fire, the shimmering of the invisible—were bent toward one, centripetal end. Everything wound around something hidden within. A zone that persisted by sucking things in, using them up.

Valeria made her way through the crowd of neighbors who were keenly interested in the way a corona of flames, jumping up through the beams of the neighboring house, threatened to re-ignite the Lenehans', now merely smoldering. As water was pumped in, the fire in the neighboring house flared up, sparking and crackling as if the water were a chemical fuel. She paused. A woman in the crowd looked familiar, though hard to place. She was big, but graceful. Dark, wavy hair flowed back in a full mass over bare shoulders; arms were round, tanned in a white sunback dress; a white evening bag over her shoulder. Something about her style of dress, or the way she wore her hair, was out-dated—from several decades back, if not from another century.

As Valeria approached her, with no clear idea what she wanted to say, she moved off through the crowd with a gliding swiftness. This was the moment Liam saw her. Something flew open in his face like a box when the lid is lifted. A little enigmatic emotion gleamed in the depths like a gold button. He came forward as if to intercept her. His face looked like a shattered dinner plate.

He turned and went inside and his sister-in-law followed him. Valeria looked at the smoking house. The fire had left it with an unfriendly expression. She wanted to leave as much as she wanted to have a look inside.

As soon as she stepped through the front door, Valeria was aware of an odd kind of disorder that had nothing to do with the fire. In one cavernous room after another, heirloom highboys and vast tv consoles stood back against high, pale green walls, each thing adrift in a sea of greenish light and not one thing bound to another by the peculiar coherent density that signals family existence.

All the rooms were empty except one. A big guy with a tremendous face, clayey lumps between yellow sideburns, red at the cheekbones and damp at the forehead, was sitting deep in a faded green-and-ochre-striped settee, watching color tv with the sleepy, mystically satisfied expression of someone who's able to watch the same program a couple of thousand times.

She came to the kitchen but didn't go in. Liam and Nora were in there with some policemen and firemen. It was crowded and noisy, almost cheerful against the yellow-and-orange-flowered wallpaper. The big man with tufty yellow sideburns who'd been wallowing in the settee came in by another entrance, went to the refrigerator then the stove, set a couple of little fish sizzling in a cast iron skillet.

Nora was saying to the police that these weren't the first things that had happened to Ambrose or to their property. One night Ambrose was attacked outside the bar. He had seven ribs broken and he got cut up pretty badly. He was positive that a guy named Tom, a family friend, was behind it. When he got out of the hospital he took his gun and went to Tom's apartment. But nothing happened. After that they became buddies. Ambrose had always been into bowling. Bought himself a new bowling ball every year. Now Tom had taken up bowling and they went bowling together. They'd sit on the porch and argue about foot positions and follow through.

Then other things happened, she said. Hundreds of windows were smashed in the bungalows. Gas jets were turned on in vacant apartments. They had a series of holdups at the bar. Minor fires. A boiler exploded, completely gutting a basement. Desmond was beaten severely on two separate occasions. The second time he had a concussion and was in coma for two days. Pat was run down by a car, had her leg broken. The dog was poisoned. A scaffolding gave way under Liam at work. Ambrose had three or four minor driving accidents, then went through a railing on a bridge up near Miller- ton. Broke his wrist and injured his neck. And now this stabbing in the subway and the fire. Could all these things just *happen?* Could they all be accidents? Did it all just *grow* like mold on bread?

One of the firemen said that her fires weren't the only strange fires. Strange things were happening not only in the neighborhood, but in other neighborhoods, other cities, and not only in the States. The papers were full of stories about Europe and South America. There was an epidemic of arson. Whole districts were going up. Billions of dollars were probably being lost and made.

The poisoned dog was nothing, a policeman said. There were loonies everywhere. Neighbors were always poisoning their neigh- bors' dogs. Always had and always would. Same with a lot of that other stuff.

The man at the stove said that it reminded him of *Mannix.* They were just showing the famous episode where patients in a fancy Baja sanatorium are getting systematically knocked off and Peggy goes undercover as a nurse. The head doctor's been in coma for months. His office has been converted into a hospital room and he's been lying in there all this time flat on his back—can't move and can't talk, but his *brain* is probably ok—though they can't tell for sure because he can't *communicate.* Eventually it turns out that the guy in there isn't *really* the head doctor. The head doctor's been murdered long ago. The place is being used as the headquarters of some top secret organization, but what or why exactly he didn't know because he'd fallen asleep.

"What does this have to do with that?" Nora said.

The big man dumped the pan of little fish into a plate, fetched a can of beer from the refrigerator and cleared a place for himself at the table.

"Well, look at it," he said. "Ambrose comes out of the men's room. Platform's deserted. Two guys come out of nowhere. Can't come from in front of him, cause he'd see them coming, obviously. And there's nothing behind him but a tile wall. The only other place is the roadbed and the track leading into the dark tunnel. So where did they come from? Then there's the way they did it. He wasn't really *stabbed*. They hacked away at him with the *point*. The way you use an ice pick. His legs, his back, his shoulder, they're all hacked up. One ear's in bad shape and an eye is just about shot. He's lost a lot of blood and he's in shock. Nerves were severed. He'll lose the use of an arm or something. But *no vital organs*. So were they trying to kill him or what? And where did they go? No one really knows. Someone says they ran into the tunnel. But does that make sense?"

"A man spends his whole life working," Liam said suddenly. "Being what you'd call a perfect American—a model citizen—all the things you're supposed to believe in—he works hard—he buys property and builds himself up out of nothing—he raises a family— he's good to everyone—he doesn't *cheat* anyone—and then he can't get *justice*. He finds out there *is* no justice. And it does something to you! Something you can't know about until it happens to you. There are only two kinds of people: the ones it's happened to and the ones it hasn't."

A couple of people seemed like they had something to say. But they didn't say it.

"No one knows!" Liam said. "But I *know* the sacrifices my brother made! I lived through it! I know the kind of shitty jobs he held! I know the *holes* the family had to live in! I've seen too much! They're not going to murder my brother and get away with it!"

After that he seemed to calm down or to get depressed. He sat down at the table where the big man with the tufty sideburns and big lumpy face was now working on a wedge of pie and a glass of milk. Nora sat down and so did a fireman and a couple of policemen. They all talked quietly back and forth about Ambrose and debated possibilities without appearing to believe any of them.

Nora said that he hadn't been the same since he fell off the porch. The physical changes had turned into personality changes, if that made any sense.

Liam said it was because everyone let him down. When he lost his job the union didn't lift a finger. And the whole time he was laid up not one so-called friend showed his face. Naturally he began to turn a little bitter. Then when he got back to work and things were looking up a little, he was beaten up outside the bar. A couple of crumbs were arrested, but somebody got them off. Meanwhile Ambrose was in the hospital. It was a joke. He lost his job again. And after that you couldn't talk to him. He just about gave up on everything. He wanted to go after the guys that did it, but Ambrose said no, there was no point. Those guys were nothing. He knew what it was all about. Someone big was trying to grind him into the dust. Somebody up there wanted to get his hands on a particular tract of wetland he had a piece of. He wasn't the only one they were after. "Stay out of it," he said. "They've already murdered one guy. There's nothing we can do."

The terrible thing was, Nora said without much emotion, that now Liam's friend Roger had introduced Ambrose to some people and he was working again. And now this. . . !

"I don't think he can survive another setback!" Liam cried. He had his face in his hands. It seemed like he was weeping. Nora made an effort to comfort him, said that he was wrong to feel responsible. *They* were wrong for *giving* him so much responsibility. He didn't know the whole story, she said. She put an arm around him, but his shoulders looked bony with resistance.

Valeria began to feel worn out by all this. There was a peculiar sort of weariness induced by other people's lives, she thought. A certain region of the brain was exhausted by spending too much time listening to things that had nothing to do with *you*.

She slipped back the way she'd come.

"EVERY SOUL A TELEVISION"

Valeria opened the door to Roger Muller's apartment with her borrowed key. She was looking from the dark hall toward the living room, where a lamp brought the red and yellow Navajo rug to life on the wood floor.

Laura came into view, pink as bubble gum and wearing nothing but gold earrings and fluffy pink slippers. She did a shorthand dance step while examining the red label of a record and switched off the light. A blue indicator light and an orange turntable light made the stereo glow like a miniature airport. A woman's voice sang urgently about love, about a lover who'd become a space traveler and was lost in another solar system. "I'm going to take a spaceship and search for you forever!" she sang. The flight of her voice was supported by a deep, propulsive rhythm, a black jam of passion and rocket fuel.

"Roger?" Laura sang out.

A minute or more passed. The blue and orange stereo lights were eclipsed once, twice, three times by someone passing in bare feet or slippers.

"ROGER?"

Her voice clashed with the sensual urgency of the record.

"HEY ROGER! WHERE THE FUCK *ARE* YOU? *ROGER?* HEY—CUT IT *OUT!*"

Sounds of scuffling and then a man's hoarse whisper.

"Scared? Watcha scared of?"

"No, seriously, where *were* you?"

"Where did you look?"

"*Everywhere!*"

"Couldn't have looked *everywhere*. . . ."

"Well, *almost* everywhere."

"I was in the bathroom, dummy!"

"You were *not!* I *looked* in there! That's one place I definitely *did* look—and you weren't *anywhere!*"

"Well, I was."

"There's no place to *hide* in there. I even opened the *shower curtains*."

"Did you open the bathroom door?"

"Of course!"

"Did you turn on the light?"

"I turned on the *night* light."

"Well, what did you see?"

"I *told* you what I saw! I didn't see *anything!*"

"That's what you *didn't* see. I asked you what you *did* see."

"What?"

"You saw an empty bathroom, right?"

"Right."

"'Right.' Dummy! Did you see *behind the door?* Huh?"

"Are you trying to tell me you were behind the door?"

"If I wasn't behind the door then where was I?"

"But there's no *room* behind the door. . . !"

A yellow bit of wall got lit up, a door opened into a bigger block of yellow, the door closed again and the shower began to run. There was laughter and squealing.

Valeria went into the living room, turned on a lamp and sat down on the zebra-striped couch. There was too much reality in the world, she thought. It was flat, over-illuminated and literal, like videotape. It wore you out.

The light of the lamp touched off a flameless match in everything. A red telephone gleamed in the kitchen. She thought of Nadja (minor pang of guilt); of her mother (news of the Guras); and of something more desirable but less nameable.

She crossed to the kitchen and turned on the light. The fluorescent bulb buzzed, filling the room with flat, inhospitable rays. She began to dial, but heard odd noises coming from the bathroom. It sounded as if something was being scoured with paper toweling. And at the same time it sounded as if quilted ski parkas were rubbing together. Could they be making love through the shower curtain?

A woman's voice cried out in a deep, strenuous way. The familiar cry of agony struggling toward a singular, irreducible thing in the distance.

Something bumped against the door.

The woman was whimpering in real earnest and the man began to groan.

Now it sounded as if a cotton sheet were being pulled back and forth across flesh.

The paper, the nylon, the cotton, the occasional violent thumping, the whimpering and groaning added up to something at once mysterious and prodigious.

Then it went quiet and the shower started up again.

Valeria dialed Nadja's number. A man's voice came on, crackling with static, before the phone had a chance to ring. "Yes?" the voice said politely.

"Andy?" she responded, though certain that it wasn't him.

"No. This isn't Andy. Andy is visiting his folks, I believe. And your sister is downstairs, waiting for me to drive her to the hospital. Since Andy took the Saab, naturally she's without any means of transportation."

Why would Nadja be visiting Liam's brother in the hospital? she thought. That was dizzying. Alarming. Or beyond alarming.

She demanded to know who she was talking to—what he was doing in her sister's apartment—what he was talking about.

"I'm offended," the man said. "We all like to imagine that we're remembered. That we leave an indelible imprint. That we've populated the world with our reproductions."

She recognized the dinner guest, Humberto Vilanescu.

"Don't be alarmed," he said. "Everything is under control. It's just that your mother is in the hospital."

Some drapes had been taken down and cleaned, he explained. Her mother had repaired their hems and had then undertaken to re-hang them herself, using a kitchen stepping-stool for a ladder. She'd fallen with a sewing scissor in her hand, cut her lip and gum rather badly and broken off two teeth. She'd suffered a concussion, but it was too early to tell how serious that was. Frankly, when he'd first entered the apartment and found her lying unconscious at the foot of the stepping-stool—with one leg still in an awkward position on the second step and her forehead against the decorative radiator cover—the drapes fairly twined around the body (apparently her heel catching in the drapes was what had sent her falling)—a deep bloodstain on the portion of the drapery that had fallen across the injured mouth—he thought the poor woman was dead. Happily, that was far from the case. What's more, the phone had begun ringing at the very moment he'd bent down to examine her. It was Nadja.

Valeria asked for the name and address of the hospital.

He answered by saying he would come for her. He clicked off without bothering to ask where she was.

She called back, but he was gone.

***   ***   ***

Valeria snapped awake. The apartment was as quiet as a hospital ward after visiting hours, when two hundred people lie sleeping and breathing on audible electronic waves and pulses. A dry blue flood of television light washed under the bedroom door, varying rapidly in brilliance and intensity so that the switching of images, shifting of planes and volumes from here to there, was just about discernible, along with the suppressed modulation of voice tones.

Someone was standing over the couch, staring at her closely, poised uncomfortably as if afraid to make a sound.

Liam whispered her name. She shifted her legs so that he could sit down.

He explained that when he got back from the hospital he conked out in front of the antique Magnavox despite the noisy explosions of *Merrill's Marauders*. Every program on that thing was the same mess of stewed fruit, so it never failed to throw him into a trance.

He had a horrible dream (that a murderer was after Valeria) and woke up terrified. Couldn't shake the feeling that she'd been murdered and rushed over. Even now, when he knew that she was ok, he felt poisoned by the dream. He began to give her a plot summary of the dream, which had to do with an elevator and a death ray. She didn't want to hear it, she said, and went to the open window.

She looked out toward the ocean where scattered lights hovered below the sky and above the water. It gave her the feeling of being situated at an odd, middle altitude between Earth and Cosmos. "Up there" and "down here" were equally distant, equally abstract, beyond entry. Even the spicy breezes, with their earth-and-flower fragrance, might have flowed down from space on one or another boundless stream of rays, picking up a flavor of the here-and-now from parks and gardens.

The vista sucked something out of you. Bombarded by coded messages, you couldn't help transmitting something in return. Every soul a television.

Far beyond the hovering lights she saw a tiny red point, a minute gem chip, a tiny red spider like one that lands, along with leaves and shadows, on the open pages of a book being read outdoors, under trees. It followed a remote, slow arc as if it weren't moving at all, yet managed to cross the sky quite swiftly, dwindling by sub-measurable degrees into the close-knit fabric of things.

Liam came up behind her. He still wanted to talk about his dream. In the dream the one who was threatened was his nephew, Desmond. He looked like a tiny, prematurely aged Mickey Rooney. But he knew it was her. And then at the end he was climbing some Roebling cables up through the ceiling of the elevator into the sky. That meant that their only salvation lay in escape. He knew it sounded stupid, but she had to remember that salvation usually came through something stupid.

She said that he was making her feel like George Hamilton in *Crime and Punishment, USA,* the one where Raskolnikov was a student at UCLA.

He knew that she could accomplish something far beyond anything he could imagine, he persisted. He'd work for her. Support whatever she decided to do.

Men were already saying things like that in tv movies, she said. And whatever had appeared on television could no longer be taken seriously as a destiny. Television was a vacuum cleaner of possibilities.

They stared out the window.

"Tell me why I can suddenly see myself in a garden, on a glass bench," she said. "A long, sloping lawn, a deep green dish facing the sky like the vast dish radio antenna in Arecibo, and tall hedges that still have a thin screen of leaves—leathery and purple-black with frost, more like grapes than leaves. I see a white lampshade glowing in someone's window through the hedges. And I think: 'the beautiful lamp of the sky.' I look up—and sure enough the sky is white and glowing, shedding late afternoon light on everything just like a lamp with a thin, fabric shade. A few birds fly overhead making sounds like transistor radios and a brown-and-white dog barks in a yard four houses away. Her barking reaches the cold sky and it begins to snow. What does it mean?"

"It means that there isn't a second to lose!" another voice said.

She turned and looked into the dark apartment. Something was visible in a dusky, infra-red way.

Humberto Vilanescu came up beside them, between the zebra-striped couch and the open breath of the window, just as Liam switched on the lamp. His head was larger, more powerful than she remembered it, the body not quite so soft in its blue suit and red shirt.

She introduced the two men. They shook hands and gazed deeply into one another. Or one gazed through a magnifying glass while the other took an X-ray.

It was only when she was already in the street with Humberto Vilanescu and everything, dense hedgerows and black plastic garbage sacks, fragile windows trembling in their frames and twenty-one story building blocks of sparkling limestone, seemed about to cartwheel away in the dark gale blowing off the ocean, that Valeria remembered that she hadn't asked Liam about his brother.

She thought, as she climbed into the safe harbor of Humberto's limousine, that it was as easy to pass from one reality to another as it was to have your picture taken.

SEVEN

BORNE AWAY

As summer advanced to the point where a discerning eye could see a scorched orange in the green tunnels, Valeria went to more parties than there were days. She felt borne away not so much by Humberto Vilanescu as by the torrent of his life. A cascade of people, ideas, projects, deals and possibilities. A downpour of faces, parties, meetings, dinners and dwellings, hardly the same one twice and, apparently, none of them his own. He knew so many people, and from such diverse realms, that it was impossible to figure out what he did. Many things were puzzling. Or one, essential thing was puzzling and kept cropping up in a confusing number of superficial ways.

How did he earn his money?

Was he wealthy, as it sometimes appeared?

Why was she now convinced that she was going to achieve the unique and significant thing she longed for?

One evening, at a party in a blue and black apartment far above Fifth Avenue, Valeria was surprised to see her old friend George (formerly Georgi). He was far away, on the other side of a spiral nebula of guests talking triple in order to be heard above those talking double, in front of a black upholstered couch under a black-on-black-in-black vista.

As she made her way toward him, she saw that he looked utterly different. To the degree that it was hard to account for the fact that she'd recognized him at all. His stiff crop of hair was gone, replaced by a soft, short, slightly wavy hairdo, still wheat brown. His pale blue suit was slim and expensive. Similarly, shirt, wrist-watch, rings, cuff links, shoes were altogether of a different, far more costly variety than anything George had ever worn. Joining his immediate circle (deep in conversation, he didn't seem to notice her) she saw that he'd lost an incredible amount of weight and seemed oddly smooth-shaven—as if he'd discovered a new kind of razor and had finally succeeded in shaving all the darkness out of his furrows. The weak, dark look of the unhappy (the unsuccessful?) intellectual had fled him. Now he had a weakness that suited him in a new way, like the forty-year-old boyhood of a new life.

The woman George was talking to had a clear, almost transparent face and unusually opaque coffee-brown eyes, a surprising but not unattractive amount of gray in her dark, flat and silky hair. While her companion, with a small, pointed nose and a somewhat fishlike mouth, was nevertheless quite handsome, the twin of an actor seen now and then in dubbed French murder mysteries.

"He was only able to give me thirty minutes of his time," the handsome man was saying. "And of that thirty minutes I only understood *ten* minutes of what he said. But it didn't matter. Those ten minutes had such a profound effect on me. . . ."

"I felt that too!" the beautiful woman with the transparent skin and coffee-brown eyes said. "*His* dream was *my* dream. How could he know my dreams so *vividly?* Did he dream exactly the same thing? It was a little *frightening.* . . ."

"You know him better than we do, George. What is he like? Is he the way he seems—or is he something else in private. . . ?"

George said that, to put it simply, the man had changed his life, almost with a wave of his hand. But beyond that he really didn't care to talk about it.

The handsome man said quite seriously: "The thing that amazes *me* is how quickly he knew I'd had a breakdown. He took one look at me and he said: 'You inherited money and now you're using that money to make *more* money, but you've had a breakdown and you're *still* half in and half out. You're creative. You're inventive. You're *brilliant* in many ways, but you've never been able to *do* anything.

You haven't exactly led a life of significant achievement. And, unless you get yourself harnessed to something you believe in, the same fantastic internal pressure is going to build up again.' It really shook me."

"How *could* he know that?" the beautiful woman asked, a note of anxiety creeping into her voice like Cremora in strong coffee.

"What *I* want to know is: what exactly does he have in mind for me? What is it that he's *offering* me? Would you know, George?"

"No."

George chose this moment to notice and greet Valeria, making a fuss about wanting to hear news of mutual friends and steering her toward a brass helix stairway that, he said, led to more private rooms upstairs.

Buttonholed by a tiny man in a black suit, George lagged behind on the landing while Valeria waited in the bedroom.

George seemed annoyed. "I don't know anything about that and I'm not *interested* in that! Why do you *bother* me with these things?"

The tiny man (who was virtually engulfed by George's pale blue foreground blot) insisted that he only wanted George's opinion and nothing more.

"It suddenly occurred to me," he said, "we're being too *lenient*. Why should *we* pay? Let *him* pay! I want to give him a call and say: 'We're not paying. *You're* going to pay. Everyone has to pay for his sins *some* time, and this is the time for you!' I can do it in a very nice way, believe me. 'It's all mud. I have nothing against mud. I'm a guy who *likes* mud. I like the feel on my skin of a damp day in November. I like to crawl across the ocean floor. But, let's face it, you haven't exactly been on the up-and-up. You know the sort of buildings we need to put up, yet you try to palm off this swampland. I want you to remember later that I didn't *threaten* you. I just explained to you, as a friend, that you aren't the first cretin we've had to send back to kindergarten. We're very good at teaching guys like you their ABC's, believe me!'"

George turned to close the bedroom door, momentarily exposing half of the tiny man's countenance, a sharp-featured fox face. He was eclipsed too quickly for Valeria to be certain she recognized him.

She sat down on the enormous black cube of the bed, leather-upholstered like an automobile interior. Other biting touches of the industrial—of an astringent minimalism that fell between a worn-out idea of the modern and another idea which had yet to be conceived or which was inconceivable—were out of tune with a densely floral wall covering. A bottle blue wall mirror faced the bed, so that Valeria appeared a second time at a slightly dizzying tilt.

Several large books were lying on a bed-side table, as if for late night reading. Valeria opened a quarto-sized, morocco-bound volume and read:

> What is a monster? A monster is patient. That's what's monstrous about it. It waits. It feeds on the happiness or the unhappiness of others. Everyone is a tiny meal for it. It sucks them up like algae. It grows larger. It swims in circles, like a tumor with fins. In general, people don't understand the depth of hatred they create in others. There are pools of it everywhere, in round, calm faces. Monsters waiting in their pools everywhere for something to happen. We quickly forget the faces of the monsters we've seen. Our ability to forget things, not to *see* things, makes it possible for monsters to walk easily in our midst.

Not very grown-up reading matter, she thought. Childhood tastes persisted throughout life, only less cleanly, more self-consciously. A very few lucky ones found ways of living a life-long childhood. A limited immortality-in-life that only wore out biologically. Collectively these lucky ones were a reservoir of preserved childhood. Toward which one yearned, as toward a real afterlife.

The so-called "growing-up" of normal life was nothing more nor less than the wadding in of the original personality and its desires. When the necessities of normal life fell away, acquired habits fell away with them, the preserved child returning to its original pursuits. As if the goal of all that hard work and money-earning were the freedom to play in the open air again. You saw this cycle in your own family, but still you did the same. It was one thing to grumble about passing time, to have blue moods; it was another thing to jump off the edge of the everyday.

She continued to leaf through the book and on another page she read:

Isolated instances of mass-hallucination are not uncommon—Le Bon[2] cites many, and a good example was provided recently by the imaginary aeroplane-crash witnessed off Shoreham[3]. . . .

The footnotes read: "*Psychologie des Foules* (Paris, 1895)" and "[3]12.i.34. Several persons believed that they saw a single-seater plane, 'painted white, with a red stripe,' plunge into the water about 500 yards from shore."

George came in, sat down on the black bed. He'd lost even more weight than she'd thought, like an old chair that's been re-upholstered, modernized. And the lost weight was like the space in a doorframe, both there and not-there, a mirror panel of some unfamiliar anti-substance.

He talked about himself freely and intimately, in a way that didn't at all remind her of the George she knew as George.

Humberto Vilanescu had saved his life, he said. Lucky for her, she didn't know yet what happened to you as you approached forty. A melancholy set in that was unlike anything you'd felt before, soggy and dangerous. He remembered vividly the day he decided once-and-for-all to stop struggling to secure a foothold for himself somewhere in the university system. He set fire to all his research notes and unfinished manuscripts. He was in shock. To have done something that irreversible, that *real*, was like committing a crime. Like *killing* someone. No going back. Something was done that couldn't be undone. His life could never be the same. He thought: "I'm no longer a producer, only a consumer."

He took a civil service job, as she knew. That turned out to be ideal. A sort of high (or maybe only middle) level idiocy. Those in the grade above him had something serious to do. Something resembling work, even thought. Those below him did a lot of scrambling and legwork. While he was in the realm, the *non*-realm, of paperwork and interviews. What was required was to place your brain in a jar of mild antiseptic, like false teeth. After a short time you found yourself writing and talking automatically. This was quite relaxing. And they kept you enormously busy. A relaxed, brainless busy-ness. He'd often listened with contempt when others spoke of their jobs that way, as a sort of active, local boredom that kept a more cosmic, vacant boredom at bay. Now he supposed he'd discovered that the margin that separated us from any and all unthinkable conditions was much narrower than we preferred to imagine.

At last he was living a life he didn't care about, like others, without guilt and without ambition, and which therefore had no power to torment him, as his various failures to reach the academic heights had.

After a few weeks he began to feel depressed in a way he'd never experienced before. Sitting at a table he would suddenly burst into tears. He began to think incessantly about all the mistakes he'd made. How badly he'd lived. And, still worse, how badly those he loved (only one, in reality) had lived because of him. Where he'd dreamed of giving happiness, perhaps wealth, even fame, he'd only succeeded in passing on his own incurable deprivation.

It dawned on him that the best moments of his life had already passed. The moments when he and Charlotte were first in love. Love was no longer possible. Neither with Charlotte nor with anyone else. Love was only possible once, before you knew too much about yourself. Conventional wisdom had it that love grew impossible with the years because you became cynical about others. The truth was quite the opposite. Love was only possible in ignorance of what you were about to impose on another. This couldn't be done twice. The idea of a second love was an obscenity. It required the ability to re-live what you no longer believed was true. To accept sympathy for injuries you'd long since passed on to innocent others. To re-enact the drama of one's emotions as if for the first time. To ask and receive—this time knowing the consequences full well.

Charlotte left him, just as he deserved, taking the children (who were of no consequence one way or the other) with her.

One night, after a week of rediscovering the specific gravity, the frightening visibility of the darkness that can fill an apartment, he dreamed that it was hot summer. A certain fragrant weight of night air, the exact instant of total blossoming and perfume, leaf size and tree mass.

He was driving an old car along a road that was torn up, a mine field of pot holes, craters, jagged rocks. It was taking a lifetime to reach his destination: a distant building, white and monumental in a Washington, D.C. sort of way. He arrived, looked back and saw that he'd done something incredibly stupid. Many people were arriving by way of a service road, smooth and pleasant, that led to the same place. He was the only fool driving on the torn-up one. Those on the smooth road were white-haired, in their eighties or nineties. Hordes of them were entering the building. He got out of his car and entered along with them. Inside it looked like the International Arrivals Building at Kennedy and throngs of old people were struggling up a broad plane something like an escalator without steps.

He panicked. Had to get out of there. Spotted an archway on a distant mezzanine that could be reached by a long flight of steps. The people were younger up there, a few familiar faces among them (Valeria may even have been there!), and he ran toward them. But it became clear that whatever was drawing him toward the youthful faces on the mezzanine, whether fear or longing, was not permitted. He felt a searing pain in his left leg, as if he'd been branded or shot.

He woke up, switched on the bedside lamp. His leg was throbbing. He pulled up the leg of his pajamas and there on his calf was a bloody wound, sickle-shaped and puffy. He felt all around the bed, the wall and every object within reach. Nothing sharp enough to inflict that wound.

He sat on the edge of the bed, exhausted. "I've used everything up," he thought. "There isn't another ounce of anything left in me."

He had to get out of his apartment. He dressed, went down to his car and started driving.

He ended up on the Verrezano Bridge, possibly on his way to see Valeria, since he didn't know anyone else in New Jersey. He stopped the car on the bridge, got out, clambered up on the railing—teetered there—felt an enormous rush of air as if the world had launched away from him like a rocket.

The next thing he knew he was a boneless bundle of flesh, a

filleted flounder, in the back corner of a blue-toned limousine. The man next to him was enormously forceful and reassuring, but in an unfamiliar way. That was the man he now knew as Humberto Vilanescu. He'd never forget what Humberto Vilanescu said. "Everyone perishes, in every age. It may be that no one has ever survived or ever will. But the weak always perish while trying to hide themselves in the comfort and pathos of a bygone age. While the strong perish in the effort to cross over to the future, in terror and isolation. This is not your time."

She didn't need that from Humberto Vilanescu or anyone else, Valeria said. Didn't need to be resurrected. So far she was impressed only in the limited sense that she understood and sympathized. She felt the allure of all the suggestions Humberto Vilanescu had made about the future. But she needed something more definite to go on. She was a scientist, not a magician. She'd heard from a friend who worked at Fermilab in Batavia, outside Chicago. If nothing happened here soon, she might go out there, though she'd never planned to spend her days waiting for a proton to fly 200,000 times around a 6.4 kilometer track.

These things weren't his province, he said. But he could assure her that Fermilab was nothing, CERN in Geneva was nothing compared to what was happening here. He'd heard her name mentioned more than once in connection with something of revolutionary importance. Unfortunately, it was completely beyond him.

There was a rap on the door and it sprang inward. The woman who was ushered in by Humberto Vilanescu (he somehow succeeded in dominating the moment from behind) hovered between the familiar and the unfamiliar. She thought of the loft party where she'd last seen George. But a little too familiar to be one of those talking faces, dancing or slouching bodies who were known to someone but never to you, like the people who occupy nightclub tables in gangster movies, mouthing conversations, weaving a world for the characters in the foreground. And too unfamiliar to be someone she'd spoken to.

Whoever she was, Valeria didn't like her looks. Bony face and bony wrists in several floral shades of silk. Horsy, with a stiff, yellowish wave of hair. A somewhat aged debutante, Valeria thought, who'd been set up in business, perhaps after a collapsed marriage or two, and who'd surprised everyone by making still another fortune.

Humberto introduced her: the hostess, Bente Fog. Once-upon-a-time *Baroness* Fog. Or *was* it Fog at that time? Happily or unhappily, the baron had, one drunken evening, taken a stroll down an elevator shaft—his parachute failed to open, poor chap—and so Bente had been abruptly restored to democracy. In any event, Bente was extremely eager to make Valeria's acquaintance.

"Yes," Bente Fog said, extending a bony forearm, wrist and hand. Her long face unfurled a few surprising folds of warmth.

"I know one of your sisters quite well," she said, her voice dry but friendly, her words sending a slight billow of vertigo through the black-carpeted floor.

IMMORTALITY ON A SCIENTIFIC FOOTING

The room began to fill up. Dozens of those from downstairs (bringing drinks, bottles, trays of food) had followed Humberto Vilanescu and Bente Fog up the helix staircase, as if expecting to find god-knew-what. A thousand conversations were multiplied by a hundred.

Humberto had one arm around George's shoulders, easily encircling the narrow blue shaft of the body, while at the same time directing the removal of the large blue mirror from the wall facing the bed. Valeria tried to keep close to Bente Fog. Which sister did she know? she asked. And how did she come to know her at all, let alone "quite well"? Did she know her sister *before* Humberto had come to dinner at her parents'?

"I'm more than just your sister's *friend*," Bente Fog said, cupping her mouth and talking at the top of her lungs, yet with no danger of being overheard. "A friend is *nothing*. Friends come and go. Friends have a vested interest in your failure. The more they admire you, the more they're hungry for what you have. What you need in life are good *business* partners. . . ."

"Are you saying that you're my sister's business partner?" Valeria shouted back across the short noisy space, through which objects flashed like dislodged electrons.

Bente Fog nodded.

"Then you must mean *Martina.*"

Bodies and voices surged into the gap, toward Humberto Vilanescu who was holding forth in a corner.

"People have always wanted to live well," he was saying. "However, in the past, the idea of an after-life dominated our sense of what constituted 'living well.' Christian moral philosophy held sway for so long only because of the promise of resurrection. The moral philosophy which we think of as Christian is nothing but a system of codes and tasks mastered in order to gain entry into that other realm of second life. Thus, the idea that life is utterly biological and death unbridgeable brings all moral philosophy to an end as something that can influence mass behavior. Moral philosophy now enters the limited, aesthetic realm of poetry, art, mathematical reasoning. More and more it becomes unacceptable that moral behavior doesn't help one live well—that it prevents neither anxiety nor depression, cancer nor poverty. Moral behavior is now functionless, an emotional museum piece or an irrational spasm on the order of a *petit mal* seizure. Thousands of self-help movements and commercial therapies are more effective and more popular. On the other hand, this phase too is merely historical. The necessary precondition for a truly new historical phase (one in which philosophy, actual life, art and the generalized will and fervor of the mass of humanity are harmonious) is the full acceptance of science that has not yet come to pass—the dissolving away of all sentimental resistance to the things not only of one's own time, but of the future. This can only come to pass as succeeding generations actually live in intimate harmony with the effects of our discoveries—as, of course, earlier generations have with the debased 'miracle' of television. The advent of the home computer was a small step precisely in that direction. But, of course, we live in an age when it's possible for something like the computer to be both a cliche (seen everywhere, duplicated and pictured a billionfold, the source of a whole new realm of boring careers, symbol of almost anything) and yet remain universally mysterious in its fundamental principles.

This is exactly our task: to begin to initiate the young into our mysteries.

"The one who comes along with a new guarantee of immortality, immortality on a scientific footing, will automatically send new tasks, rules and codes of behavior sweeping through the world. . . ."

He stopped speaking or his voice was engulfed by the clamor of other voices.

Bente Fog reappeared at Valeria's shoulder.

"I didn't know that Martina *had* a partner," Valeria said.

Oh yes, Bente Fog said, a woman named Minou von Riper had been Martina's partner from the beginning. They'd founded MvM together. But, unfortunately, despite Minou von Riper's considerable talents, she was an idiot in certain ways. It was Martina's idea to bring her in as a third partner. Minou von Riper opposed this arrangement bitterly. Tried to persuade Martina that she, Bente, was playing a double or triple game of some kind. But she'd put them on a sound commercial footing. And Minou von Riper was *out*. Back to her dolls and coloring books. Now it was Martina, Bente and an associate of Humberto's. Humberto was the one who'd seen that there was money to be made there. And the need for money around here was just about insatiable, as Valeria could probably guess.

Valeria said that she was surprised that Martina's business needed to be put on a sound commercial footing. She was under the impression that she'd been successful for some time. And what precisely did it mean when Bente said that Minou von Riper was "out"? Where was she exactly?

She felt that her questions were fundamentally stupid. That they wouldn't be answered. Didn't *deserve* to be answered. It might very well be true that one either chose to reline oneself with a moral Lexan, a spiritual Silverstone, or chose life in a pre-historic swamp in Jersey or Colorado.

Bente Fog receded into the crowd as if on purpose just as Humberto Vilanescu re-appeared facing the black bed, against the wall where the blue mirror had been. His red shirt and large head showed up with electronic vividness against the frame of freshly exposed floral yellow wall fabric. All available attention was bent toward him like a beam of charged particles by a powerful electromagnet. Bente Fog's crimson smock had made its way swiftly to a far corner, alongside the weak, watery blue of George's suit and above a smoky crystal vase that held a magnified aquarium of green leaves, green stems, a creamy froth of enormous pink roses, a solid nugget of carmine, a frozen raspberry at every core.

"There are people in this room who've dreamed the same dream," Humberto said. "Last night three people dreamed this: On a wide thoroughfare, sunlight without shadow, more dazzling than quartz, a tropical afternoon. Something blue flashes in the distance. You can't tell if it's someone in blue, a blue object hovering over a distant roof or an unfamiliar vehicle whose blue side panel flashes like a crystal as it banks a turn.

"Someone approaches, demands the names of all witnesses. Others hurry off, but you remain, supplying your name in full despite the fact that you've noticed a starved little wolf of a man (bony features and curly hair) standing nearby, noting things down (a heavy script like inkblots) in a leatherbound album.

"The starved wolf tells you with pleasure that you've been unbelievably careless. Hasn't anyone ever told you that you must never, never give your name to a stranger in the forest?

"But you're *not* in the forest, you protest. You're in the middle of a thoroughfare, in broad daylight. But then you see that it's no longer true. You're in a beautiful gold-green meadow surrounded by woodland. You see a cool thicket of birches in the distance and you feel an overwhelming desire to be there. You have no idea why the impulse is so strong, as if you'd been there in childhood. You find yourself on a woodland road the color of chewing gum. You pass fields, forest thickets, stands of trees, but the longed-for birch copse remains hopelessly in the distance.

"As you walk you begin to regret that you *had* given your name. You become so frightened that you think: if only you could find that little wolf again you'd give him a *false* name, or the names of others, of friends and relatives—you would betray anything and anyone in order to save yourself. You're assailed by feelings of guilt, a moral frenzy that quickly develops into a splitting headache.

"You feel the need to get off the road, where the sunlight now seems to bear down with tremendous pressure through the wide rift between the trees. You realize that you've come a long distance and that it's already deep into summer. Life is merciful, as always. No matter where you are, there's always someplace else you can go. While terrible things are going on in your own life and in the life of the world, for example, it's possible to go to a movie, dine in a restaurant. A round, dark, cave-like arch opens up in a dense stand of evergreens. You go in. Within a hollow cone of green light and purple shadow people are watching color television. A variety show of the kind you would never dream of watching. Something like this."

He turned to the frame of yellow wall covering that had been exposed by the removal of the mirror. She had the impression that he was preparing the wall in some way by making rapid passes over the surface with his hands. He stepped back. The room went dark and a tremendous image appeared on the wall without any detectable projector, projector beam, mechanical whirr or electrical hum. The image was so flat and brilliant, it looked as if high energy particles were being dislodged from the wall, made to arrange themselves into shapes. What was pictured was a spectacular Las Vegas-style production number. Against a backdrop of screens, flamingo plumes and bright strings of women in tiny, tinsel-bright costumes tripled in banks of angled mirrors, a half-reclining dancer was revolving on a large circle of mirror glass. Her coral orange, silver-spangled leotards were cut out on both sides in naked ellipses that extended above the powerful, smooth hips. And a heavy silver tassel cord dangled down from a loop around her waist and rested between her legs, from the bent knees down to the soft, exposed double curve of the buttocks. While she was going through the usual athletic abstraction of four dozen intercourse positions, the enormous floor mirror whirled slowly under her like an ice rink.

"'Did I leave the meadow for *this?*' you think," Humberto Vilanescu went on. "But the image flips and you see an elderly couple being interviewed on a talk show. You recognize your parents, though they seem to have aged dangerously, to the point of death."

The elderly couple on the screen resembled Valeria's parents, though she wasn't the only one to take a sharp breath.

The man who resembled her father (at least as he might look twenty years from now or through the premature aging and shrinkage of illness) said that he'd suffered a total blackout recently, fell and ripped open his face. This explained the dark glasses and the awkward way he was sitting, turned away from the camera. He was worried that he'd re-injured his eyes. The doctor had warned him that the next time they had to perform eye surgery they'd use a laser. Use a laser and put a *buckle* in.

After the fall his eyes began flashing and now the world looked like a blackish cloud through which a bit of dull lightning occasionally flashed. Impossible to make out anything in a dark room. Even with a lamp on, people were phosphorescent ghosts. It affected his mind too. He kept thinking that his wife had died seven years ago, after fourteen years of marriage, one of four-hundred-and-ninety-six killed in a supersonic plane crash in California, the largest in history.

The woman who looked like Valeria's mother cut in and said that he was always feeling sorry for himself. He dramatized everything that happened to him. While the truth was, nothing dramatic had happened to either one of them. Everyone dreamed that this or that would earn immortality, fend off death *in reality*. But things passed very quickly, in a peculiar way, as if you were on the swiftly moving train of things, and also standing quite still on the platform as things went by without you. Sooner or later you vanished into some black tunnel or other, as if you'd made the mistake of dozing off at the wrong moment.

You simply vanished and that was all there was to it. Things vanished and people vanished.

Not long ago her sister came to visit, walking, as always, with the aid of her walking stick. It was a sturdy Alpine walking stick, with an animal head, German lettering and a spiked tip, a souvenir not only of her Alpine honeymoon long ago, but of her dead husband, who invariably brought back such keepsakes from their travels. Her husband's utterly real ghost, sealed up in a tube of wood and metal, carried everywhere, a pet mummy. So there was no forgetting that her sister had arrived with it or that she herself had placed the walking stick in a certain spot. When it came time for her sister to leave, the walking stick had disappeared. And it never turned up again, neither at her place, nor her sister's, nor anywhere else.

Then just the other night (or was it twenty years ago?) one of her daughters dreamed that she woke up from sleep and called her mother. She called and called but her mother didn't come. Another woman appeared, wearing her mother's green nightgown. It didn't have the feeling of a dream, her daughter said. She was certain that something had really happened and she questioned her sharply. How could she be sure that she hadn't wandered in. People did that sometimes. And, in the darkness, she might have looked like someone else. She had her wondering if it was true. Sleepwalking or something else. Wandering out of yourself, beginning to vanish in that way.

The woman fell silent and Humberto said: "You call out to them, but, of course, they can't hear you—since you're only watching color television in the cone shade of an evergreen thicket. You feel, without knowing why, that you must find your way to the birch grove across the perpetually receding distance. Everything depends on it, though you don't have the faintest idea what that 'everything' is.

"On the road again, between tall and beautiful ranks of eucalyptus, you're accosted by the horrible little wolfman. Now that they have your name you'll never know a peaceful moment, he says. Anything can happen. He tells a story about a man who was recently murdered in the States for no apparent reason. And many other deaths, a wave of murders, seemingly random or looking like accidents. From now on, you're either in or out, he says.

"You're really frightened, for the first time. . . ."

The image brightened to a blinding degree. The wall was like a sun.

Valeria fled the room.

She stood outside the door, more than a little shaken. Hushed voices, the tinned, precise murmur and blue violet flashes of a large television washed up through the brass rods of the helix staircase.

A mild gust of crazy laughter drew her attention to the end of the long hallway, where a deep, lusterless red was visible between door and doorframe. The laughter turned to bestial snarling, like the sounds heard at dusk in jungle pools and thickets, the awful cries of things eating one another.

She slipped down the passage so that she could see into the red interior. She saw a bare back, a bony ladder of vertebrae down to buttocks sunk in glossy rose sheets. Bente Fog's blonde, jaw-length hairdo. A bony wrist and hand blotting up a bloodstain from the back of the shoulder, the arm straining to reach the wounded spot with a thick wad of cotton.

A man's voice could be heard, spitting, guttural, grinding consonants. "Save that song for someone who hasn't heard it before!"

The man paused as if listening, though Bente Fog was silently tending to her wound. Valeria guessed that he was on the telephone.

"You people all talk the same way. Meanwhile, it's guys like me who have to take care of things. Yeah, I know you're not stupid like her. So what? She's stupid her way and you're stupid your way! But one way you're stupid in the same way is you're not willing to get a little blood on your hands!"

He fell silent again. The Fog woman stood up. A magenta robe sailed around her as she disappeared from the funnel vista, as if into an enormous silk handkerchief.

"Hold up your end, my dear, or we'll arrange something for you!" the man barked. "Anything can happen to anyone at any time! You won't even suspect it's happening!

"Like Gaby Cherteau. I think you know old Mariella Cherteau, don't you? Gaby is her daughter. Gaby married some Portuguese dummy and six months later they were divorced. Mariella Cherteau had trouble swallowing the divorce. In her century it was a big deal. Then, just when she was getting used to it, Gaby went off someplace and a couple of years later she brought home this guy who looked like a tiny, stuffed crocodile. White hair, narrow head, fat belly, maybe five years younger than old Mariella herself. Minus one arm. Divorced several times over and with a flock of awful children. It took old Mariella five years to recover. But now they're all happy. It's cozy. The husband keeps the mother company while Gaby's out making an ass of herself. What they don't know is that he's eaten the foundation out from under them. And that he's one of us! I can't help laughing every time I think what the old woman would do if she knew where her money was going! In another year or two they'll be picked clean. We'll dream up something else for you, of course. Something you've never heard of. Even *you* must realize that there are more ways of creating unhappiness and destruction than there are seconds in a lifetime."

The red telephone receiver that flashed into view cradled a horrible, vulpine little face like the face of the man on the landing except that the flesh seemed to have been stripped from half of it. She caught a glimpse of a white jawbone and white double row of needle teeth like two hair combs. The door flew shut as if kicked.

She retreated swiftly down the quadruple twist of the helix staircase.

"WE OURSELVES, NOT OTHERS, ARE LIVING IN THE FUTURE"

The dark planes of the city arrived through the windows in the usual mysterious way. And other, darker planes from far beyond that. Space travelled to us easily, a lucid, inexplicable diagram, while one's image hovered at a tentative, indeterminate distance, just a bit further than it did in a bar mirror, amidst green bottles and red gleams. We hadn't ventured far enough, she thought. We were timid and it would take centuries before anything like true inter-galactic travel could happen. For that we'd have to test certain speculative proposals with all the possible horrors of failure. But what was there to be afraid of? The most horrible thing that could happen out there was better than job, house, even love, whose essence lay exactly in hammering you down into a specific plot of time. That meant living in history, like everyone else. History gobbled up all those who acknowledged it.

Humberto Vilanescu (in a black suit and red shirt) came up on one side of her and a woman came up on the other. The slight wave of her hair was cut to frame the longish oval of her face in a clear way, neither assertive nor non-assertive, neither too cold nor too familiar; her skin had a smooth, lively pallor; her lipstick was a soft heather; she was dressed in pure electronic shades of turquoise, mauve and yellow.

"You were eavesdropping in the hall," Humberto Vilanescu said matter-of-factly.

"I heard a little something," she confessed. "As I was passing."

There was no need to turn one's head, since it was possible to see the others' faces in the window above the obscure circuit of the street.

No, he insisted, she didn't just hear "a little something." She listened. It would take a moron *not* to listen. What was a moron? A moron didn't eavesdrop. A moron didn't read other people's correspondence, diaries, private memoranda. A moron didn't go through other people's drawers and closets. A moron had the idiotic power to short out his senses by way of discretion. A moron, in short, refused to taste the tastiest portion of the human stew. Nothing was more repugnant than this lame-brained piety.

The fact that she *had* listened only added to his already high opinion of her intelligence.

On the other hand, there were a few—a *few*—occasions when you could create a lot of misery for yourself that way.

Once he was staying in a hotel. He could hear a couple making love in the next room. They were speaking a foreign language, which sounded to him like Greek, but which might just a well have been Arabic, Latvian or any other language with too many right angles, double consonants and detours in it.

Music was playing in the background, simple and rhythmic, a few dark, seductive phrases rotating like the disc itself. Nothing but the deep, violet-shaded vibrations of a woman's voice, eggplant smooth, trilling over a regular pattern of drumbeats. The body singing through the throat, the lips hardly bothering to shape the sound into words. The sound of a profound sexual longing that would inevitably bring another longing body slithering or loping swiftly toward it.

Then there were happy kisses, playful patting, a little coughing. Laughter from the woman, a bass murmuring from the man.

Then the woman began to sing along with the voice on the record. The hoarse yet childlike timbre, her phrasing and timing, matched those of the voice on the record so exactly that he wondered if the woman on the other side of the blue-flowered wallpaper, to which his ear was fastened as if with the little suction discs of a red starfish, might be the woman on the record.

His longing to be with her was unbearable. He imagined that that would be a different sort of happiness than anything he'd known: to be on the other side of the wall, lying where the Latvian or Turkish guy was lying, inside the embrace of the woman whose singing made your body ache. The woman's sighing was a simple exhalation without a trace of painful moaning. The arched back, the long belly exhaled arrow after arrow of breath and pleasure.

For ages he felt an intense, wolf-like prowling in himself. He became extremely attentive to women's voices, women's laughter, to Balkan and Middle Eastern accents. He sought out women who sang. But nothing captured what he'd overheard that night in the hotel.

He began to have some weird dreams.

He dreamed that he was falling along the face of a black glacier. He smelled the cold mineral breath of the rocks. And through the glacier, clear as through a watch crystal, he could see the typed pages of a paper he was scheduled to deliver at the International Time Technology Conference in Lucerne. "Dreams of falling," the paper read, "are dreams about time. Time is the one involuntary dimension. You move through it, it moves through you, without your will. It propels you. It adds weight to your body, like falling from a height. Gravity is only one of time's many manifestations, another name for it. All destinations are attempts to veil this involuntary plunge with optimism. It passes alongside us through life, passes *under* us, as if every step we take on gray sidewalk or black macadam were actually a step downward. Nothing so alien as that vertical sheet of ice, that black mirror we step onto in our dreams, as if on skates."

In another dream he was in Veracruz, where they had (just as they did in Havana) what they called the Malecon, a water-side esplanade, a place to stroll, to meet people in a casual way and for men to accost female tourists.

Well, there he was on the Malecon, walking along, gazing vaguely over the water like any other idiot, admiring the fishing boats and the familiar Mexican sunlight in which something yellow as a wax cheese casing always shown. And he saw a small, dark woman in a mint green linen skirt, who, like every other tourist, was staring at things Kodak-style, not so much to see as to fix things in memory.

He went straight over to her and told her about the dreams he'd been having.

"Yes," she said, as if her thoughts were his thoughts, "when we're younger we imagine it has to do with this or that trivial psychosis that happens to be plaguing us. But the truth is that in those dreams we're living at another rate. Falling is a plunge into the inner acceleration of existence. In these dreams life races through us, we race through our lives, possibly from beginning to end, with the velocity of protons through the doughnut tunnels of accelerators. When we wake up we retain a terrified sense of rushing across wide avenues, under trees, above long retaining walls. Flying toward death as surely as the planet is moving through space at speeds none of us perceive."

A moment later he found himself in bed with the woman, her mint green skirt nowhere in evidence. He opened her blouse. Her body poured out over his hands. A long human animal, smooth and hot. Not *quite* the woman on the other side of the wall, but a wonderful sensation nonetheless. An antidote to what had been said. Not a thought in his head. No body either. A feverish cloud with a vicious appetite. And the body springing back into existence out of this fever like a panther, one bounding muscle. The feelings of beasts. What we imagine the feelings of beasts to be, which is: nothing. A beast acts, produces effects, its "emotions" the inner tides of its movements. What it feels is: the rush forward, the rush back, the body sinking through the skin of another, emerging into the clear. To *smell* something is the same as to *feel* something. At the height of things they were in the so-called animal position. She was face down, her knees outside his, quite wide open, the ass heart-shaped and full, expressing the body's insatiable swelling. Lust, but sublime.

Something was said about the hunger that had to be satisfied again and again. No end to it. One had to walk up and down on the yellow bricks of light, find someone.

He had this last dream shortly before running into old Lupeni on Fifth Avenue, which led directly to his visit to her parents. For a few brief seconds he saw something of the woman in the mint green skirt in Amy Gura. Until she spoke, that is.

Valeria started at the mention of Amy Gura's name. The cosmetically perfect woman on her right chose that moment to ask if Valeria felt the way others did, that there was a "disintegration of values," from a moral standpoint. Or from the standpoint of Nature, as if chlorophyll and ethics were one and the same. People found it hard to accept the fact that things went forward without regard for our feelings or the names we attached to them. History cared as much about us and our high-flown notions as the dark facades of office towers or the mineral plasmas of the Cosmos did. Was Valeria one of those people?

She might have meant those gathered around the 100" television projection screen, or everyone in the room, everyone in the apartment, upstairs and down, or everyone in the world outside their little band at the window.

Valeria was struck by the harmony of the woman's voice with Bente Fog's. (And of both their voices with someone else's?) The lengthy oval of the face (long jaw, long forehead) and the bony wrists were also in harmony. But that was all. Everything else was too different to be accounted for by clothing, jewelry, makeup, hair style or any other superficial means of altering the identity.

Valeria said that she believed that there was no turning back from anything. Every new thing changed every other thing irrevocably. No matter the lapse of years before its effect was felt. More powerful than the entrenched resistance to new things that had always existed, was the hunger for the new. Each new thing, new site, new utterance a sign that we'd passed on to a new age. That we ourselves, not others, were living in the future.

Yes, Humberto Vilanescu agreed, no age resembled another, despite the platitudes one continued to hear about the constancy of human nature. The need to be recorded, projected and transmitted, for example, had replaced the need to be remembered by intimate loved-ones. The new unit of life was extremely brief. The sense of what made life significant could now be measured in seconds or hours. Thirty minutes of televised existence was now felt to easily outweigh an invisible lifetime of treading water.

"You'll agree then," Bente Fog or her dissimilar duplicate said, turning toward her, "that there is now only one enterprise that matters. What might be called the business of inventing the future. Or, I should say, this enterprise is a business for some of us, for others something else entirely."

A number of possibilities were laid before Valeria, some of which ("The Internal Television Capsule," "The Dream Projection System" and "Video Gel") were referred to as supermarket ventures. And others that, perhaps, would fulfill her desire to go beyond all others, along lines that were barely suspected.

The essential thing was to begin.

Valeria wondered if there was a name for the sensation she felt, as if there were such a thing as a purely material emotion. Her whole being, accelerated beyond imagination, splitting off into heretofore unknown particles and broken traces of energy.

She thought: "all those others *are* the invisible ones who weave the world for the visible few."

EIGHT

SPACE STATION

Her mother's jaw, broken when it cracked against the window-sill, was clamped shut by a gruesome chin brace. She was barely conscious. Or, god alone knew, unconscious yet with her eyes open. They seemed to be pleading for help. Imploring Valeria to do something. Only what was it she wanted?

Her mother's face was slightly puffy and with an odd discoloration, yet younger, like a child with a grave illness. A somewhat aged and strange-looking child, in whose eyes one nonetheless saw the pathos of abandonment, the knowledge of having, through the hospital, passed over into another realm. It was as if her mother had already died and she was looking at a photograph in a family album, feeling an agonizingly useless affection. This was the woman others had known in a different way, she thought. Her sense of regret was unbearable. Only she couldn't imagine what there was to regret or what could have been done differently.

She pulled a chair up to the bedside, fell asleep while holding her mother's hand and dreamed that she was in a vast greenhouse on a country estate. The plants were enormous tropical varieties she'd never seen before. But something was seriously wrong with them. They were dying of an unknown form of radiation poisoning, someone said, caused by the recent mini-hole explosion over south-eastern Canada. "The whole other sector is on fire again," he said. . . Someone else suggested they go on a picnic and she and several friends set off in an old convertible, with picnic hampers and an odd television-like contraption on which they intended to follow the progress of the fires that were burning out of control in the other sector. "It's being razed," someone said, "so that the imaginary future of the architects and science fiction writers can come to pass. So that we can begin to see it cover the Earth before we die." They drove across vast, rolling fields and then around the edge of a lake so wide and dark it was an inland sea. . . . Marika was there but didn't look like herself. Her hair fell more softly around her face, which seemed young and unaffected. Nevertheless, they argued, as usual. It was impossible to remain friends with the woman Marika had become, she said. After a certain point the events of life were *not* reversible. Things became more definite, all but unalterable. Impossible to keep shifting one's ground, to forget, as if one had no memory. . . . A small, yellow plane appeared from behind a screen of orange trees, roared overhead, dangerously low, skidded speedboat-style across the lake, lifted off and barely cleared the trees on the far shore. When it was out of view there was an explosion and a hot cloud of flames. People near Valeria were shrieking and sobbing as if their loved-ones were aboard.

She woke up. Her mother was looking at her more imploringly than before. Now she thought she understood. Her mother was pleading with her to travel toward her. To bring her back from the outer space of the hospital, which was imperceptibly spinning toward the dangerous external boundary of the solar system.

A CREATURE NEVER KNOWN ON EARTH

Denise sounded shrill, not exactly like herself. She was desperate, had to see Valeria, she said. But refused to talk about it on the phone. She acted as if the phone were tapped. Valeria couldn't figure out how Denise had tracked her down through all Humberto's shifting of location. She was now living in a dead financier's estate on the Hudson, with suites of offices and laboratory buildings on the wooded grounds. No telephone was listed under her name.

"How did you find me?" she asked. But she couldn't get an answer to that either.

She agreed to drive out and visit Denise at Noel's condo complex in the country. Maybe she'd stop off on the way and say hello to a few people in her old neighborhood, she said. "Oh no! Don't do *that!*" Denise said. Since most of the neighborhood had burned down in one of those mysterious fires that had become an accepted part of the daily round of misfortunes, it was dangerous to stop there. At least that's what they were saying on tv. Though she wasn't at all sure if it was a matter of vandalism or of some sort of strange radiation.

Despite smoldering ruins and blackened lots, the bright eclipse of small town life, a sort of calm and open interment in time, still reigned. Here and there a house was miraculously intact, a green strip, a white patch inexplicably untouched.

Her street seemed to be the most severely devastated and her house seemed to have been the focal point of the devastation. Trees were like dried up fountains, houses were shadows, hedges piles of charred newspaper.

Valeria got out and stood on the sidewalk. Where her house had been she was able to look through to the next block, directly at a white shingle facade streaked with charcoal in a downward pattern that suggested an overhead explosion.

Things were erased for you, she thought. Memory, feeble in itself, was aided by the world, which periodically scoured itself, erasing all traces of your existence. The biological economy that relentlessly made room for new biology also appeared in the world of things. Nothing was more stupid than the desire to have memories. Forgetfulness the natural order of things. Each thing one forgot helped one travel more swiftly into the future. As if the fire had saved her a tedious job of packing.

An airplane rumbled remotely overhead. A little bright ball-bearing. Tiny, silver-blue, with a red streak along the side, it turned the sky bluer than tinted cake frosting.

Someone called her name. The voice sailed toward her, a dense little cone like the compact quasi-musical cry of a bird that comes shooting toward a target over roof after roof.

Something orange fluttered beyond a glowing white fence visible in the rift between gutted houses.

An old woman, waving an orange leotard, called out to her again. "Oh Miss! Miss Florescu!"

Orange cloth, black straw gardening hat with green ribbon hat band, coffee-colored dress stood out against the deadened shades of oxblood shingle.

The woman's house was untouched. Summer reigned in her back garden quite pleasantly. A continuous sheet of light extended from green lawns and dark beets on poles, shining eggplants, heavy tomatoes on vines to lusterless white towels and dull clothing sailing in the blue between two roofs.

A red-haired child with a long, surly face sat on the ground in a worn green dress, digging with a red toy shovel in the dark soil at the base of a tree.

"You're wondering how I know you," the old woman said. "But it's natural for everything and everyone to be known. That's how a neighborhood exists. It knows itself to the point of suffocation. You don't know *us*, but we know *you*," she went on while cutting a number of enormous red-in-deeper-red roses from a bush with mirror-bright garden shears. "I suppose you're all like that nowadays. You want to *be* known, but to *know nothing*. As long as you've lived here, you haven't gotten to know a single soul in the long-lasting, trivial and suffocating way that weaves a neighborhood. I know *you* because I've seen you coming and going in your little yellow car. I've had your *mail* mis-delivered to my house. Sometimes my phone rings and the call is for you. Our telephone numbers are just about anagrams of one another, if that's the right way to put it. I had a conversation with your boyfriend. He wondered where you'd disappeared to and he was trying to track you down.

"Known but unknowing, is what you are."

She didn't *want* to be known, Valeria answered. Our families, for example, became repellent to us for exactly this reason. They imagined that they knew us. Their supposed knowledge of us was an obituary. She didn't want to be known by others or to know herself. She didn't understand the mania for self-knowledge. She longed for nothing more than the chance to go on generating herself blindly, for centuries.

It wasn't that sort of knowing she was talking about, the old woman pointed out.

She'd finished cutting her roses and gathered them together in the crook of her arm, a fountain of strawberry and blood crimson.

She barked something at the child (her voice had an animal's flat tonality and sharp projection) and the child, an angry bulge in its forehead, came running across the uncut grass, taking hold of the old woman's hand with docility.

Valeria followed them along a dun-colored and flower-bordered path that led to some gray steps and a screen door.

The night of the fire, the old woman said, she'd put on her robe, gone down into the street, around the block and watched Valeria's house burn. She'd even salvaged a few of her things. But Valeria hadn't asked about the fire. So maybe she wasn't interested in it.

Valeria followed her into a green walk-in cupboard and through another door into the kitchen. The doors were the color of peanut butter, the cabinets alternating panels of burnt sienna and luster-less orange. We talk about the future, she thought, but the past is everywhere. It really does exist, and in a stubborn way, with deep roots, like thick tree limbs that heave up paving blocks. It refuses to disappear. It's what we call the present.

"What happened was this," the old woman said, bending into an old crib where an infant—sparse red hair and a tiny white face, a withered little apple that had fallen prematurely to earth—sat placidly chewing on a red and blue plastic toy that resembled a crude model of the planet Jupiter. "I was asleep and dreaming. Orange leaves were burning first in an oil drum, then in a dozen gigantic mounds in a meadow under trees. Then it smelled like a barbecue, but not so pleasant. Something rotten on the barbecue grill. I sat up, pulled up by the roots of my hair, flung out of bed. People were screaming in the street. 'Get the hose! Get the hose!' 'Help! Oh help me!' 'My *dog*! Someone save my *dog*!' and similar nonsense and other shrieking.

"That one in there," she motioned with her head toward a

peanut-colored door, "*never* wakes. There's no explaining why there are sleepers who sleep like sparrows, restless and alert, flying from branch to branch of some other life, and others who sleep the sleep of the dead, of blue metal steamer trunks lost in the darkest corner of the cellar. Better off not knowing where they are or what they're dreaming. Hard work doesn't explain it. No matter how many hours she spends on her feet in the diner, that doesn't explain it and nothing explains it.

"Nothing woke her. Not the screaming, not the foul smoke, not the wail of the fire engines neither. Through everything I could hear her ugly breathing through the door. My own daughter, but her breathing made me sick. Wheezing and sucking as if someone were forcing a pillow over her face with two strong hands.

"And these two are just the same. Exactly like their mother. More asleep than awake, and when they're awake you could kill them. You could kill them both. The little one because she's so stupid and the other one for her crankiness and whining. Lori and Lisa. They all have names like that now. Thank god it isn't Melissa and Jennifer. If they were Melissa and Jennifer I would have killed them both a long time ago!"

Valeria looked at the child at the table, whose glowering eyes, eyebrows and forehead, working along with the little mouth, looked back at her from a compressed whitebread sandwich, one large bite outlined by a ragged, peanut-colored half circle. A railroad loaf of Silvercup, a three pound jar of Ann Page grape jelly, a tall glass of ketchup-red fruit drink stood on the table.

The infant in the crib, with its withered little face, its white and red little walnut head, made no sound, as if it were a creature never known on Earth before, one that thrived on molecules of dye and plastic.

"You have no way of knowing how easy it is to kill a child," the old woman said. "Sometimes you feel you'd better tie your hands to a towel rack, you're coming that close to doing it. You have to restrain yourself. It makes you dizzy. You think to yourself: 'her brain is no bigger than a sunflower seed, she's bad-tempered from morning to night, she'll end up exactly like her mother, miserable and stupid, with her ass sticking out of her uniform in some coffee shop. Why not nip it in the bud?' But you don't. Those that do, cross over the line into another world. We guess what that world is like, maybe worse than this one, and we stay here.

"There's this side and then there's the other side. We call it 'the other side' because instinctively we know that others belong there, not us. We see those others on television, on the movie screen, in magazines, a tiny handful, but never-ever us or those we know. If one of those we know seems headed for the remotest outer boundary of the other side, we inwardly feel that we no longer know them.

"But you don't want to hear about this, you want to hear about the fire. . . ."

Valeria said that she didn't want to hear about anything. Life was only so long, the number of stories one could listen to endless.

"After I'd knocked on the door and called Paula's name," the old woman went on without pause, "I realized that nothing would rouse her. 'Only death can wake her up,' I thought, put on a robe and went out the back door to see what was what. Things were blocked by the peaked roofs of the houses, like trying to see something from the wrong slope of a mountain. I could see black smoke rising at two or three points, much darker than the sky, which looked almost blue and thin by comparison; an orange moon, really tremendous, rising over the roofs. The house directly behind mine was already like a burning ship. Fire, having eaten away everything else, was eating itself, while the black bulk of the house seemed to be sinking into the ground.

"The roof of your house was crawling with little flames, as if following the sprinkled trail of something flammable.

"I went around the block.

"It looked as if they'd dropped a bomb. Houses that weren't on fire looked toasted. Broken windows everywhere. Hedges scorched, in some places flattened. You could feel a flat wall of heat all the way over at the intersection. Your hair felt like it could burst into flame.

"Someone in the house next to yours had lost a dog in the fire, imagined she could still hear it barking and whimpering though nothing could be heard, and was weeping inconsolably. You'd think it was her mother in there. But a bird had been saved, a tremendous thing with green and blue feathers and red claws. It sat on the sidewalk in a big cage making a jungle's worth of yammering. Things were piled up all along the sidewalk. Old trash, but people had saved every stick, as if the idea of continuing life without those miserable things was unthinkable, like beginning life anew in a space colony.

"One idiot heard a loud explosion. Another saw a tremendous red flash high above the trees and gutter."

Now Valeria was interested and wanted to know more. But the old woman remembered Valeria's things stored in her basement.

"Come and have a look," she said.

She led Valeria through a door at the nether end of the kitchen into the front hallway. Sunlight falling through a rank of potted plants on a window shelf made weak rectangles on a thin layer of vermilion carpeting. There were several doors and stairways. She opened one with a skeleton key. The open door frame was perfectly black. There might have been a hundred steps or none at all, a sheer drop. Even after a light was switched on, very little was visible in the sharp powerless sparkle of the tiny bulb.

Valeria took a few steps down, to a level just below a ceiling overhang that blocked the further reaches of the cellar from view. A second tiny light twinkled in the distance. She made out something large, square, of low brilliance, the tawny hue of a wooden shipping crate; the red glow of upholstery; the iodine gloss of an old portrait.

She retreated to the sunny front hall. She couldn't imagine what had made her think of going down there, like an animal with a tiny brain pan lured by crumbs of bread.

The woman was welcome to what she'd found, she said.

The old woman protested but locked the cellar door with dispatch. Her face looked more human.

Simple greed after all, Valeria thought with relief, and left.

"HER NAME REPRODUCED HOW MANY TIMES!"

Heat was smeared like Crisco from one end of the sky to the other.
In the west, where the road was headed, a round white sun burned
through a blinding cloud cover, against which the low roof level of
the houses, the withering tree masses and the windshield offered
only the weakest resistance. Every pedestrian who managed to drag
himself/herself from one end of the windshield to the other seemed
to be running a fever. A distant, abstract suffering like the suffering
of someone glimpsed from a hospital corridor.

It struck her that it was now late afternoon. Yet she hadn't spent
enough time with the old woman for morning to pass to late
afternoon. Where had the day slipped off to while she was in the dim
apartment?

Outside town the sun was one long, blazing inch away, as near
as a winged insect that descends on you in a dream.

If you kept driving along this way, she thought, between half-
hearted meadows and woodland remnants, you could poison yourself with unknown rays and waves, a thousand deft injections
straight through the iris.

A few miles out of town she saw a fluttering row of trees. It looked
both near and far, above the red clay roof of a gas-station-like
dwelling. Cool air seemed to be circulating through their thin
stalks, as if from shaded woodland, and she veered off into the
narrow secondary road that headed in the general direction of Noel's
condominium.

After several miles the red-roofed garage was still nowhere in
sight, despite the flat, open landscape screened by a see-through
border of shade trees. The only dwelling that appeared was a two
story shingle house, yellow with red shutters and trim, on the
left-hand side of the road. Two broad, neatly clipped wings of lawn
split by an S-curve orange path. A small, round fruit tree dotted
with ruddy orange fruits. A blond boy with a large head, all in blue
(blue polo, blue shorts, blue socks), squatted on his haunches under
the fruit tree, hacking up a tiny plot of green sod with a red toy
shovel.

"Hello!" Valeria called out. "Is your mother home?"

The boy neither looked up nor answered.

"Is *anyone* home?"

The boy continued digging, only a little more violently, as if the stubbornness of the ground had gotten him angry.

On the point of getting out, Valeria thought better of it and pressed two short blasts from the car horn.

The glossy, red-varnished front door opened inward. A woman with a round, pink-cheeked face, curly blonde hairdo and fluffy pink short-sleeved sweater, leaned out of the doorframe and gazed in the direction of the preoccupied child with a slightly troubled expression. The expression of a mother who isn't certain if the muffled, distant sound she'd heard inside the house might be threatening to the safety of the child left out-of-doors.

Valeria leaned out her window and sang out a friendly hello. It seemed to her the woman turned toward her and that encouraged her to ask how to get back to the highway.

The woman didn't answer. She looked past her, way into the distance.

Valeria called out another time and sounded her horn again, but nothing happened. When the yellow-and-red dwelling was a good distance behind her she saw, in her rearview mirror, mother and child watching with dismay the flight of her car toward the nearest horizon.

The road was a quiet and empty straightaway, where both residential and commercial structures had long since slipped away into yellow-brown acres of water meadow, here and there a hot, roughly-spread paste of green. One long stretch was taken up by a country club with its idealized, persuasively real heaven of golf greens, and another by the intermediate stages of construction of still one more industrial park, a blueprint-like zone that modelled research and something resembling thinking the way a shopping mall modelled the idea of buying-and-selling.

Not one other vehicle was to be seen. Still, she could hear the gummy rush of tires along the smooth, slightly melted macadam, sense the presence of another car keeping its distance just beyond every curve. She switched on the radio to blot out this and all other possible feelings (the anticipation that at Denise and Noel's, for example, she would be compelled to listen to still one more tale of life-gone-wrong). A rapid cross-section of frequencies brought her to a deep voice that couldn't belong to anyone but Humberto Vilanescu.

"I'd like your answer to a simple question," he was saying. "When light from a star reaches us, when we see a tiny blue or orange-yellow twinkle, is that the same as seeing someone in a red coat in the distance along with a blue awning and a birch sapling?"

The host mumbled that he'd never given the question any thought, but it seemed obvious that in one case you had light *rays* and in the other, well, you still had *light*, but *reflected* light. . . .

"Either of two possibilities must be followed to its conclusion," Humberto Vilanescu said. "Either sight is a peculiar suggestion of immortality (the fact that things travel in a coherent, transmaterial way across limitless distances) or else everything is visible as the result of variously energetic emissions. In this case seeing is the name we give to one human intersection with the universe. Light particles, or photons, travel in waves. Things are visible because they are continually giving off these waves of particles. In this sense there are no classes of things. All things are on the same plane. 'Life' is not divided from 'inanimate matter.' Things and beings generate waves of particles at varying frequencies and with varying degrees of intensity, all within the narrow, visible section of frequencies. The 'deterioration' of things, the 'death' of beings may be the direct result of this perpetual attrition and exhaustion. Vision may be a sort of metering of the electrical activity of things as they vanish. If nothing were visible (or detectable in other ways) everything might be eternal. My brilliant colleague, Valeria Florescu, is currently investigating various means of impeding the rate of transmission and deterioration and the results of such alterations on longevity."

"Fascinating!" the host said with enthusiastic stupidity. "But we're used to that! Every time you've been on the show you've told us about some weird thing that came true later on. And we'll all be looking forward to your series of demonstrations on our local interactive television system."

She'd heard her name over the car radio while casually spinning the dial, as countless others might be doing. Her name reproduced how many times! She tried to get hold of herself. It was no big thing, she told herself. This was trivial, unworthy of her. Much bigger things to come. Still, she felt that a noiseless rocket was taking off and she was on it. The large poison tablet of the sun, dissolving perpetually into the atmosphere without effervescence, receded to a cool distance. The road was nothing but a runway, a worn-out reality falling away into invisibility on either side of it.

THE DIARY

A paved area and stadium-sized circle of lawn separated the parking zone from the white building. The white shafts of the condo complex, perfectly commonplace, indicated a smothered yearning for a zone where things were, at last, truly different than they'd ever been before. What were you supposed to see? A blue, white and green disc, perhaps, hovering above the ground like a hydrofoil. And, covering the ground, a second, mirror sky across which you could walk. While the first sky drifted, as always, over every single place you happened to be.

The light in the corridor leading to Noel's door fell in radiant, corrosive blocks. White walls and blue carpets, emblematically nautical (the condominium as a ship motionlessly sailing some-where), were bleached away along with the lyrical pseudo-nature that ought to have been visible in the panoramic vistas.

At Noel's door (also a nautical white) she couldn't make up her mind whether to ring the bell or leave. She heard a woman's voice inside.

"Come on now! Be *nice!* Be nice now! Don't hurt me!"

The sound of thumping on the floor. Upright struggling of torsos of unequal strength, legs wheeling and feet pounding, struggling to maintain balance. Then there was a loud thump, dull and frightening, as if a body had been flung against a couch and rebounded, striking the floor.

Valeria couldn't decide whether to ring the bell or go for help.

"Listen!" the woman pleaded, breathless. "Do you want a blow job? I wouldn't mind giving you a *blow* job. We could do *that.* . . ."

The sound of a television surged up in the apartment and through the minute crevices around the white door. An announcer's voice and then the throaty, tonally-averaged voice of a crowded stadium.

"You wanna rape me? Is that it? You feel like *raping* me?"

"What's got into you?" the man's voice said without aggression.

Valeria continued to listen.

"If you wanna *rape* me, you rip off my panties—then you *take* my panties and you. . . ."

"Would you knock it *off!*"

"Am I annoying you? I'm not trying to *annoy* you. I'm trying to figure out what you *want.*"

"You *are* annoying me."

"How about *this* then? I could do *this.*"

A leathery sort of creaking stopped a minute after it started.

"No!" the man said.

There was another terrible thump and another surge of the television. The announcer sounded excited, as if the crowd was going to tear him limb from limb.

It was all pretty confusing. She began to suspect that Noel and Denise were playing a game, something like Roger and Lana. No public clues to private actions. What you took to be revealing moments, confessions, were just a subtler kind of lying.

"Stop it!"

"No!"

"I said *stop* it!"

"You *know* you deserve it!"

"Stop it, or I'll slap you!"

"*You'll* slap *me?* You'll slap *ME?*"

"I've got two hands, same as you!"

"How many hands have you got now? You've got *one* hand! Have you even got one hand now? You've got *no* hands!"

Thudding against the walls, stumbling and cursing right up

against the door.

Valeria took a step back toward the corridor and the elevator.

The door jerked open, slammed shut, jerked open wider. Denise's face lurched out. It was swollen, livid, yellow-red, blood on one cheek, eyes like boiled egg whites and the skin under them black. A man's arms were holding Denise's, trying to pry her loose from the doorframe. The arms were slender and muscular like Noel's, the torso angular like his, but the face was obscured in the blinding glare of windows remotely behind them. Denise looked at her as if struggling to figure out who Valeria was. "Help me!" she cried, losing her grip on the doorframe.

Faster than the speed of thought Valeria was with Denise in the doorway, pulled inside, the door slamming behind her. Noel wrenched Denise away, spun her against the wall, grabbed her throat and hit her hard with an open hand.

An unintelligible hash of words poured out of his mouth.

Denise couldn't stop sobbing and the more she sobbed the less she seemed able to struggle. She sagged against the wall while Noel slapped and punched her as if there were something he wanted to beat out of her or as if she were an inexhaustible taffy he could push and twist into shape.

It struck Valeria that Noel could kill Denise without realizing she was alive. She punched and kicked at him until he left off beating Denise, turned toward her, his face a weird sightless cone. He stared at her in a way that was less human than purely optical, like a closed-circuit camera mounted on a swivel, turned and hurried down the hall, disappearing around a corner past the dining alcove.

Valeria made for the entrance door, but Denise was already motioning from a door in the hall. She heard Noel coming back, hastened to join Denise and saw with dismay that Denise's hiding place was nothing but the bathroom—behind a thin door and flimsy lock.

Denise caught her look. She'd been hiding in here all week, she said. "He doesn't try to get in."

After a few minutes there was a tap on the door, then more taps, like the pathetic scratching of a household pet.

"I'm sorry!" he cried. "Sorry, baby!" He was sobbing. "Something's wrong with me! I don't *mean* to do these things. I want to be *good*. . . ." He was barely audible, snivelling.

"Come out, honey," he pleaded. "Send your friend home and we'll talk this thing out, ok?"

Denise was sitting in a white garden chair. She looked up. Her face, so swollen and discolored she didn't look like herself or anyone else, begged Valeria to open the door.

Outside the door it was quiet in a peculiar way. As if Noel had slipped away yet remained lurking there. Valeria could feel a ghost of anger and misery through the wood.

She got some cotton and peroxide out of the medicine cabinet and tried to do something for Denise's face. Denise jerked away and got up to look at herself in the mirror. She dabbed at the raw wound with an orange washcloth.

That seemed to calm her down. She stared at herself for several long minutes as if she were looking at something Valeria couldn't guess at, a region the deep exterior plane of the mirror was perfectly suited to lay before her.

Valeria put her ear to the door. Nothing was audible but the hum of waves and particles travelling in the walls. She tried opening the small, stamped-glass window, but it seemed to be nailed shut. It would have to be smashed, but that would attract Noel's attention. The situation was as hopeless as it was ridiculous.

She asked Denise why she'd dragged her into this. Wouldn't it have made more sense to call the police?

By way of answer Denise sobbed for minutes. When she gained control of herself she tried to tell Valeria the story of what had happened.

It seemed that a few months ago Noel said that he wanted to give Denise a present. "Choose anything," he said. She chose sailing lessons. Okay, he said. But instead of sailing lessons he took her on a windjammer cruise. Things were ok until they got where they were going. It didn't bother her that the whole thing was synthetic, a floating diorama of an adventure that was once real. You could sort of screw your head around to the point where you saw yourself as the heroine of *The Sea Wolf* or *High Wind in Jamaica*. If there was a weird kind of distance to things so that you felt neither happiness nor unhappiness but an unknown something that resembled both equally, that was okay too.

One night, sailing toward an island through the depthless blue X-rays of the tropics, travelling along with dark waves and mild breezes toward the island's tree fringe, drink in hand and feeling something arriving from the infinite distance, Noel said that he knew she hadn't stopped screwing other men. Roland and some tall, skinny guy named George. He'd had her watched.

She was too stunned (too stupid?) to deny it. "Spying on people is disgusting!" she said. It was all she could manage.

He knew it was disgusting, he said. If it made any difference, he hadn't *hired* anybody. He'd done it himself. A pretty weird experience, actually.

That scared her. He was beginning to remind her of Joseph Cotten in *Niagara*. She tried to convince him that the whole thing with Roland had fizzled out. And as far as this guy George, he was wrong. He was just some guy she'd met on vacation. They'd gone out a few times and they'd talked. They hadn't slept together. She didn't know *what* he wanted, but it sure as hell wasn't sex. (She gambled, figuring Noel hadn't actually been looking through this guy George's *window*.)

"I realize that you need to see other people," he said reasonably. "There's something you're searching for in life and I can't stop you. But it makes me unhappy."

The thought crossed her mind that he meant to kill her. Had brought her up here for just that purpose.

He proposed to her for about the two thousandth time. The longer you lived the more you came to value the eternal verities, he said. Marriage and family. This architecture of life had a purpose: to give life shape. Others had devised the well-made plot of life, we had only to live it. Any other decision was a decision to prolong the sloppy existence of childhood.

The crazy logic of his proposal was lost on her. She was so shaken that she told him something she shouldn't have. She confessed that she'd been thinking of moving out. A terrible mistake not to have a place of her own.

She saw in his eyes, which reflected every black billow swimming toward shore, that she'd only succeeded in confirming his craziest suspicions.

She tried to cover her tracks. A lot of couples maintained separate apartments, she said. If they did get married, and they moved in together, it would be an adventure. She thought the word "adventure" would appeal to him. So many cliches came to her lips, freely, without any effort, that she had no idea if she was lying or being stupidly sincere.

He mentioned her ex-husband, Don. She'd tired of Don, left Don, and now she was tiring of him and leaving him. He remembered only too clearly how she made fun of Don after she'd left him, how she refused to see him.

After that he subsided.

The next day they were sightseeing on shore. They were alone on a beach and they weren't talking. She lit a cigarette. He asked her to put it out. She gave him a look and went on smoking. "Put that out!" he said. He looked like a disposable razor. She ignored him. He made a grab for the cigarette, knocked it out of her mouth and gave himself a little burn.

Shaking, she lit another.

He slapped her hard enough to loosen a tooth, grabbed her, began to wrestle her around. His nails dug in so deep he drew blood.

She left the cruise, took a plane back to New York. Noel caught a faster flight and was waiting at the terminal with flowers. He begged forgiveness. No need for her to look for an apartment, he said. *He'd* move out. It was hers. She took him up on it and lived there for a week without hearing from him.

One day he called and very politely asked if he could come over.

She said yes.

The separation seemed to have melted something in him, like a crusty heel of French bread in soup. There were tears and apologies. Something welled up in her. Not exactly love and not pity either. A geyser of unidentifiable lava like the stupendous one, ragout of a thousand sunsets, Debra Paget leaps into at the end of *Bird of Paradise*.

He moved back in (though she secretly intended to begin searching for an apartment in Manhattan). And since then it had been hell.

She fell into a fit of harsh coughing and after that Valeria wasn't able to get anything out of her beyond the fact that she'd kept a diary, which was concealed in the linen cupboard. Maybe she'd feel less sick if someone else read it, she said.

Valeria found the diary easily, sat down and began to read it. The smallish, red-ruled pages were dated, the black handwriting surprisingly graceful and deliberate, shaky or blotted in only three or four places, never illegible.

July 17

Noel was sitting and staring at the television. I tried to talk to him but he didn't answer. It was odd. Like one of those cases that were reported in the early days of television, a catatonic state induced by the flickering of the image. His face had a greenish tint from the green radiance of the picture. I was standing next to him, very close to his chair, in an apricot robe. I could feel the warmth of his body and I'm sure he could feel mine. It should have warmed his whole left side like the glow of a lamp globe. But he didn't move or say a word.

"Watchawatchin, honey?" I said, dumb and friendly, knowing full well he was watching baseball, his latest passion. The tv screen (a new Sony VideoScope projection system) was the size of a baseball field, an electric green more alive than anything in nature.

He must have had the remote control in his hand, because suddenly the camera was cutting its way through spinach-green vines, tropical underbrush, waist-high saw grass.

"What are you watching *now?*" I asked, stupider than before.

"Some kind'v thing about a human ape monster down in Louisiana."

"You mean like one of those fictional documentaries, honey? I saw a scary one once called *The Legend of Boggy Creek.* . . ."

He shrugged.

"A monster is a monster," he said. "They make something up, the stupidest thing possible—only they don't know and no one knows how close to the truth it might be. . . ."

I wasn't sure what he was talking about, so I said: "Anyone can tell the difference between an actual *monster* and some dumb thing on *tv*, Noel."

He went on watching a little longer, his face still as green as lime jello. In one scene a big farm dog went bounding across an open, darker-than-twilight meadow toward the edge of the forest that ringed round the backwoods cabin. You could just about make out some sort of big blot waiting where the trees began. You could see the dog go for the blot and you heard it scream and then give out six or seven little whines.

"Hey, you know, honey," I said, "I think this might be the one I saw!"

Without switching off the set, Noel said: "You're always after me to be honest, so I'll tell you exactly what I detest about you. I've thought about this, I've worked it out carefully, and I know that it's true. I want you to listen to this, because, if you take it *seriously*, if you *work* on these things, it will do you good."

I didn't like the way he looked or sounded. As calm as a brick that doesn't know it's about to fall on your head. I started to leave, but he grabbed my arm so tight I could feel it in the marrow of my bones. Tears came to my eyes, the way they do under a dentist's probe.

"Invariably," he said flatly, as if he were delivering a paper, "you lie about what you're doing. Over the years, your lies have become increasingly desperate, pathetic and far-fetched. Your overblown romances, your exaggerated sexual adventures. This affair with Roland is simply the latest, most absurd example. But always, inside the lie, *I* feel the truth. The hollowness is only too apparent to *me*.

"Sometimes (particularly when we were younger) I had the feeling that you had an inkling of the truth and were only waiting for someone to put it into words. But I was wrong. While you're living the lie you know nothing. Want to hear nothing. Far from waiting for the truth, you compel your friends to collaborate in the lie.

"It's only later, when things fall apart (as they always do) that you become eager to hear the truth, as if you heard me all along and were storing it up till the expedient moment. You know how to *use* the truth when the lie collapses. The lover who was a fool and a nobody before becomes a fool and a nobody only *now*. Now you say that it was this truth that made it impossible for you to go on with the lie. You're so used to lying, so comfortable with whatever comes out of your mouth, that your face looks like a puddle of oil in a teflon frying pan."

Between the painfulness of his grip and what he was saying, I began to cry.

"If you *think* that, if you *hate* me so much, then why are you after me to *marry* you? Why don't you just leave me *alone*. . . !"

"I don't *hate* you—I want you to *change!*"

He stood up. I got scared, ran in here and locked the door.

July 20

Another argument, for no reason. I *must* find an apartment. Sheer inertia! This morning I got dressed, began to make breakfast, preparing to leave for work. Noel was still in bed, cover tucked under elbows and armpits, reading a newspaper.

I was moving around in the kitchen and the round little dining alcove—using the sink, the toaster, putting breakfast things on the table—disappearing, reappearing, disappearing, into and out of the opening of the bedroom door.

"Getting up today?" I asked, annoyed that he wasn't helping.

"No."

I was searching for something in the refrigerator, so that I felt more-or-less divided into the visible/invisible, human/mechanical.

"Wudja say?" I called out.

"I said *no,* I'm *not* getting up and I'm *not* going in to work today."

"Are you *sick* or something?"

"I called *in* sick. . . ."

"Does that mean you *are* sick. . . ?"

By now I was standing in the doorway with a chilled quart of reconstituted orange juice in my hands.

He was still lying there, his face hidden behind the paper, which, from a distance at least, looked like it was in another language.

I sat down at the dining alcove table, started to eat my toast and eggs.

Noel came in, sat down at the table in his black bikini shorts, and started to read me a Sunday-supplement crime feature about a series of strange disappearances—people who'd jumped off bridges or last been seen on bridges—not only in the States, in New York, San Francisco, Mackinaw City, Pittsburgh, Niagara Falls, but in London, in Sidney, in Denmark, Sweden and in other places.

I said a few things to him—don't remember what exactly—probably nothing more original than suggesting therapy—he'd been toying with a fork and threw it down—it struck the table—bounded off like a bullet straight into my face, just missed my eye and left red little welts on my forehead.

I left for work.

July 24

Woke up in the middle of the night, the time of other planets, whether dreaming or awake. I lay there for hours, afraid to move because Noel might wake up. The room was swampy. Eventually I inched my way out of bed, went to the window. One of those nights when the trees look exhausted. You can feel their suffering. A terrible thirst despite the wet breezes blowing over from the poisoned water meadows.

I sneaked out of the room to the bathroom, where I am now, sitting in the garden chair. Tried to open the window and found it impossible, as always—so that it dawned on me for the first time that there was no air conditioning. No electric lights. Nothing visible along the walkways. The familiar white, contained glow in the glass-globed ranks of imitation gas lumps had been absent all along. Might have been a blackout. But the windows had already been opened. That meant Noel was awake, moving around the apartment while I was asleep. That scared me.

I do not know at this moment who I'm living with. There was a moment tonight when he shared some things with me, intimate things I didn't know, when I felt close to him and sympathetic— though even these confessions surprised and disturbed me. The thing of it is, Noel, who *hates* his father, is beginning to show some of his father's worst traits. Violence, obsessive jealousy, and something worse and harder to name. He confessed that he'd always known that his mother had a lover. (Whether one lover or many lovers over the years I couldn't make out.) I said that with her drinking problem and pill problem and everything else I didn't think there would be much desire or interest in anything like that. But I could be completely wrong. I'm beginning to see how little I understand *anything.* As if there's a part of me that's just very *dumb.* Or not exactly dumb—that *doesn't want to know.* Something that isn't alive along with the rest, inserted in me like a plastic heart value. *Resents* knowing. Wants to be *left alone.*

August 2

My life doesn't seem real even while it's happening. The opposite of a dream, I suppose, where the strangest things seem *super*-real if anything.

Noel has, at least, been going to work. At least it *seems* as if he goes to work. We leave together in the morning, he returns at the time he would return if he were working. No reason to doubt that he's actually working, and yet. . . .

Today, when I came home, wet as a watered flower pot inside my business costume of skirt and blouse, Noel was already there, sitting on the couch in old jeans and gray work shirt, sleeves rolled up, watching a re-run of *The Man with The Golden Gun*. The room should have been brilliant, the tv light dissolved in sunlight. But the silver Bali blinds were drawn, so that there was a peculiar twilight that made the television light unnaturally intense. Colored shadows of images revolved across Noel's face. I couldn't help thinking of that science fiction film where the naive young bride senses on her wedding night that her husband, George, is acting strange. Not at *all* like the darkly handsome, smalltown insurance salesman, the fun-loving guy she fell in love with. *This* guy is some kind of *zombie*. She's waiting in bed in the seductive nightgown she bought for this all-important occasion, while George remains by the window in his dressing gown, his back to her, off on the shadowy side of the room, looking down into the dark street or the even darker hotel garden. It's raining, a small storm in fact. Thunder and lightning. There's a flash and (I don't remember which) the bride sees reflected in the dark glass or *we* see from the dark garden, through the storm and the window, the husband's real face, a strange, fleshy tubing, something like a heart with its valves and arteries, or a tropical plant with bizarre, animal-like roots and leaves, or even an insect's mandibles right under the surface of the skin. It isn't until months later that the young wife discovers that he's really a creature from another planet, a being with superior intelligence and X-ray vision who knows everything you're thinking and has the power to transmit messages to other aliens nesting in the bodies of friends and neighbors.

The swift flight of images across Noel's face, a green X-ray, a blue X-ray, a red X-ray, looked horrible in a similar way.

"Come here and sit on the couch," he said.

I lied and complained that my clothes were soaked and that I needed to change.

"Look," he said tenderly, "don't think I don't know how you feel. I *know how you feel*. I've been like a *zombie*."

I was amazed to hear him call himself a zombie. "You haven't been yourself," I said.

"It's just that sometimes you get into these moods—you get into *them* or they get into *you*—and you can't get out. *You* get in, *it* gets in—and you just can't get out! My aunt Judith had some squirrels in her attic once. They'd gotten in somehow, *gnawed* their way in I suppose, and then couldn't get out. Horrible scrambling and scratching could be heard from below. And when the exterminators went in to kill them, they switched on their flashlights and saw these strange-looking creatures, gaunt and huge, like enormous furry *rats*.

They made horrible noises, dashed forward, climbed the walls. They didn't back off, they *attacked*—seemed to be trying to *fly*—managed to claw someone's face—to inflict bites. The exterminators ended up having to climb a ladder, break the attic window and gas the squirrels from the outside."

"There *have* been a few times lately when you've been sitting in your chair watching television—I saw the back of your head and I thought to myself: 'Who *is* this man sitting in our apartment?' It didn't *look* like you."

I didn't say that I'd had that same sensation just two minutes earlier. Now we were *both* sitting on the couch and he was too close for the tint from the tv to make him look strange. Or was it because I was tinted too?

"Am I your baby?" he said.

"What?"

"Am I still your baby Noel?"

I didn't know what to say so I said: "Yes, you're my baby. . . ."

"And will I *always* be your baby Noel. . . ?"

"You'll always be my baby Noel."

He had his head on my shoulder and it seemed to me he was crying, though just about noiselessly.

I started crying a little too.

My voice sounded peculiar to me, throaty, like someone else's. Noel's voice tone was close enough to mine (to the one I didn't recognize) to blend with it and form a vocal outline just above us.

Feeling a little blended in tears, as well as in the Lifesaver colors washing over us from the television, I was able to snuggle up to him, allowing my face to rest in the deep hollow under his jaw, which is rather sharp and a bit protruding.

"I've heard you crying when you lock yourself in the bathroom," he said. "I feel *awful* about that. . . ."

"Well, I *have* cried a little. I've cried a little and I've scribbled a little nonsense in my diary."

"I know," he said.

I went cold. I pictured him standing there in the middle of the night, holding the diary.

I was frightened again, but he said: "You know what went through my head—the first time you went in there and locked the door? When I heard the bathroom lock?"

I shook my head.

"I was thinking about the first trip we ever took together. Remember?"

"Of course I remember," I said. I laughed: the same unrecognizable voice as before. "We were in a little hotel down in the Yucatan," I said. "I was taking a shower and you came in on me and then we made love."

Noel was silent. *The Man with The Golden Gun* was still on. An endless sequence of actions whose only purpose was to bring on more actions. A livid tide of cars, guns, flights and chases, lasers, bodies, fires, kisses, explosions, rockets—nothing more important than anything else—beamed through us and every other porous thing.

"I wonder if I can really be honest with you," he said.

"Of *course* you can be honest with me."

"Don't be stupid!" he snapped. "No one is honest! Everyone is hiding some little thing and everything else winds around that little thing till you've got a *spool!* Then these spools of lies get together and talk like everything is normal!"

"Well, maybe there are some things we're better off not knowing," I said. I was probably thinking of my secret search for an apartment in Manhattan.

"Maybe I don't completely trust you. Maybe you're still a stranger. Maybe you'll *always* be a stranger. Maybe the only people you ever know, the only people who ever know *you*, are your family, the ones you hate most because they're exactly like you."

I didn't at all like the drift of things and I tried to steer him back to the memory of the Yucatan.

"I remember you washing me with that French lilac soap your mother brought back for me from her last holiday abroad."

"I made you bend over. . . ."

"My only problem was that I was afraid of *slipping*. . . ."

"The tub *did* get slippery—*really* slippery—because of the soap. Or it wasn't just the soap. It was us. *We* were in a lather. Our pores were foaming. We weren't human. We passed through one another's skin, like water through a strainer. *Delirium.* The only thought I had was—at one point—while you were bent over and I was looking at the soft cleft of your ass—and below that a sort of face, a strange elongated countenance, like the narrow, dark and bearded one that shows up on the Shroud of Turin."

I laughed, but he didn't at all seem to see the humor in it. He went on quite seriously.

"In everything and everyone there's a hidden face. The faces that we see are nothing but frozen aggregates of energy. Frozen energy is what we call matter. How do we see the true face of things? Lower the temperature to within 0.001° C of absolute zero. Raise it to one hundred million degrees. Accelerate things to 400,000 million electron-volts. Do you understand what I'm talking about? Do you have any idea why there are gigantic accelerator complexes in Switzerland, France and the United States?"

I *didn't* know what he was talking about and I didn't think he knew either. The more he talked the more disturbed and confused he seemed, as if he'd picked up these ideas somewhere and was in over his head.

The weird thing was, the *horrible* thing was, that I was getting aroused. My panties already felt like so much seaweed. I began to kiss Noel with everything I had.

Noel was excited also and we went into the bedroom.

I was still wearing the eggshell blouse and coffee linen skirt I'd worn to work. He asked me to lie down exactly as I was.

"You mean, just like this?" I asked, lying down full length on my back.

"No, like *this*."

He knelt on the bed, his knees between my calves. Slipped his head under my skirt (which was lightweight enough not to cause suffocation), began kissing me intimately at once. I felt myself pulsing right away. Not really against my *will*, and yet so rapidly and without control, that my agreeing to it or wanting it didn't seem to matter.

Everything rushed to that one spot, as if a live animal had been caught between the teeth of a larger animal which proceeded to play with it, nip at it, pick it up and put it down, push and pull on it, suck on it, rather than deliver the deep bite that would draw blood. While my arms and legs were about as useful as a pair of pajamas drying on the line.

I was aware, of course, that he'd reached under my skirt, pulled my red bikini panties down to a point only a little above the knees. Trying to accommodate him, to open wider, as if he could slip in and get around behind some deeper sensation in that way, I heard the thin fabric of my panties tearing.

This went on for a bit, with decreasing effect, as if tongue and lips didn't have the power to escalate the body out of the neutrality of the everyday, didn't give the mouth-to-mouth resuscitation they once did. I complained. And before I knew it, without giving me a chance to remove my skirt or slip off the torn panties, he was on me and we were fucking with our clothes on! Old-fashioned legs open, up and down fucking. The more we went at it, his jeans swelling into the cradle of my skirt, the more insanely stimulated we became.

There was something about it that got him wild. Knees wide apart, trembling in mid-air, skirt that couldn't help sliding down to my hips, shoes still on my feet. An off-center desire I'd never felt in him before. He looked as if he'd swallowed a potion, couldn't fuck me hard enough. I began to feel a little frenzied myself.

"Wait," I croaked, reaching down with one hand to try and pull off the skirt. Figuring he'd do the same with his slacks.

"Not like that," he said, holding my wrist. "Like *this*."

He unzipped his fly, grabbed the thin material of the skirt at the belly and tore a flap off like a sheet of paper towelling. There I was, ready and glistening, like a Japanese lunch box. He began thrusting through the opening and I thrusted back up against him, pushing my hips up off the mattress, just about doing a shoulder stand to increase the depth and force.

I felt his ribs against my thighs.

I warmed up his prick like a muff. A quiet swarm of furry bees, delivering and receiving a thousand wet stings of pleasure, their buzzing turned into something else.

My orgasm just sort of bounded out, like something let out of a cage. Noel started off groaning, as usual. But then he lost steam, seemed to be going through the motions.

He began talking in a screwy way. "Every time I fuck, I try to fuck away the right angles, but I can't!" I didn't know what he was talking about. It was bizarre to hear him cram as many "fucks" into a sentence as Roland. "Like the right angles where two walls meet. A vertical cleft of shadow from head to toe that looks almost soft. If I could fuck away that cleft I'd be *healthy!*"

He'd swung over to the side of the bed, head in hands, looked desperate. Began to talk about his mother. How he used to watch her at her vanity mirror, powdering her breasts with a large powder puff. On the bed, removing or pulling on her stockings. Lying in bed next to his father, naked because it was summer, while the father lay there half-dressed, in pajama bottoms or shorts. Hiding in the dark, looking into the lighted depth of the bedroom, sometimes directly, sometimes from the sharp angle of a mirror. He remembered imagining he'd discovered certain principles of perception. If you could not see someone's *eyes*, for example, then the eyes could not see you. The misconception that if nothing is visible to *you* (from inside a lighted room, for instance) then you can't be seen by others. In this way he learned to position himself so that he rarely saw his mother's eyes or face. She was no longer his mother, he imagined, but simply a woman's well-proportioned body. The breasts wide discs, fragrant with powder, the dark-dark tuft of hair a path that leads down from the lower belly between the swelling of the thighs, something like Denise's.

He described in detail a time when he saw his mother sitting on one of her lovers, with her back to the man's face. A double negative of anonymity: Noel positioned in such a way that he could only see from the neck down, the woman facing the man's legs and the wall, the man facing a rippling back. Rear entry, but from below, with the man reclining. A complicated message. The man not actually in the so-called feminine position, because the woman was facing away, not sawing away between open legs, but with her knees *outside* his legs. Yet, while he *was* thrusting up into her both from the rear and below, he was nevertheless lying back while she rode him like a rocking horse. She swivelled, she pushed, slowed things down, sped them up, exerted pressure, eased up, just like a man screwing a woman. The image of a man's hand on a woman's (on his *mother's?*) ass stung him with a permanent cigarette burn of sexual agony.

"I should've figured your mother was mixed up in this," I muttered.

His face went black: from head-in-hands desperation to something unnameable.

Did he want to hide somewhere and watch me undress? I asked. Was *that* what he wanted?

No, he wanted to tie my hands to the bedposts, he confessed. He looked a little shamefaced.

"I don't know," I said. I couldn't think of anyone I knew who'd done that, not even Holly.

He began pleading with me. How he never-ever asked me to do anything out of the ordinary—while he was absolutely certain Roland or one of the other jerks I'd been with *had* to have asked me one time or another to do something weird. He'd tie my hands loosely, or with a slip knot, so that I could free them easily. He couldn't explain it, but he *needed* this! He'd never ask me to do anything again! His voice was agonized.

I acquiesced.

He tied my hands; removed my blouse and panties, but left on shoes and torn skirt; turned on the red bulb and the stereo. I didn't feel real. Or "real," but in a way that's hard to talk about. Pre-recorded? A little like the feeling when you visit someone and they videotape you playing with their kid or something. Minutes later they play it back through the tv set. "As if you're on television." You resemble yourself. You but not you. A strange abstraction of the human. A real person, and yet. . . .

My legs were lifted, pressed back, my knees against my shoulders. I was powerless, but had agreed to be powerless. That idea has always excited me. Like the dream where you're overpowered, struggling and squirming while feeling with humiliation that your squirming is becoming a source of pleasure. Folded small, compressed, a cradle someone is free to rock in, wallow in. And the more they rock and wallow in it the squishier you feel, a kind of living mud.

By this time I was dripping, a shrub in water, a swamp with beds of spongy vegetation. My body felt the way it does on humid days in summer: any place there's hair and two warm surfaces of flesh it turns to mud. You can stick a finger into the warm stuff like a cake thermometer. While the rest of the body is as pale and weightless as a rice wafer.

If he'd plunged into me then he'd have gotten everything he wanted. But he didn't. He lifted me up by the ankles! So easily, with one hand, that it reminded me how strong he is.

He began spanking me. One stinging slap and then another.

"What are you *doing?*" Trying not to show fear, I sounded stupid.

"Bad girls get *spanked!*"

I gave a little laugh, trying to get into the swing of it. I remember thinking: "If I *consent* to this, then it's not the same thing. There might be something to it. A Victorian father and his daughter. She's done something naughty and she's being punished. She lifts her skirt, pulls down her panties and drapes herself over his lap. Papa has a strap, a paddle or he uses his hand." Whenever we resist something, I reasoned, it's because it transgresses some boundary. "The only way to grow is to give yourself over to it, especially when it goes against your grain." But it didn't work. I lost my desire. No matter how hard I tried I couldn't get it back.

Meanwhile, Noel had lowered me to the bed again and was talking about a Colonial punishment device. Two wooden blocks, matching half circles carved out in each to accommodate neck and wrists. He speculated that there must have existed a lesser known, more profoundly humiliating device designed to lock in place and expose more private parts of the body to public scrutiny. The ass, in particular. Why was it that the ass, both in terms of punishment and exposure, was the crux of humiliation? He thought it would be interesting to study that. Lock me up that way and maybe write something about the role the ass played in the psychology of punishment. Then he went on from that to some crazy theory about dreams and machinery. The smallest implement and the grandest feat of engineering, the stock and the submarine, the rack and the rocket, the strappado, the nutcracker, the bridge and the tunnel, all carried nightmare states into the upper world. And daily returned new forms to the nether world, altering our dreams and shifting our terrors toward alien territories.

I was too worn out to follow him, I said. It was either too complicated or too stupid. I just wanted to be untied, to take a shower, warm up a frozen potpie in the microwave, eat it while I watched a *Twilight Zone* rerun and go to bed.

"I told you it was a slip knot," he said. "So you *should* be able to slip right out." His voice had no inflection, in the same way the room's red shadows made his face look expressionless.

I tried to slip out, but the harder I struggled, the deeper the cords bit into my skin.

I began to cry. Deep gulps swallowed my face.

"Basic rule of life," he said.

He sat down on the bed, kissed me on the mouth. Then on the breasts, tenderly. On the mouth again. My lips were open. Desire rebounded in me. The desire that had fled with the first sting of the spanking had been gathering force somewhere and returned to overwhelm me.

My head bent back. My neck felt long and exposed. Mouth open. My body wanted to levitate. Legs wanted to rise over my head again, of their own accord, without being pulled up by the ankles. Body seemed to want to curve around completely, make a circle. As if it could just float up there.

But Noel turned my body sideways, lay down next to me. He'd shed his clothes (when?) and entered me quickly.

A hand on my breast. And the other buried in and fingering the dark path he'd compared to his mother's!

Violent tremors erupted between two fingers. It didn't seem to matter that there was coercion. Violence, humiliation—the body didn't care.

My whole body shook.

Legs trembled.

Head was so far back it was looking down into the dark gap between mattress and headboard.

Mouth open wide enough to swallow a face.

Involuntary convulsions with every caress, cries with every thrust.

Suddenly Noel rolled off the bed. Maybe he'd fallen. It happened so fast he might have been shot.

He jumped up.

"I'll get something to cut the ropes," he said and left the room. His voice was even flatter than before. While he was gone I twisted and struggled some more, only succeeding in rubbing my wrists raw. I drew blood and gave myself a nasty gash on the skin, sickle-shaped like a tiny animal bite, kicking against the sharp edge of the tv.

The set was catty corner to the bed for late-night ice cream and the second or fortieth viewing of *It Came from Outer Space* or *Day of the Triffids*. The black matrix picture tube was dark. There I was on the screen, small and complete, a miniature figure dyed red, the light odd and unreal, like light in a storm cloud. The swelling of the hip, the tapering of the leg, subtle red shadows in place of ordinary shadows in every crease of face or sheet: everything both beautiful and alarming. It crossed my mind that the set was positioned there as a mirror.

"How did I get here?" I thought, on the verge of crying again. "And how can I be *there too*, lost in space like an astronaut in a red suit who's fallen overboard, pulled away from the gliding shuttle by unknown forces, a vacant and endless sort of drowning. As small, as utterly isolated, as much an object among objects, as if viewed from the perspective of death."

While I was staring at my red image, concentrated like tomato pulp, in the black screen, something else appeared at an optically improbable spot in the screen, at first a little gold-tinted cloud, an amber sail, a candle flame, and then, quickly swelling, a leg, a naked torso gradually reddening as it advanced into the lamp glow.

Noel came close, bent over me, covered my face with his hand, my nose and my mouth covered by the palm; fingers covering my eyes and reaching across my forehead into the hairline.

I thought with complete lucidity: "He's going to murder me."

Something long, straight and black was raised above his head, just about touching the ceiling, as if he were hanging from it. I don't know what it was—maybe the bar he attaches his weights to—though it looked thicker than a weight bar.

I lost myself completely. Don't know what came pouring out of me—words and tears—felt like I was throwing up—but I think I was begging for my life, saying I was sorry about this, sorry about that, pleading, blubbering, making myself into so much shit. . . .

He threw the rod across the room—hit the dresser—broke the mirror and zillions of perfume bottles—an incredible explosion—and a smell like the Hanging Gardens of Babylon in Odorama. (Not one neighbor said a word or called the building manager or the police, the way they do when you're having a party.)

He undid the ropes by giving a sharp pull on each knot and sat down on the bed, a dead weight. I had the impulse to strike back, but my hands were like rubber gloves. I thought: better leave it alone. And I locked myself in the bathroom.

August 3

Woke up at 6 am. Idea was to get out of here before Noel woke up. Come back some other time with the police or with friends to pick up my stuff.

Noel was dressed, pacing back and forth, cursing. Eyes looked weird and a crazy expression on his face. Voice much deeper than I'd ever heard it, like an announcer on an all-day news station. "I should have kept going!" he said. "Why didn't I keep *going?* Why did I turn *back?* I'm so *stupid!"*

More pacing and then: "No one *knows!* I didn't tell you—I didn't think you'd understand—maybe I *should* have told you but I didn't—that I started to go somewhere—I had the opportunity—someone made me an offer—offered me a *whole new way of life*—that was so fantastic I couldn't believe it! I should have taken the risk, but I didn't! I came back. I was too much of a coward to keep going—and now I'm one of the living dead, like everyone else!" He stopped, looked straight through me, and said: "It isn't true. I didn't *come* back! I was *thrown* back! I saw—I don't know *what* I saw! They showed me things! They asked me to study certain things—and I couldn't do it! I just couldn't do it! I *wanted* to, but I couldn't grasp it! What was it that I wanted? I had no *knowledge* of those things. I had no *capacity* for those things. But I wanted this one thing they were offering. They held it out to me like the one thing that makes the victim unlatch her window night after night in all those vampire movies. But as soon as my money ran out, they dumped me like so much garbage! They'd kill me, but they know I'm too stupid to know what I saw! Or maybe they *will* kill me!"

"You're talking nutty," I said. He came over and punched me in the face. Went crazy and beat me very badly. Eyes swelled up so much I couldn't see. Nose was bleeding and felt like it was broken. Blood from one ear. Loosened two teeth and split my lip. Side hurt a lot so maybe he broke a rib or something. I tried to plead with him. Said all sorts of useless crap. But he just kept beating me and beating me like he wanted to pulp me into jelly. I broke away and made it into the bathroom.

After a few minutes I heard his footsteps. He came close to the door and said that he'd just figured it out and he knew what was wrong. Once you were left behind you were left behind. No such thing as standing still. If you missed your one-and-only chance to go forward then you had to go backward! Had to *choose* that and find a way to do it! This was not, repeat, was *not* the same thing as nostalgia! Nostalgia was the half-emotion that came from lacking the strength to do either one thing or the other.

"We're arrogant," he said. "Arrogance is the fundamental facial expression of our age. We assume we're correct. A billion little differences add up to two or three opinions. We argue and argue to hide the fact that we agree. Tv programs, magazines, movies are dreamed up just to let each other know that we think the same thing and that we're correct. This is how culture exists: superficial variety and fundamental sameness. But a few of us—a *few* of us—are beginning to suspect that we're *wrong*! That all those jerks we make fun of are *right*. We secretly long for the frame house, the picket fence, the bicycle and the elm tree. Frank Capra and Douglas Sirk, Mickey Rooney/Judy Garland, the Lane Sisters, Deanna Durbin, Jane Wyman, *For Me and My Gal*, *Alice Adams*, *Meet Me in St. Louis*, *It's A Wonderful Life*. It's as if that's real life and it's already happened. We visit it in films the way we go to a museum. How can we re-enter it? We restore old houses, we plant gardens, we bake muffins, cover the sofa with chintz.

"Not long ago I was visiting my parents in Connecticut. Walking down a quiet old tree-lined street I heard two women talking, saying goodbye, one inside the house, holding the screen door open, and the other outside looking in.

"'Thank you again for the eggs,' the woman inside said in the most naturally friendly way, clear as a lake 1/4" deep.

"'Oh, that's nothing.'

"'Well, you helped make a wonderful *cake*.'

"It went right through me: the conviction that this was *right*. A basic goodness, modest and simple, we've wasted our lives making fun of. 'How crazy it is,' I thought, 'that we thirst after these images, but don't have the sense to look for them in *life*.'"

I couldn't believe what I was hearing. My head was reeling. After everything that had gone on, while I was barricaded in the bathroom with terrible bruises on my face and body, bleeding, in pain, he was standing out there raving about June Allyson and homemade cake!

"Have you gone *crazy*!" I croaked with the little nub of a voice I had left. "What do the Lane Sisters and chintz slipcovers have to do with *us*?"

He left the corridor.

After a while I had the feeling things had calmed down. I felt no tension radiating from the apartment. I unlocked the door and went out. But he started in on me again. . . .

Valeria replaced the diary, Denise looked like so much unrisen buckwheat dough. Valeria looked at her with new-found disgust. Reading the diary hadn't made her feel closer to Denise, but further away. Or, at least, the desire to *be* further away.

The sealed window radiated heat into the airless bathroom. It was quiet in a peculiar way, as if the electricity was dead and an unidentifiable background hum along with it. The murmuring of the outer world, its minute twittering and gross rumbling, flowed in.

The apartment was silent, permeable, with not one sound in the foreground.

Valeria ventured out, looked both ways. To the left there was a short length of corridor, a set of louvered closet doors and the front door. To the right, light of polar brilliance blazing from the living room through the round dining alcove. She saw no one. (She guessed that Noel had slipped out, humiliated, and could now be found pacing and waving his arms in the wooded periphery edging the condo complex or driving on some interstate highway, looking normal.) Denise clung to her, as she would have if Valeria had walked straight up.

She started toward the front door, sensed something and went the other way without knowing why. As she crossed the dining alcove she turned and saw a blue shadow in the vicinity of the louvered closet doors, its blob head and blob body revolving swiftly around two corners.

Noel ran into the living room only a few steps behind them, pointing a revolver so thick and black it looked like it was made of cast iron. He stopped short. They all turned toward the wraparound bank of windows and stared at the corona of flames darting up beyond the distant tree fringe. The white chairs, couches and carpet were tinted orange. Denise tried to hide in full view on one of the couches.

Noel recovered himself and fired. A lamp right in back of Valeria exploded. He came closer, looked at the gun, at the shattered lamp, placed the barrel in his mouth and pulled the trigger, as if expecting a sort of phantom bullet to slip through him the way it had through

Valeria. A shelf of knock-knacks that had been hanging on the wall just behind his head crashed to the floor as he fell.

THE FAMILIAR FEELING
THAT THINGS ARE INCONCLUSIVE

Billions of tiny electron guns buried in the paving blocks and building fronts fired into the atmosphere. The crystal structure of the universe dazzled as if it were bobbing at anchor off a tropical port. Vivid banks of purple-violet immortelles, pillows of white fraxinella and blue-and-white sails of monkshood stood out clearly on the building's green border of lawn. A foil wrapper scraped across the plaza.

Noel was dead, the police had departed, and Denise, already subtracted to next-to-nothing, was about to disappear, taken away in a white family Cadillac as if by ambulance. Valeria followed the car's earthbound flight out of view. It struck her that all resolutions were vacant and absolute, unlike the more familiar feeling that things were materially stuffed and pathetically inconclusive.

NINE

"THINGS STIRRED IN THE VACUUM. . . ."

Far from the place where Valeria was at that moment, after weeks of fruitless searching for her, Liam dreamed that he was lying in bed (as he really was) in his basement apartment. No curtains, blinds or shades on the windows. A terrible, white daylight ate through the atmosphere, his body, the bed, the floor, the ground below. Light collected like water, setting the bed afloat.

It buoyed him up into one of the second or third story bedrooms. An odd scraping sound woke him. He opened his eyes and saw a dark shape against the screen. A large squirrel was fastened there with four bloody sets of claws and bloody mouth. The creature stared at him, its glassy orange gaze both alien and penetrating, like a tv camera. It clawed at the screen. His body twitched violently. The creature bolted upward. Why would it go *upward*, he wondered with alarm. The normal thing would be to escape *downward* or *sideways*, toward trees, hedges, telephone lines.

Tiny claws scratched swiftly across the roof.

He approached the window cautiously, opened the screen, looked down into the sprawling bank of evergreen shrubs. The shrubs were dotted with bright red berries, not quite opaque, a little light transmitted through each fleshy globe. Not a deep enough crimson, he thought, to be the stuff sticking in gooey clots to the squirrel's claws and mouth.

The scrambling receded to the far side of the roof, faded out. He looked around and saw for the first time that he actually was in Nora's yellow-flowered bedroom.

*** *** ***

That afternoon (having spent most of the day patching up Ambrose's bungalows) Liam arrived home in the middle of a bitter argument. He sat down on the searingly hot green plastic cushions of the porch swing, reluctant to go in. Something in the pitch of their voices told him that it wasn't just another argument about money. Or, perhaps, the usual argument about money turned inside out. During their frequent arguments about debts, household expenses and real estate losses, so much emotion surged in their voices, enough to blot out everything else, as if lack of money could erase the human slate, that he always wondered if money could be the real subject.

If this real subject had broken through, he didn't want to know what it was. One's identity trembled, threatened to come apart, in the presence of such eruptions of truth in the lives of those one loved.

"We didn't actually *lose* anything, Nora!" Ambrose shouted at the top of his lungs. "What did we actually lose? The thing was *worthless*! Look at the goddamn figures, for christ's sake! The taxes *alone*. . . !"

"You killed us! You *finished* us! We're wiped out *completely*! But you don't care about that! You don't care about *anything*! You're *happy* about it. I can *see* it! But you won't get another cent from *me*! You'll have to kill me before I give you another *penny*!"

Nora went on. He couldn't quite make it out. Something about her earnings. And then clearly, as if she'd moved closer to an open window: "Drained *me*, drained my children! But never again! I'd *kill* you if it weren't for *them*. . . !"

This was surprising. Or more than surprising. He didn't want to hear it. He went and sat at the bottom of the porch steps, where their words were hard to hear.

Fifteen minutes or more went by.

The screen door banged. Liam turned his head. It was Tom, the family friend, the pork butt on two legs. Apparently things had reached the point, Liam thought glumly, where they didn't mind airing their secrets in front of the likes of *him*.

"Jesus, what a doozy!" Tom said, mopping his forehead and sitting down next to Liam. "Christ almighty, have they been going at it to*day*!"

His meaty face had a small red smile crammed between its cheeks.

"Shut up," Liam said.

What the thing was about, Tom persisted, was that Ambrose had gone and given away the bar. Gave it to some ugly little weasel for nothing but an assumption of debts and back taxes. This hyena (who had just about the ugliest kisser you'd ever want to see, like they'd torn up half his face and forgotten to replace the cover) acted like he was doing Ambrose a *favor*.

He was there when it happened. Ambrose's lawyer was ten minutes late, so he signed it over without him. Craziest thing he ever saw. Didn't even claim this month's *rent*. The hyena was getting that too. It was as if he couldn't wait to sign the paper!

"'Some people have a talent for business and some people don't,' the little guy said (with some kind of accent), showing plenty of teeth. 'For some it's a salvation, for others a lifelong disease. A dummox like you is better off with a salaried job. You were told what to do, but you didn't do it! A dummy who doesn't know how dumb he is is a curse not only to himself but to his family. Now you're in a hole you'll *never* get out of! *NEVER!* Do you understand me? You and yours are finished. Is this perfectly clear? The bar is nothing. The bar cancels nothing. You might say that you've mortgaged not only yourself and your wife, but your grandchildren.'"

The guy went on and on, but it was impossible to repeat it. One thing screwier than the next. Ambrose seemed to know what he meant, so they'd had dealings before.

All Nora knew, he said, was that Ambrose had given away the bar.

The argument inside hadn't died down. On the contrary, while Tom warmed to his subject, rolling his sleeves up in two tight coils at the shoulder to tan the pale hams of his arms, it sounded as if Ambrose and Nora had gone and gotten themselves a couple of microphones. It kept building up and then there was a crash, something tremendous hitting the floor and a lot of glass breaking along with it.

Liam rushed in.

Ambrose's voice was thick with everything that couldn't be expressed.

"You don't need *ME!*" he said. "You have your *SON!*"

"I don't ever want to hear you mention my son again! He's been your *slave* for fifteen years! I should be *shot* for letting you use him that way!"

"I'm taking the Buick, I'm driving to the airport, I'm getting on a plane and I'm never coming back! But before I go, he's gonna find out just what kind'v whore you are! I'll tell'm about Tom and every other bum who's had his finger in the jelly!"

"I'll tell you something I never told you, Ambrose," she said. "I met a guy at a bar out in Lynbrook who said he knew you. This guy knew your whole lousy story. And he offered to kill you for $500! 'Do yourself a favor,' he said. It was a good deal, but I was frightened and I said no. When you were stabbed, I thought it was him! But now I'm going to make a phone call. . . !"

"You do that! While I talk to Liam," he said.

"I *want* you to talk to him! I want you to tell him the *truth!*" she screamed. It seemed like blood was going to come out of her eyes.

Ambrose started toward her, fragments of broken crockery and fluorescent ceiling fixture cracking on the yellow imitation brick linoleum.

"Do it!" Liam said. "Lay one finger on her." He'd taken a long bread knife from the cutlery drawer. "I'll finish the job they started! I'll open every stitch!"

Ambrose was both dead white and waxen red, like half a domestic Edam cheese in a supermarket display case. He took a step forward.

"TOUCH HER AND I'LL *KILL* YOU!"

Liam's voice wasn't human.

"It's alright," Nora said. "I can handle him."

"No, it's *NOT* ALRIGHT! I'll knock him on his *ass*, if he isn't out of this house in one *minute!* I want him out *NOW!*"

Ambrose looked like he was going to say something, but changed his mind.

"GET IN YOUR CAR, KEEP DRIVING AND DON'T EVER COME BACK!" Liam screamed. "CAUSE NEXT TIME I SEE YOU I'LL KILL YOU!"

Ambrose read his face and went out the door. Tom followed.

Toward evening Liam was sitting in the overgrown back garden boxed in by run-down tool sheds, sagging porches and the back walls of shingle houses the color of dogfood. He was drinking a beer and the beer was muddling his thoughts instead of helping him think things through.

The sun was going down behind the low roofs. Things stirred in the vacuum, the weight of sunlight, pinning things back against walls and sidewalk, slipping off as always.

Smell of wood smoke drifted in: barbecue, burning house or bonfire.

Aqua-flowered bedsheets and slender white nightgowns of adolescent daughters flew up, lashed by the cold, invisible current of evening.

What difference did it make what happened? he thought. No difference between the most and the least one could say about things. They occurred and that was all. Of no significance to anyone but the victim. People looked at you and saw your life as something tiny, a passport photograph. No such thing as an individual destiny. Dumb to imagine that your blob of habits-and-opinions, the coherent clump of self you recognized in the mirror, what others knew as your "personality," had a superior sort of importance to, say, the blind usefulness of a molecule of glue sealing the flap of an envelope.

Now he knew (he told himself) what others had discovered with crushing certainty long before him. The shallow yet infinite well of everyday depression and everyday optimism. If you remained in it too long, like Roger, you couldn't help but develop a worshipful hatred for the others, the tiny handful of celebrities whose faces you saw over and over, till they were more familiar than your next door neighbor, whose names you heard so often you mistook them for your own, duplicated so many times any one of them could populate a continent.

He wondered if there was any sense in which he'd just won a victory over Ambrose. Or if, to a real and awful extent, he'd just succeeded in turning himself *into* Ambrose. There was always some way one's victories were actually defeats. No salvation. This was the reason no one lived forever. It never happened because no one *wanted* it to happen. No use dreaming of how he and Valeria were destined to meet again in a so-called other life. The guarantee of eternal death was born in life. First you became a normal jerk. Then a little mote of antagonism swarming with other motes. Then you felt like someone who'd already died and returned to Earth. No one heard you or saw you, present in life but without weight or value. As good as dead though you'd continue to walk around on two legs for another thirty or fifty years.

There were only two conditions on Earth. And you were either in one or in the other. It pushed you along, as if there were a hand behind you. It pushed you all the way through life. It never stopped.

The evening thickened, as if a sort of black flour were mixing itself into it. Soon it would be too thick to breathe. A man could be found suffocated, sitting upright in his back garden at the coolest hour of the day.

He went inside, sat down on the striped settee in the cavernous living room, facing the pea-soup mirror of the switched-off tv screen. He imagined himself fleeing with Valeria as if pursued. At incredible speeds by car at night on country roads. Desperately, with tremendous difficulty, through crowded cities. An endless pursuit with hairpin turns. As if the soul were a motorcycle shooting out from under them. They could barely hold on. The soul was fleeing—but from whom? And where was it headed? He guessed where Valeria would like to land, but couldn't figure out how to get there. Nothing seemed adequate, not even Astronaut Training School. One dumb idea replaced another. You lived at least two lives. And the stupid, dreamy one in your head dominated the other. He thought of all the times he'd longed for the moment John Garfield dreams of after he's blinded in *Pride of the Marines*, when Eleanor Parker embraces him on an elevated subway platform above a deep local vista of streets and trees. Her hair so wavy, her eyes so warm, her hat and coat so laden with memories that an unshed torrent of tears sweeps him back from death.

He made up his mind to find Valeria. And if he found her, he

resolved, he'd forget Nora, forget the property, the debts and
everything else and flee with her, just as he'd pictured on the dead
tv screen.

THE HUMAN ELECTRONIC CREATURE

Valeria's mother reclined on the soft green and yellow ribbing of
the new chaise lounge, her upper body at a 45^0 angle, sunbathing
like the others. She'd removed her brown skirt and coffee blouse
and stretched out flat in her brown one-piece bathing suit. Now
Uncle Sylvan had helped her tilt the chair up so that, with the aid
of a hospital straw, she could join in drinking some of the frothy,
egg-nog-like drink Nadja had prepared.

Her jaw was still in a brace. Her mouth couldn't open beyond the
little tunnel of the straw. Both chewing and speaking were impossible. A thick pad of notepaper and an orange plastic pen lay on a
small glass garden table beside her, so that a message could be
scrawled on the spur of the moment.

It seemed to Valeria that it was taking an awfully long time for
her mother's jaw to mend. No one else seemed to notice that. Or
how ugly the brace was. The grotesque leather harness compressed
the mouth into two pale, slightly moistened lines. And the difficulty
of sucking in sustenance through a straw had caused a striking
weight loss, forcing a certain latent profile to the surface: hawk-
like, predatory, horrible against the round green blocks of the back
gardens.

With parental solicitude the others nurtured the pathetic spark
of childhood that seemed, as always, to be rekindled in the invalid,
while Valeria looked on in horror. Left unattended for an instant,
she shot Valeria the same pleading glance as in the hospital.

Valeria went over and sat next to her and her mother set down
glass-and-straw, picked up the pad and orange pen.

Valeria rested her arm on the hot aluminum of her mother's
chairback and twisted her neck around to read what her mother was

writing. "We're blind. . ." she began. Nadja bent down between
Valeria and her mother. Smiling, she proffered refills with a
brimming glass ladle, a heavy punch bowl cradled in the crook of
one arm. Suntanned, in sand-toned halter and blue shorts, she
looked like her mother's younger, prettier and dumber sister.
Burdened. The burdened-looking friendliness found nowhere but
on the faces of spineless children at family gatherings.

Nadja filled Valeria's glass cup and her mother's tall glass. A bit
of liquid brimmed over the lip of the ladle, dripped on the pad. A
blue-stained goo ran down from her mother's unfinished sentence.

"Mmm, this is very *good*, Nadja," Aunt Elena's voice sang out
from the other end of the porch, where she was hidden in a cluster
of sunbathers. Uncle George was over there and two adolescent
cousins Valeria hardly knew, the blond boy a dead weight in the
deep pouch of the woven Mexican hammock and the blonde girl in
a halter and white shorts, tanned legs and white sneakers up on the
railing, crossed at the ankles, the glossy magazine supplement of a
Sunday newspaper stared into by features cut so short there was
nothing for life to snag on.

"Oh, this *is* good," someone else chimed in.

"What *is* this?"

"Isn't it yummy?"

"Oh, yes!"

"*Wonderful!*"

"I think we're going to want *more*."

A weak tide of laughter swept Nadja across the porch to the picnic
table, where she busied herself at once with a blender (a yellow
cable ran from the blender through the kitchen window), measuring
cup, and various bottles and containers.

"This tastes like a pina colada."

"It's *related* to a pina colada," Nadja said over the blender's
churning, a tiny, muted sound out of doors. "But it *isn't* a pina
colada. That has pineapple and this doesn't. This doesn't have any
liquor at all and a pina colada has rum. It just *tastes* like it has liquor
because of a trick Andy learned in Tahiti. Just about the only thing
this has in common with a pina colada, I suppose, is the coconut
cream."

"Is that what it is? Coconut cream?"

Without lowering the sound of the small-screen television where a soccer match had been surging through the afternoon, Valeria's father said that he wanted everyone to know that he welcomed this marriage for one reason only. It was the idea of marriage they were sanctioning and renewing, not only as a contract with one another but with the ages. Every new marriage wove the present with the past—the common vessel in which we all sailed, rocked now forward, now backward—like the enormous ship of woven reeds that Scandinavian chap had attempted to sail from Egypt to South America. Parents sailed on in the marriages of their children. And not only through the doubtful immortality of the genes.

No one said anything. But Valeria's mother began scribbling fiercely on her pad.

"What's your mother saying?"

"'Blind and stupid,'" Valeria read aloud. "'If everyone talks about something, then that's history. Mass agreement = History. It happens. Again and again. There's no resisting it, though it takes you by surprise every time. Now everyone is talking about marriage again. . . .'"

Her mother had written more, but Nadja came out with platters of mangos, grapes, oranges, bananas, pineapple and other fruit and the family went back to its business of being a family having a pleasant day by the shore. Shirts on and shirts off; lying on towels or on chairs and hammocks designed not to intrude on one's suspension in the distance between emptiness and solidity. Everything was suited to the half-language, the blurred focus of family being.

Nadja motioned with her head for Valeria to follow her into the kitchen. But Valeria pretended not to notice. She preferred to stay out-of-doors watching her family across the vast sun-filled distance that lay between her and everyone. While the porch was not the tiled villa terrace, its Mediterranean vistas hedged with cypresses, that showed up so well in *Susan Slade* and *Love Has Many Faces*, still the compact, infinite ball of space boosted the family beyond its particular super-reality. Ordinarily, she thought, each family member was an utterly opaque clot of self. And all these opaque clots twined and packed together to wedge out other realities. Here the family seemed peripheral to something else, like a television laugh track, whose function is to provide a steady chattering frame of unreality around the action, just as the action suggests a border of unreality around the life of the viewer. An atmospheric bubble-dome, like the charged gases bathing a planet.

"Ooh! This is *sticky!*" the blonde girl cousin whined in a cute and winning way. Trying to drink her strawberry drink while lying down in the hammock, she'd spilled it on the electromagnetic turquoise cotton of her tank top and on the tanned scoop of skin above.

"I didn't bring a *bathing* suit," the blond boy cousin pouted, half-sitting, one leg up, on the raw wood railing. "No one told me we could go *swimming*. . . ."

"I'm sure *Andrew* has something you could wear," Aunt Elena said while sweeping the porch with vigorous strokes, sending dark motes and sparkling grains of silica flying into the deep trough of sunlight beyond the railing. Aunt Grete looked up from her hand of cards with their woodland-and-covered-bridge backing and called loudly toward the screen door and windows:

"DOES ANDREW HAVE A BATHING SUIT PETER COULD BORROW? HE'S *BORED* UP HERE ON THIS 'CRUISE TO NOWHERE' WITH THE OLD FOLKS!"

"Yes," Uncle Sylvan murmured from a concealed point at the card table, where a dark plane of sunlight was stuck to the green surface. "He wants to get away from us and I don't blame him. He sees the corpse that's always travelling with us like a coffin in a baggage car, a rigid horizontal.

"Of course, it isn't hard to see that he's just as stupid as we were at his age. Stupider. They're stupid in new ways now. A clever kind of stupidity that wasn't on the market then. If you think he looks dumb now, just *give* him a couple of years! He'll be a real *moron* then! Still, he has the right to avoid the dead, I suppose, to paddle across the lake as fast as he can."

"There's *nothing!*" Nadja sang out from the interior in a tonelessly lyrical soprano. "Andy must have all his spare suits down at the locker!"

Valeria's father (his white business shirt blazing against the white wall) raised an eyebrow and shot his wife a look as if to say he'd known all along that something was wrong out here. But the look was lost on her. She was staring fixedly over the railing, focused on something as if longing to spring up and fly into the trees, seize hold of something that was perched or crawling there.

"How many *strawberries* did you put in this. . . ?" someone who was sipping strawberry drink through a straw called out to Nadja.

No answer.

"Nadja?"

"Yes. . . ?"

Her voice seemed to come from much further away than the kitchen.

"How many strawberries *are* there in this?"

"Let's see: five, six, seven—eight-and-a-half, I think. Eight-and-a-half per glass. . . ."

"Oh—eight-and-a-half per *glass*. . . ."

The Mexican net hammock tore loose from its hooks and the blonde cousin shot straight to the floor with a thumping crash. More spilled strawberry drink and a little trickle of real blood too, the glass punch cup cracking and slashing a finger.

Gasps, cries of dismay from the older relatives, titters from the blond brother.

"Television at its best," Valeria thought.

She stood up and crossed the porch to the screen door. The atmosphere behind her was smoky. Between slate red roofs and slate black roofs a band of ocean boiled with pinpoints of radiation. Steam rose into a blinding white sky. Birds jumped from branches as if their feet were scalded. Shadows ate other shadows, building up an enormous black box of shadow, whose image inched across a white wall in the middle distance.

Voices came from the bathroom: the blonde cousin's childish sobbing and the cooing of those tending to her injuries.

Nadja walked back and forth between white kitchen and pink bedroom, folding articles of clothing and putting them in the cartons that lay about, shifting objects from one place to another without reducing the total volume of things.

"I don't know what they're all *doing* here!" Nadja whispered. "I thought we'd be *alone*. But they just show *up!*"

She said that her big mistake was visiting Mother yesterday. She looked so hideous that she invited her out. But she didn't stop to think that someone would have to drive her. So Mother showed up toward evening with Aunt Grete and Uncle Sylvan (who'd gotten wind of it and come along for the ride). Then Father, Aunt Elena and Uncle George showed up today with those awful children. It had been like this since the engagement. As if there was a chute through the window. As if she'd been reclaimed by the family in some boundless, fathomless way. Baron Pauli said that all families, experienced *en masse*, were a strange mixture of the intimidating and the ludicrous. Meeting your family was a wonderful chance for the loved one to see you magnified, shrunken, deformed and parodied in four or ten different ways. If a speck of the romantic, what someone had called the "infinite strangeness" of love, remained by the time of the engagement, meeting the family was bound to kill it.

No use blaming the family for your own weakness, Valeria said. Within the family there was no such thing as individual identity. The family's function was to gobble up anything inside it. The family was a collective creature whose goal was a sort of low grade immortality, like an amoeba. Larger forces swallowed smaller forces: that was how collective immortality worked. The family swallowed you only when you were weaker than the family. There were now only two conditions on Earth. . . .

The bathroom door opened and the blonde cousin, still snivelling, shirt stained strawberry, hand and knee stained red with mercurochrome, made a big show of hobbling through the kitchen toward the porch door, supported on either side by Aunt Grete and Aunt Elena. Nadja disappeared into the bedroom, where sunlight stuck to the walls in blocks of chalky pink.

***   ***   ***

Nadja made a quick change into blouse and skirt and bent down over an open cocoa suitcase. Towering, primary-colored layers of folded clothing stood on bed, dresser, chair and three-legged stool. Three or four pieces of blue canvas luggage on the floor.

Someone was bound to come in and interrupt them, Nadja said, grabbing things off the towers of endless colored units and stuffing them into one suitcase, then another. So she'd come straight to the point. There wasn't going to be a wedding. Andy was gone. On his way to New Zealand or already there.

She saw now, Nadja said, that it was going to be hard to account for what happened. Her life with Andy had always been lazy and functionless. But that never bothered her. What others called laziness, she saw as a pleasant, prolonged childhood. The daily grind wasn't for her; she had no ambition; no talent; and she was never attracted to the up-dated Pioneer life, the post-post-60's mystical farm life of children, domestic crafts and vegetable gardens that still persisted with a certain attenuated vigor among the wives and lovers of men in so-called creative or culturally marginal professions. Baron Pauli always said: very few were capable of achieving great things. Very *very* few. If you couldn't do something fresh and startling, lead a life that hadn't been used up by others, then you had to find your way into the safe harbor, the eternity-in-life of pleasure. Here too you found a small band—a band apart from the mass-after-mass yoked to History. . . .

Andy knew that too. But not so clearly as Baron Pauli. Andy *didn't* know that poverty would one day eat up his way of living a pleasant, prolonged childhood. It hit her after Becky Andropolos committed suicide. Exactly three weeks after her party, Becky jumped off a bridge in Puerto Rico. Or not a bridge exactly, but a catwalk suspended 500 feet over the valley where they had that giant radio dish or radio telescope. No one ever found out what she was doing down there. Or what happened to her body. Her body was never recovered, like the bodies of the other "Mystery Leapers" the newspapers were talking about. So maybe it *wasn't* a suicide.

It depressed her. She lay in bed for two days watching tv. Then Baron Pauli called. Some restaurant was throwing a banquet in his honor (something to do with his new vineyards in California) and he wanted her to accompany him. The desire to go was very strong. Andy didn't like it and they had a big fight. But she went anyway.

Reporters and photographers were waiting at the restaurant. She hadn't realized that the Baron was a celebrity. The weak force from the tiny explosions of the flash cameras coated her skin with an electric desire that flashed back to the film waiting for precisely that image. The next day she showed up in newspapers with the lit-up, super-excited look she'd seen ten million times in photographs of celebrities going to parties. Her eyes were two bright minnows swimming toward god-alone-knew-what. Her face blazed like a vanity mirror with twelve high-intensity bulbs. The photograph caught the Baron whispering in her ear romantically. But what he was actually saying was: "If you didn't know it before, now you know that the Unreal really does exist!"

They ran into a little problem at the banquet. The Baron's feet weren't permitted to touch the ground while he dined. She didn't know if it was a question of protocol, of having to be elevated above mere mortals, or if it was a phobia of some kind. There was quaking and scurrying. Finally they inverted two tremendous roasting pans and placed his chair on those. The Baron nodded his approval and the staff rejoiced as if they'd discovered a cure for death.

After dinner there were interviews, more photographs. Baron Pauli asked her to pose with him. She sat there, more or less on his lap, laughing, champagne glass in hand, blending with a cliché. She'd seen the image so many times that she couldn't really call it *deja vu*. It was more like the inverse of *deja vu*, if such a thing were possible. As if you sometimes slipped into a state that was lying in wait.

Then they took a long drive up along the Hudson, almost to Rhinebeck. The Baron invited her to Deauville and lost a little of his awesome composure. He hinted (something she'd always suspected) that he'd been taken with her since she was twelve or thirteen.

She was trembling, like a scrap of paper lifted toward a reality we call unreal because we never expect to experience it.

When the Baron dropped her off Andy wasn't there. He came home the next day and they argued. A superficial argument but it wouldn't drain off. One argument after the other. The basin of things, which is tolerable when it's empty and we don't notice it, filled up. Their life together was spoiled. Then Baron Pauli—

"NADJA? OH NA-DJA!" a woman's voice sang out, clearly and thinly, the ringing vibration of a crystal rim. "IS YOUR *SISTER* IN THERE WITH YOU. . . ?"

Valeria marveled at the disembodiment of the crystalline voice, which logic told her had to be travelling from the hot, tree-circled porch, through the window where a puckered jade plant in its clay pot was soaking up heat like a miniature adobe dwelling.

The blond boy cousin slouched in, radiating adolescent boredom from the doorframe between white kitchen and pink bedroom.

"Your mother," he yawned with an offhand truculence, "or rather your *father*—your father *says* that your mother wants me to give you this *note* that she wrote. *He* says that *she* says it's important."

He handed Valeria a sequence of green, mauve, blue, yellow, red and turquoise slips of notepaper on which hard-to-read blue sentences were scratched out at a difficult diagonal.

The cousin, having nothing left to say, slouched back to the porch.

Valeria struggled to read the note aloud.

"'Evil arises from the subverted longing for. . .' something—or something-something—one long word or two short words close together. And then: 'I think you know that I've never watched much television. I've always felt that your father, with his dull passion for sports and comedies, easily watched enough for two. But, since my "accident," I've had so little freedom of movement that I've found myself watching afternoon television (soap operas, an occasional film or game show), evening television (news, crime melodramas, tv movies), and films all through the night as well. What with the horrible brace your Mr. Vilanescu persuaded the doctor to substitute for the usual one, I'm so uncomfortable at night I've forgotten how to sleep. I sleep a few minutes here, a few minutes there, no more than two-three hours all told, and I'm never truly awake during the day. I know very well I've entered a twilight land, neither healthy nor sick. Sometimes on a pleasant afternoon Grete will pick

me up and we'll go back to her place and sit out on the patio or
whatever word they're using now for a little plot of colored paving
and a striped awning. We'll rig up a portable television out there,
play cards, Grete will eat a salad, I'll suck in some blended goo that
looks like it came out of the garbage disposal and we'll drink some
iced tea.

"'I've watched so much television that I sometimes expect to see
my name on the credits. I say to myself: "these stupid dreams are
yours!" Two things happened to me, one after the other. And those
two things are really the *same* thing. Television is another king-
dom—I was going to say, like illness. But since I haven't been "ill,"
is that really what I mean to say? Reality wears History as a mask.
We're always afraid of the same things. We've learned certain
names and no matter what happens our fear is bound by those
names. Even our paranoia is out-dated! I feel a little like Elizabeth
Montgomery in that movie where she's a young, neurotic socialite
who gets involved with a mysterious gangster played by Henry Silva.
She's on her friend's yacht, waking up in the dark after a horrible
night of drunken partying and a day's lifeless sleeping and she says:
"I met a man and I spent ten hours with him—it couldn't have been
more than ten hours all put together—but I *saw* terrible things and
I *did* terrible things! 'The Underworld.' It really *exists!* It really is
out there, right now! There *is* an underworld and there are *monsters*
in it. *Monsters!"* She's only talking about gangsters, but I know
exactly what she means. She *doesn't* say: "in the company of
monsters we *become* monsters. At night something leaves our bodies
and goes out hunting. . . ." I want to give you some advice. You're
not immune! *There is no cure!* "Neither this nor that will fend off
death!" Only one salvation. YOU *MUST* GIVE YOURSELF
ANEW TO THE AGE-OLD PROJECT OF RENDERING HU-
MAN AID. . . !' There's another half line, but it's completely
illegible."

"Yes," Nadja said, "Mother has gotten a little strange. Last night
when she, Grete and Sylvan slept over, I gave them the beds and I
slept outside in the hammock. After what seemed like a few hours
I woke up with a violent jerk—as if I were having a nightmare. It
seemed to me that I'd dreamed that something had descended on

me from the overhanging trees. Mother was standing there in her nightgown, looking awful. Grotesque, of course, because of that contraption on her jaw, but frightened and desperate too. I could tell that she wanted to say something, so I guided her inside. At first I thought she was sleepwalking, because I had no other way of explaining the bizarre mixture of remoteness and hysteria; but later I became convinced that she wasn't and gave her a pen and some paper.

"'I'm going to *die!*' she wrote. Apparently *she'd* had a nightmare. She'd dreamed that she was lying in bed, not quite asleep, in a palace of some kind. Her dead mother appeared, dressed in a gown from that era—with her hair done up quite high—like this. . . ."

She outlined a tall cone above her head. "A style something like a white, elongated beehive, what Mother called *la coiffure du roi.* Very frightening. Apparently much more so to her than I could appreciate.

"Her mother held out a beautiful, gold-speckled green shawl wrapped round something and tied like a package. Mother undid it and inside she found an enormous dead fish. Mother knew in the dream that this meant death. Joining her mother in another realm. She woke up with a start just a few minutes before she came out—waking *me* up. . . ."

"VALERIA!" one of the aunts called. Then two other voices, more urgent and shrill, and three or four more in a blended chorus called in to her from the porch. *"VALERIA! COME OUT! COME OUT QUICKLY!"*

The cousins were sulking in sunlight, Uncle Sylvan was playing solitaire, Valeria's father had dozed, melting into the hot wall, and all the others were gathered around the plastic-ribbed chaise lounge where Valeria's mother was stretched out, leather-tanned and rigid-looking, her arms and legs at awkward angles. A tiny foam of would-be language stained her lips, which were fixed in an expression of hatred.

"Is she *dead?*" Valeria asked with an intonation that was hard to read.

"Quiet!" someone said, motioning toward the portable tv that had been blathering away all afternoon.

"THE WORLD IS SUFFERING FROM AN OVERDOSE OF ITS OWN SUPER-REALITY."

Valeria was surprised to see herself.

"A DEPTHLESS OVER-ILLUMINATION, LIKE VIDEOTAPE, AND, IF THE WORLD NOW LOOKS LIKE TELEVISION, A BRAND NEW CATEGORY OF REALITY, THEN A COSMIC WAVE OF LONGING FOR UNREALITY CAN'T BE FAR BEHIND. TO PARAPHRASE WHAT I SAID IN *NOTES TOWARD A GENERAL THEORY OF TELEVISION*: EVEN IN TELEVISION, BURIED UNDER MOUNTAINS OF VULGARITY AND SILLINESS AS IF BY DESIGN, THERE ARE STARTLING INFERENCES TO BE DRAWN ABOUT THE NATURE OF MATTER. WITHIN THE LONGED-FOR OTHER WORLD THAT TELEVISION ESTABLISHES, MEANING-FREE AND CONTENT-FREE, REALM OF MESMERIZING DUMBNESS, PICTURE OF NOTHING BUT ITS OWN INFINITELY REPEATABLE CONTINUITY, THERE ARE REAL GHOSTS OF MATTER TRANSMITTED FROM ONE PLACE TO ANOTHER. TELEVISION IS HAUNTED BY A COSMIC RADIANCE, INTIMATE AND INDIFFERENT TO HUMAN LIFE."

Humberto Vilanescu's enormous head above the collar of a soft red shirt and lapels of a baby blue raw silk suit replaced Valeria's.

"IN THE PREFACE TO THE *REVALUATION OF ALL VALUES*," he said, "WE READ: 'THIS BOOK BELONGS TO THE VERY FEW. PERHAPS NONE OF THEM ARE ALIVE YET. ONLY THE DAY AFTER TOMOR-ROW BELONGS TO ME. SOME MEN ARE BORN POSTHUMOUSLY.'

"ONLY VERY FEW HAVE PROPERLY UNDERSTOOD WHAT THIS MEANS. THERE IS A VERY REAL SENSE IN WHICH, IN EVERY AGE, A TINY HANDFUL ARE LIVING IN THE FUTURE, TALKING TO THE FUTURE FROM THE CEMETERY THAT SURROUNDS THEM. 'THE DEAD HAND DEATH ON. THERE MUST BE NO SURVIVING.' THE ONLY WORK THAT MATTERS IS THE WORK THAT LEADS US BE-YOND DEATH. AND THOSE OF US WHO ARE DOING THAT WORK CONSTITUTE A REAL SECOND COMING. THE WORLD WILL ONE DAY COME TO US FOR ITS BREAD. WE'VE ALREADY SPOKEN, AT AN EARLIER FORUM, OF THE CURSE OF BEING EARTH-BOUND. THE

IGNORANCE OF THE HISTORY-YOKED MASS IS EXACTLY THIS CURSE, THIS FALL OUT OF THE FUTURE.

"THE HISTORY-YOKED MASS KNOWS NOTHING OF HIGH ENERGY STATES, MICRO-PARTICLES, SUPER-CONDUCTIVITY, SUPER-GRAVITY, THE WEAK FORCE, STRANGENESS, COLOR, CHARM AND SPIN. AND THOSE STUDYING THESE FORCES AT THE MAJOR CENTERS IN STANFORD, CHICAGO, BROOKHAVEN, LOS ALAMOS, HAMBURG, PASADENA, BERKLEY, GENEVA AND COPENHAGEN ARE THEMSELVES DRINKING THROUGH A STRAW AS NARROW AS THE HOSPITAL STRAW THROUGH WHICH MRS. MARIANNA FLORESCU WAS ONLY MOMENTS AGO STRUGGLING TO SIP A FROTHY TROPICAL DRINK ON HER DAUGHTER'S PORCH NEAR THE ATLANTIC."

The perspective simultaneously tracked out and zoomed in to frame a panoramic close-up of Valeria and Humberto Vilanescu standing side-by-side on an elevated rostrum, something like a divingboard platform, in a large amphitheater. The dark sky above them had the dizzying, near-distant super-clarity of the cosmos in the lens of a high-powered telescope.

"IT'S NO LONGER SUFFICIENT THAT A TINY, ADVENTUROUS HANDFUL IS ROCKETING FORWARD FOR ALL THE OTHERS," Valeria began to say, but her voice was drowned out by the arrival of a car, its engine noisy and infarcted, spluttering with arhythmias in the earth-and-gravel drive. It kicked off and for seconds nothing could be heard but the little burning engines of the cicadas in the trees, a concentrated drilling at innumerable sites, here and there a drill bit flying out of its socket and shredding leaves.

Valeria's father, her uncle George and the boy and girl cousins tried to carry her mother's rigid body indoors, out of the terrible heat, but she weighed three or four times more than usual and they couldn't help letting hands and feet scrape across the porch boards.

Liam, looking wild and sprouted, like a potato after it's begun to shoot its long tubers, saw that no one had paid the slightest attention to his arrival. Everyone who hadn't gone inside with Valeria's mother was staring at the little tv screen where Valeria and Humberto Vilanescu seemed to be taking turns fielding questions not only of a narrowly scientific nature, but about the so-called "Mysterious Leaper" phenomenon, the world-wide epidemic of arson, suicide and missing persons.

Liam grabbed hold of the television and heaved it over the railing. It thrashed through the trees, still getting juice through its long yellow extension cord, jerking to a stop only when the cord looped around a particularly antler-like branch. It twirled, swung back and forth, banging hard into the somewhat spongy tree trunk, made noises like something burning in a frying pan, but continued to play.

"THE TASK OF ART, SCIENCE AND ALL OTHER FORMS OF KNOWLEDGE AND COMMUNICATION IS NO LONGER TO ILLUMI-NATE EXPERIENCE OR TO PROVIDE IT," Humberto Vilanescu was saying. "THEIR ONE FUNCTION IS TO *USE UP* EXPERIENCE. USE UP EVERY-THING! GOBBLE IT ALL UP, LEAVE NO GROUND TO STAND ON—FORCE EVERYONE INTO THE FUTURE!"

"MILLIONS, ALMOST AS MANY AS PASS THROUGH THE TELEVI-SION SCREEN, WOULD ENTER THE FUTURE GLADLY," Valeria said, "WOULD THROW OFF EVERYTHING, LEAVE EVERYTHING BEHIND, IF ONLY THEY KNEW HOW. HOW MANY ARE ALREADY STRUGGLING TOWARD THAT ZONE LIKE FLIES IN A TELESCOPE, HALF-HUMAN OR NO LONGER HUMAN AT ALL? EVERY SUCCEEDING GENERA-TION WILL INCREASINGLY FEEL THE URGE TO BECOME ELEC-TRONIC, TO BE THE HUMAN ELECTRONIC CREATURE FROM BE-YOND EARTH LIKE AN ETERNAL IMAGE OF RETURNING RAYS."

Liam looked from the sputtering television, where Valeria's image was dangling among hot leaves, to where she was standing on the far side of the porch. He moved toward her, though the look on her face made him feel hopeless.

He said that she didn't seem aware of the danger she was in. They had to leave *immediately*. He didn't know *how* he knew what he knew, but he knew that the strange experiences he'd been having were warnings. Sometimes when he was watching television or in his car, listening to the radio on the way to work, he heard her voice, lost and tiny and hidden in the sub-tones. Other times when he was in bed and his big window fan was threshing away with double force because of some sudden powerful gust of wind, he heard her voice calling his name in the low decibel chords. Very low, very indistinct, audible-yet-inaudible, one more sound among the others, a particle among billions, the voice a blue-white star might have if its tiny oscillations and spasms were sounds.

It also happened sometimes when he was using his drill or sander. He'd go on with what he was doing, not sure if he'd heard anything. Minutes later he'd hear it again, more distinctly than before. *Absolutely her voice and no one else's!* But still tiny, vacant, ghostly. And then a third time, clear but remote, as if a child were calling his name from the middle distance, the way a friend would call when he was a child himself, inviting him with a sort of everyday but urgent longing to come out of doors. He'd switch off the sander, drill, fan, radio or television. He'd listen. He'd concentrate. He'd hear nothing.

Only occasionally her voice persisted beyond its existence within a dense bed of other tones. He'd pay the sharpest attention. For an instant the minute quiver of a micro-voice created a little stir: something unnameable moved aside to a degree too small to measure, then vanished into the zillion little tones that equal the blended background murmur of the universe, leaving him with the oddest feeling of grief, inconsolable.

He broke off suddenly, looking into her eyes and seeing that all the while he'd been talking he was reflected there as an absurd miniature Gene Kelly, sliding toward Cyd Charisse or Mitzi Gaynor on one knee, pouring out an unfathomable romantic yearning disguised as a melancholy sort of speaking/singing.

He reached out to take her arm. Something prickled on his skin. He felt a slight pressure on his forearm, barely perceptible, just a few degrees more than the weight of sunlight. He felt his hand pass through her wrist.

He stared at his hand as if it had been cooked in a microwave. His face looked like a de-magnetized bubble memory bank. A negative shadow of perfect whiteness spread from his face to the faces of all those who'd remained clustered around the tv set even though Valeria's mother, dead or near-dead, had been dragged inside.

The television in the trees had a kind of seizure and came back to life, louder than before.

"WE DON'T WANT TO *MEET* CREATURES FROM ANOTHER

PLANET," Valeria said, "WE WANT TO *BE* CREATURES FROM AN-
OTHER PLANET!"

What might have been the televised amphitheater's amplified
hive of voices and applause swiftly flared up into high voltage arcing
and crackling. A white rocket plume of smoke shot up from the
television into the tree it was suspended in, which caught fire at
once, as if struck by lightning. The fire spread from that tree to
other trees very quickly, threatening the common raft of porches
overlooking them.

The table with its tremendous punch bowl, little glass punch
cups, tumblers, blender, plates, food and utensils was knocked
over. The family scrambled to get off the porch, falling over flimsy
outdoor furniture, trampling on broken glass. Screams, tears and
blood somehow blended into a certain helpful camaraderie of terror.

After they'd fled through the small kitchen and down the narrow
double flight of stairs, carrying the dead weight of the mother's body
with great difficulty, Liam and Nadja were the only ones who
noticed that Valeria wasn't with the others. They went back up,
searched the apartment, then went out on the porch and stood at
the railing, calling Valeria's name into the blazing gardens.

POSTSCRIPT

Years later Liam was living with his mother, wife and two daughters in an elevated circular green city in Texas. One day he was driving his mono-copter above the automated traffic lanes when he thought he spotted Valeria's face on the big, hemispherical screen of a blue Videomobile parked in its miniature amphitheater. He descended to the landscaped landing plaza and ran a half-mile or so along the pleasant elm-bordered path to the viewing area.

It was Valeria, though she'd changed: her face now a breathtakingly dark and beautiful sun of power, success and intelligence. It was at once the face of the woman he'd loved and a face that was no longer the face of someone one could know in the ordinary sense. The light from the screen was like a second daylight, far more powerful, more enormous than the first: the light of a human soul incandescent with mathematical certainty. From the screen of trees behind the temporary rows of blue seats Liam could see that the crowd of viewers found it impossible not to watch her. They stared at every flicker of expression, hung on every word of her brief statement about the way each system is at all times gobbling other, smaller systems, each little one formulating her or his own little system or contributing to the formulation of a little but slightly larger system as if solely to feed the next larger system. What lay at the end of all this gobbling of systems?

Liam leaned back against a tree, weeping with nostalgia and terror, then sank down to the loamy floor of the landscaped forest remnant. Valeria was still talking, the unbearable light of her face washed into the mini-forest's thin twilight, and he saw that the hovering kiosks were now doing a feverish business in the popular but expensive VHF Intelligence Enhancement Capsules, Sleep-Narrative Tablets, Camera-less Pocket Image Recorders and the Universal Strap-on Communicator Kit.

"TELEVISION OF COURSE GOBBLES UP SO MANY SYSTEMS," he heard Valeria say, "THAT IT'S FAIR TO SAY THAT IT'S STILL OUR CULTURAL ACCELERATOR, OUR CREMATORIUM."

Liam clapped his hands to his ears, but it didn't help. He fled through the artificial evening of the long path leading back to the landing plaza.

Liam was at the busy intersection of Farnsworth and Orthicon, helping to repair the glassite housing of a device he didn't understand, but which had something to do with the operation of one of the new "Air Paths" that carried pedestrians swiftly to and from higher and lower zones of the city. There was no denying that things had changed. In every burned-and-cleared-out zone it was as if a permanent illusion of magnified space had been installed. Everywhere the world seemed more open, with broad planes as clear as mirrors across which the human figure moved as if at an immutable distance from the perspective of every other figure.

While he worked in the hot sun of the open plaza with undemanding labor's neutral pseudo-happiness, he wondered if all this constituted a genuine leakage of the future into the present, or even an individual passage into one's former idea of "The Future." If the uncomfortable newness of things eliminated anything like an unconscious and natural present moment, did that mean you were in the future? Not everyone could afford the Intelligence Enhancement Capsules and all those other things. Stupidity still persisted, camouflaged and mutated perhaps, but still as powerful as gravity. Did anything that happened, even the sharp difference in one's sense of "the present" from what it used to be, matter to him or anyone he knew? Were all included? Could all *ever* be included? Except in the way the shabby side effects of things invariably seeped down over all.

A blue and white so-called Levitation-Craft (said to operate on a principle of sub-atomic repulsion) came zipping up Farnsworth and passed into the intersection, snapping a sharp turn into Orthicon faster than an electron through a super-conducted tunnel junction. A face leaned forward from the back seat which was filled with a sort of darkly dazzling prismatic shadow. It seemed to him that a woman looked out the window, that her mouth opened to say something and that the face was a round and human one, the eyes kind and friendly, the voice calling out something painfully soothing.

He dropped his tools and made for the Pedestrian Express Lane, travelling after the fleeing Levitation Craft at one half its speed, keeping it in view until it made a sudden oblique ascent, disappearing beyond the transparent dome of the Museum of Ideas.

He saw that he was at the Northern boundary of the city, very near the spot where a recent accident had ruptured the mid-level escarpment. Here, across a short gap of miles, he had a view of the foothills of real mountains, their superheated woodland blistering with vegetation as if about to rupture into another, unimaginable planet. It seemed to him he could see a steady stream of human figures making their way out through a blinding stand of birches and down the long, deep shaft of a gully.

Liam sat for a long while under a tree on the sloping bank of the lake, feeling worn out. His wife and two daughters were picnicking slightly above him, close to the point where the realm of light gave way to the realm where the forest was feeding on its own deep shadow.

The bank sloped down below him, dropping of to a muddy lip of rocks and reeds, while out on the tremendous surface of the lake a couple was rowing a lightweight canoe of a dazzling, metal-like substance, stroking vigorously toward a far-distant point where the lake narrowed then opened into a darkly shining second basin.

"WE'D BETTER HURRY!" the man called out loudly to the woman, as if she were far away on shore instead of four feet away. "WE MUST BE THERE IN *ONE HOUR!*" "CAN WE MAKE IT?" the woman asked with the same inexplicable urgency and terror.

Long minutes later a second shining canoe skimmed into view. Two women were laughing, paddling randomly, going a little forward, drifting sideways, turning full circle, narrowly escaping getting caught in the sedgy border of a forested island. Laughing, they made their way sluggishly across the lake toward the narrow opening. The sound of their laughter gave way slowly, as if time were closing around them as the hazy darkness of distance.

He wondered if the unhappy feeling that pierced him was merely nostalgia, as if he'd come here precisely to have memories, to feel worn out, to feel sick of his wife and children, to imagine that he'd once lived according to a different principle of happiness and that that principle of happiness still lay out here, away from his life in the new circular city. It struck him that while one frequently heard of others who, participating in this or that experiment, isolated in one or another guarded experimental region, were already living lives of vastly increased extension, he felt prematurely aged, haunted by memories that were easy to mistake for childhood.

Everything was still and hot. Long waves of short ripples moved steadily in one direction, altered now and then by the sudden winds that spring up in mountains. The trees bordering the far shore trembled, bent to one side, gave up the indescribable sound of wind passing across leaves, needles, rough bark and swinging boughs, through the millions and millions of shadows and tunnels of even the smallest stand of trees. It grew suddenly calm across the lake and started up in the evergreens behind the place where Liam was sitting. Something passed through the forest, where, without turning around to look, he knew his wife and children were eating and playing. He thought he heard a human voice calling his name within the forest's hive of sub-tones, and that the voice was Valeria's.